PRAISE F(

The
Christmas
Coin

The
Christmas
Coin

LINDSAY GIBSON

HARPETH ROAD
PRESS
Nashville

ALSO BY LINDSAY GIBSON

The Christmas Promise

Fly Away Summer

HARPETH ROAD

Published by Harpeth Road Press (USA)
P.O. Box 158184
Nashville, TN 37215

Paperback: 978-1-963483-17-8
eBook: 978-1-963483-16-1

THE CHRISTMAS COIN: An Enchanting New England Holiday Romance

First printing: October 2024

In memory of Agnes Lynch O'Driscoll.
May your love and wisdom forever take center stage in the hearts
of those who love you.

PROLOGUE

CHRISTMAS EVE, 1870

White Bridge, Connecticut
Ellen O'Shea

*E*llen O'Shea wrapped the long strand of red holly berries, threaded like beads along a cord, around the tabletop evergreen and stood back with a smile, admiring her work. Extra berries on prickly sprigs lay across the fire mantel, tucked close to the wall. She had just enough left for a wreath she planned to craft later. First, it was time to begin the tedious task of securing the small candles to the branches on the tree. As she picked up one of the candlesticks, she heard her baby boy, Joseph, whimper in the cradle by the fireplace. Placing the candle on the table, she fetched her baby.

Settling Joseph against her to feed him as she sat in the rocking chair, she closed her eyes, humming a familiar tune to soothe her little one. Below the sound of her humming, she could hear the wind howling outside against the falling snow. The storm promised a white Christmas morning, a far cry from the near constant rain Irish holidays always brought. She began the tune again, remembering her mother's soft voice singing the same melody.

The ocean that separated her from her family in Glengarriff felt wider during the holiday season. Ellen's loved ones were mostly likely sleeping, since it was the middle of the night in Ireland, but the thought of the Christmas feast that would occur in her parents' home the following day brought her solace during this lonely night. Her mother would surely serve her famous spiced beef with loaves of homemade bread, and potatoes accompanied by sliced broiled ham—all Ellen's favorites. She missed it all so dearly.

Gently rocking back and forth while Joseph nuzzled his tiny face into her chest, tears built in her eyes. The separation from her family was heartbreaking, but nothing like experiencing her first Christmas in America without her James.

Joseph fell asleep again, and Ellen continued rocking, the comforting motion lulling her into a trance. As she slipped into a light doze, her mind drifted into memory, and with each push of the chair she was taken back to the rocky movement of the ship one year ago, holding James as he took his final breaths.

Crossing the Atlantic had its risks, but losing her beloved husband had not been at the forefront of her mind when they got the tickets to sail to America only two weeks after their wedding. All they'd seen were visions of building a new life in America, something so many still only dreamed of. Knowing how hard their lives would be in Ireland, with remnants of the famine still holding its grip, both their parents had saved for their crossing. When they set sail, they were young, healthy, and strong, full of confidence for a smooth journey, never thinking typhus would find its way to James. She could still see his face as he stared longingly into her eyes during those last few minutes... as if he already missed her.

"*Never forget the coin,*" he breathed out. "*You will prosper, my love. And... the letter.*"

"*I won't.*" Ellen kissed his forehead as tears slid down her cheeks and whispered, "*I love you.*" Squeezing her eyes shut, she laid him gently back onto the pillow—clutching in her hand the coin he had given her on their wedding day, the one that stood as a token of him sharing with her all he possessed. It was meant to bring them luck. But when she landed in America, widowed and alone in a place where everything was unfamiliar and strange, lucky was the last thing she felt herself to be.

Yet even in that darkness, there had been a glimmer of hope waiting for her. Two weeks after arriving in America, she'd found herself with child. A piece of James to keep and cherish. Someone to force her out of her grief and make her focus on the future and all the joy it might hold.

A knock at the door startled her, waking Joseph for a moment, but she managed to shift him to the cradle and back to sleep before answering it. When she opened the door, the icy wind blew across her face and Michael Barnett stood before her, holding a pile of logs.

"Michael, you shouldn't have. The wind is roaring too harshly for you to come all this way. Please come in." Ellen ushered him inside and quickly closed the door.

"Of course I should've. Better that I take a risk in this weather than you with that little one of yours." Michael looked over at the cradle. "How's the young lad?"

"He's doing well, feeding around the clock as he should."

"This pile should last you till morning, and I will be over then with more." Michael hesitated, keeping his eyes on her, making Ellen shift on her feet. "Granted the wagon can get here. Hopefully it won't snow too much more overnight."

Since the day she arrived in White Bridge, Connecticut, after learning there was work she could do as a seamstress, Michael had been right by her side, helping her adjust to her new surroundings. He was one of the first to welcome her to town and, with the townspeople alongside him, had built the farmhouse for her and Joseph. Michael hadn't married yet and it made her wonder if interest in her was why he hung around so often. It was still painful to look at another man that way, but her year of mourning was complete, and she knew James would want her to find happiness again. Michael was a good man, kind and thoughtful, and so gentle with Joseph. And when she was with him she felt happier. Lighter. More hopeful for the future. What she felt wasn't love yet, but maybe with a little luck it could be someday.

"There's a new bundle of hay and wood shavings coming the day after tomorrow. It should be enough to enclose the gaps where the cold could still be getting in, making it much warmer in here for the remainder of the winter. If the snow keeps up at this rate, it will be a long and cold one."

"That is so kind of you. Joseph and I will be well-off in here."

They both fell quiet, Michael fixing to say something more, but little Joseph began to stir, filling the awkward silence.

"Well, I will leave you to him." Michael headed toward the door, but turned once more. "I also wanted to extend an invitation to my parents' house tomorrow for Christmas dinner. If I can get here, that is, I will collect you and drive you two over, if you'd like?"

Ellen let her gaze linger on his eyes a bit longer than usual. "That would be lovely."

Joseph began to cry, breaking their stare.

"Merry Christmas, Ellen," Michael said as he let himself out.

"Same to you, dear Michael," she called out, picking up Joseph. She shifted him over her shoulder to soothe him, listening to the crunch of Michael's boots against the newly fallen snow outside. The wheels of his wagon pulled away and she was alone with her sweet boy once again. Being on her own was hard enough, but raising her son would pose an even greater challenge, especially if the winters in Connecticut were this rough—yet Michael was always there with answers to what she'd needed before she had time to think it through.

Her mother's voice came to her as clear as if she were right there next to her, and Ellen knew exactly what she'd tell her: *Follow your heart, my cushla.* Oh, how she'd missed her, and no matter how vast the sea was between them, Ellen would always be her darling. She stood and slid Joseph to her other shoulder, cradling him. His eyes were now fully open, watching her as if he'd been able to read her thoughts.

"Don't worry, wee one. Mummy has you."

Joseph kept his eyes locked with hers, melting her heart as he cooed in response. As he became more animated, his tiny noises replaced the silence in her home and slowly began to fill her heart with happiness again.

"How about a change, yes?"

After carrying him to her dresser, she opened the drawer to fetch a fresh cloth nappy, and in the corner of the drawer, the small felt bag holding the coin caught her attention. As she ran her fingertips along the coin inside, she thought about the exchange it represented between her and her James: a love that would never die. From the moment she'd learned her child was on the way, she realized that *she* hadn't died. There was still so much life to live, a healthy son to raise, and there was Michael.

Picking up a nappy, she glanced at her little Christmas tree, the berries popping in color next to the warm, crackling fire. Like Christmas magic, her home suddenly drew her in. The light from the soft candles burning, the smell of pine wafting through the air, the logs burning in the fireplace. Michael's graciousness and a town that had held her up since she arrived showed her all she'd gained amid all she'd lost since leaving for America.

The coin hadn't lost its luck yet.

CHAPTER 1

PRESENT DAY

"*A*melia… there isn't an easy way to tell you this," her orthopedist began.

Amelia gripped the chair, bracing for what he was about to say. For nearly five years he'd worked hard to keep her on the stage as he carefully repaired her fragile ankle multiple times. But no ballerina's career lasted forever, and they'd both known this day would come eventually.

"I'm afraid it's time to hang up your pointe shoes."

"But, Dr. Reed…" She tried to remain calm against her thudding heart. "Even with limitations?"

There was a knock at the door and they both looked up to see one of his medical assistants pop her head in.

"So sorry to disturb your appointment with Miss Collins, but you have an urgent call on line two. A patient from the surgery yesterday has some complications."

"Thank you, Michelle. I'll just be a few more minutes." Dr. Reed looked back at Amelia when the assistant shut the door. "The limitations were already set before the last surgery, but we're past that point now. As we discussed a few months ago,

I had wanted to see how rehabilitation would go this summer but after reevaluating you, the injury last spring was just too much for your ankle."

Amelia dropped her gaze to her hands as the room spun, and her vision blurred behind a veil of tears. Even though she'd been half expecting this news, it still hit her hard. Ballet had been her life for as long as she could remember. She didn't know who she was if she wasn't a dancer anymore.

"I just can't believe it's over. I thought I had at least five more years in me."

Dr. Reed nodded. "You're in your early thirties, so I can understand the determination to push the career longer. But remember, every dancer is different and, for you, that ankle is just not able to endure dancing anymore. A stage-three tear of both the anterior talofibular *and* calcaneofibular is rare and serious."

"But this year's performance is *The Nutcracker*," she said, as if it would change her doctor's mind. "My brother hasn't seen me perform in it." In all the years she'd danced in the classic ballet, her twin brother, Andrew, had missed it. School, travel, work, and his diagnosis of leukemia three years prior, had gotten in the way. He was home sick from treatment the last time she took the stage as the Sugar Plum Fairy. But Andrew had been doing better all spring and summer and could finally see her perform.

"Amelia, I know this is almost impossible to hear, but you deserve my honesty. I can't clear you. After two other injuries on those ligaments, it's just not repairable and not safe to dance again."

Despair rose in her. "I really tried hard with rehab."

"I know you did, and you did everything correctly."

"I followed every exercise, never missed appointments with physical therapy, and rested fully. I can do it again."

Dr. Reed only looked at her with sad eyes, shaking his head.

When management at the theater announced last summer that they were performing *The Nutcracker* that year, she was thrilled. It had only prompted her to work harder with her rehabilitation.

But it had all been for nothing.

HER DOCTOR STOOD TO ESCORT HER OUT, AND SHE KNEW there was no more discussion. All she could think about was being carried onto the stage last spring after that tragic fall to take a bow, not knowing it was her last. It was over. She couldn't believe it. Her ballet career had come to a close.

Back outside, the scent of winter lingered in the air, a hushed stillness seeming to permeate New Haven's usual busy vibes as everyone awaited the first snowfall. It was only the end of October, but the city was already putting up festive décor, yet she'd hardly noticed. Her anxiety from the crushing blow of her ballet career ending grabbed hold of her, and she walked over to a nearby bench and sat down—completely missing the wonder of the first light flakes that danced gracefully down from the gray clouds. Closing her eyes amid the angst of the devastating news, she leaned forward to steady her breathing.

A city bus pulled up nearby, the sound of its brakes snapping her upright, and she finally noticed the snow—now falling at full speed. A cold gust of wind prompted her to stand and hail a taxi. Her apartment wasn't far, but she wanted to get home as quickly as possible. She couldn't bear to be in public any longer in her present state of mind.

Relieved when a taxi pulled up with her first wave, she got inside the warm cab.

"Nineteen High Street please," she instructed the driver.

Within a few minutes she'd opened the door to her small apartment and immediately felt a push against her legs, followed by deep purrs from below. Looking down, she saw her cat, Mocha, rubbing between her ankles as if she knew her owner was sad. After taking off her coat, Amelia bent over and scooped up the cat to snuggle her on the couch. She stroked the cat's soft brown fur, trying to collect her thoughts. The comfort of Mocha's purring helped her relax, until her phone buzzed from the front hallway. She got up, knowing exactly who was calling.

"Hey, Sam," Amelia answered, her pulse picking up again. "You have perfect timing. I just got home from the appointment." Making her way back to the couch, she tried to prepare for this difficult discussion with her lead director of production.

"I have Ms. Higgens here with me and you're on speaker," Sam said.

"The snow is picking up. Snow this early means a rough winter ahead of us. Glad you made it home safely," Ms. Higgens said in the background.

She was the theater's ballet master, but she always looked out for her dancers with her strong motherly instincts. Amelia had danced under her instruction for nearly eight years, which would only make this news even harder to share. Amelia swallowed the lump that had formed in her throat and sank onto the couch.

"I know you've been waiting all day, so I'm just going to say it—"

"Amelia, please remember we are both here for you," Ms. Higgens said.

"Dr. Reed said..." she started but couldn't get the words out. This was going to be the hardest moment in her entire career, even worse than the appointment earlier that day.

These two women had held her up through everything—challenging roles, conflicts with other dancers, a string of less serious injuries, and even personal traumas, like when she first got the news of her twin's illness. They had helped her grow and shaped her into the professional ballerina she was today. How could she say goodbye?

"Deep breaths, dear, and take your time," Ms. Higgens said.

"Thank you. This is so hard." Amelia inhaled sharply before resuming. "Dr. Reed confirmed today that the tears were too intense to rebuild and return to the stage." She squeezed her eyes shut against the brief silence on the other end.

"Oh, Amelia…" Sam said.

"We can always get a second opinion," Ms. Higgens suggested, her voice getting louder as she picked up the phone. "There's a doctor in New York City who—"

"Dr. Reed is at the top. He's the absolute best there is at what he does," Sam reminded them. "His wait list is nearly two years long and he specializes in athletes and dancers. Amelia, you could certainly get a second opinion, though, if you'd like."

Amelia appreciated Ms. Higgens's suggestion, but Sam was right. There was no one better than Dr. Reed. Dancers flew in from all over the country to see him. If he said her career was over, that meant it was over. Getting a second opinion wouldn't do anything but give her false hope.

"I trust Dr. Reed fully, and…" Amelia paused with a sigh. "And something in my heart knows he's right. It's time to hang up my dancing shoes."

"Do you need us to come over?" Sam asked.

"I could pick up your favorite red curry chicken soup from that Thai market," Ms. Higgens added.

Amelia hesitated, not wanting to be rude, but she just

wanted to sit with Mocha alone and think. "Thank you, but I don't want you heading out in this weather. I think I'm going to take a hot shower and relax. I kind of need to be by myself with this news tonight. I also need to break the news to Lucy." Lucy, a dance partner and her closest friend since beginning with Northeast Performing Arts, was going to be heartbroken.

"Good luck with Lucy, I know how close you two are. And we understand, honey. Just have a quiet night in and watch a good Christmas movie," Ms. Higgens said. "Are all your decorations up? Christmas lights always make me happy."

Amelia looked around her blank apartment. "November is still a week away."

"Which means Christmas is practically here," Ms. Higgens responded.

Amelia chuckled, knowing how much her teacher loved the holidays. She'd never forget that first Christmas season she was contracted, and Ms. Higgens began stringing lights throughout the studio before Halloween was over.

"I'm getting there," she lied to appease the woman.

"Both our phones are on if you need to call us at any point tonight. Remember, I'm only a few blocks from you," Sam said.

"I'm so grateful for your support. This has been so tough," Amelia said, leaning back on the couch, feeling fatigue begin to wash over her. The intensity of the day had finally caught up to her.

"And there's absolutely no rush, but we will need to meet with you to sign some paperwork," Sam said gently. "I'm sorry to even bring that up, but the theater management will have my head if I don't."

"I know. Don't apologize. I'll be in on Friday."

After hanging up, Amelia searched for Lucy's number and

hit call. When she got her voicemail, she slowly exhaled in relief. She knew her friend was waiting on the update, but Lucy was also in Florida visiting her parents before the busy holiday season officially began and she would be caught at the theater for endless hours of practice. Amelia hated the idea of bringing such bad news to her while she was spending time with her family.

After leaving a message, Amelia looked up at the ceiling, not knowing what would happen next. Her ballet career was *over*. Thankfully, she had more than enough money to give her plenty of time to figure out her next step. Not that she danced for the money—she danced because she couldn't imagine doing anything else. She had goals she'd still wanted to meet and leading roles she strived to get. But none of that would happen now. Luckily, after taking on extra modeling jobs in her twenties, growing a large social media following as a dance influencer, and gaining many sponsorships, she had built up a hefty savings—not to mention money her grandparents had left her and Andrew when they both passed a few years prior.

Her grandfather had owned a successful commercial and residential building company and had always told her that he and her grandmother wanted to make sure she and her brother had "nest egg" money. Owning a home had not been at the forefront of her mind during all those years of dancing, but she invested the money well for her future, knowing ballet wouldn't be forever. Suddenly, that future was now...

Her eyes began to sting all over again. As she sat up to get a tissue, her door buzzed.

She went to the intercom, hoping it was just someone at the wrong apartment buzzer, which happened often.

"Hello?"

"Amelia? It's me, Mom," Kimberly Collins said through the speaker.

"Mom? Come on up," Amelia said, quickly pressing the button to open the front door so her mother could get out of the cold snow. So much for being alone for the night...

Glancing at the mirror in the hallway, she wiped her swollen eyes and used her fingers to comb out her long brown hair that was matted from laying on the couch, but gave up. There was no hiding this from her mother.

When she opened the door, her mother took one look at her, and Amelia lost control, her emotions overtaking her. Her whole body shook with sobs as she fell into her mother's arms. She held Amelia the same way she always had when she was a child.

After a long moment, Amelia stepped back from the embrace so her mother could come inside. Kimberly set down an overnight bag and unwrapped her scarf, which had freshly fallen snowflakes all over the black fabric, and unzipped her coat.

"I can't believe how much snow we're already getting," Kimberly said, shrugging out of her coat.

"Here, let me take your things." Amelia took the coat and hung it up in the front closet. "I should've known you would have already suspected before I had a chance to call." She mustered up a weak smile. It always brought her comfort that her mother somehow knew things, even before they were on her own radar.

Kimberly stood in the living room. "Well, this is the most un-Christmasy apartment in all of New Haven. I'll help you fix that."

Amelia's smile widened, and she suddenly longed for her childhood home in Northampton, Massachusetts, that she knew her mother had already decorated to the max by now. Kimberly Collins topped even Ms. Higgens with Christmas decorating.

"I know you will, Mom. Let's go have a seat on the couch."

"Let me make you some tea first. Do you have chamomile?"

"Top-right cupboard next to the stove," Amelia said.

Her mother headed into the kitchen, her expression seeming a bit off, but Amelia figured she was just worried about her. A few minutes later, she returned with two steaming cups of tea and placed them on the coffee table in front of them.

"Now, tell me what Dr. Reed said."

Kimberly crossed her legs, shifting toward her daughter. Amelia filled her in on everything. By the end, both women were crying, and Amelia fell onto her mother's lap just as she had when she was six years old and found out she didn't get the lead role in *Goldilocks and the Three Bears*. It had taken her mother hours to convince her that it didn't mean she was a failure.

Amelia sat back up. "I don't know what to do now, Mom."

"Amelia"—her mother reached for her hand—"remember that nasty ballet teacher you had growing up?"

Amelia rolled her eyes. "Ms. Ruth? How could I forget. The woman's words still haunt me to this day."

"Well, they shouldn't. Know why?"

"Why?"

"Because you made it. All that woman did was bring you down. And you became one of the best ballet dancers the theater has ever had. I still wish you'd told me she had been treating you so badly well before you did."

"I know. Keeping that from you and Dad was silly."

"I would have had her fired in seconds. Oh, that woman still makes me mad." Her mom held up a clenched fist with her free hand.

Ms. Ruth *had* been vicious and mean—no one should treat children the way she had—but that didn't mean the things she'd told Amelia had been totally wrong. *"Pay atten-*

tion, Amelia! There's no room for laziness or distraction in ballet. I'm not going to let you waste my time by giving me anything less than perfection."

"If only she could see me now... ruining my career by getting distracted at the wrong moment." All it had taken was a second of her thoughts wandering—but that had been enough to make her fall. And now she had to live with the consequences.

"Oh, sweetheart, it was just bad luck. You're human and not built like a robot. Injuries happen." Her mother squeezed her hand.

Amelia forced a smile. She didn't believe in luck and, like Ms. Ruth always said, *"Bad luck is the excuse people use when they know they didn't try hard enough"*—but she'd had this argument with her mother before, and she didn't want to have it again. Not now.

"You'll overcome this," Kimberly insisted. "And your father and I are here every step of the way. You don't need to have all the answers right this minute, but they will come. Your professional dancing days may be done, but your life is far from over."

Amelia took in her mother's words, wanting to believe them, but she struggled with the idea. What could there be for her other than ballet?

But she nodded, appreciating having her mom with her. "I thought I wanted to be alone tonight, but having you here is really helping. Thank you for driving the two hours in this weather to be here." The silence caught her attention and she noticed her mother looking down on her lap. "You okay, Mom?"

Her mother looked up toward the window, watching the snow dance around the streetlight. "I knew today's doctor's appointment was going to be tough, so I'd already planned to come. But..."

"But what?" Amelia felt her nerves pick up all over again. "Is something wrong with you or Dad?"

"No, we're both just fine," her mother assured her. "It's… your brother, Amelia."

A familiar knot in her stomach began to form and from the look on her mother's face—she knew.

"Andrew…" She could barely get his name out.

"I'm afraid he took a turn for the worse…" Her mother's eyes brimmed with tears again. "The doctors haven't given up hope, but they're unsure at this point how treatment will go this time."

Amelia felt as if she couldn't draw in enough air. Andrew was not just her brother, but her closest friend. Even though he'd been sick for a while, and they had been fully informed and prepped by his team of doctors that anything could happen, every day she'd held hope that he would fully recover.

Standing up, she looked toward her bedroom. "Okay, I need to go pack and we will leave first thing in the morning. Did he start treatment yet?"

"Amelia…" Her mother patted the couch. "Sit down."

"But I need to be with him." Amelia hesitated, but dropped back down. "Where is Dad? Is he with him? What about Diana?" Andrew's wife, Diana, was his college sweetheart, and she couldn't imagine what she must have been feeling. She needed to get to both of them.

"Andrew is home. Where your father and I, along with Diana, can take care of him. They decided that moving in with us was the best thing for him right now so we can all be there."

Shaking her head, Amelia tried to stay calm. First the news from Dr. Reed and now this? How could this all be happening in one single day?

"But *I'm* not there. Let me just go pack. Diana has her

fourth graders to teach all day, and you both need help. I can—"

"Amelia. When I told him I was coming to see you after your appointment today, he had one request."

"So he knows?" she asked with a heavy heart. The last thing she'd want was for her brother to have the stress of her career-ending injury on his mind. But she should have known he'd sense how it would go because, deep down, *she* had sensed how it would go. They could always read each other like no one else. They called it their "twintuition."

"Of course he does," her mother said. "He knows you better than anyone and could see right through the countless times you told us all not to worry."

A memory of them as children popped into Amelia's head. They were only eight and she'd been practicing around the clock for her upcoming summer performance. Andrew had sat with her for hours watching and clapping. He'd never been jealous of the attention she got as a dancer. On the contrary, he'd always been her biggest fan. As the years went by, he had continued to cheer her on at as many performances as he could—front and center. Even after he fell ill a couple years back and he couldn't attend like he'd used to, his support never faltered.

"What was his request?" she asked, barely above a whisper.

"That you don't come rushing home. Because he's still waiting on *The Nutcracker*."

Her mother held up her hand when Amelia began to protest. How could she do that now her days on the stage were over?

"I know," Kimberly said. "I was confused, too, but he was adamant."

"I wish I'd never told him about the company's pick of *The Nutcracker* this year. I got his hopes up—"

"And you kept your head up with a positive mindset all the way until this appointment. You did nothing wrong."

Amelia stood and began searching the living room. "I need to find my phone so I can at least call him."

"Amelia, just breathe. Give yourself some time tonight to digest everything." Her mother went over and took her hand to guide her back to the couch. "He also said he knew your career in dance wasn't over because of his—"

"Twintuition," Amelia filled in for her.

Her mother nodded. "I haven't heard that in a long time."

Their connection as twins had always been hard to describe, but at the base of it was the sense that whenever one was in doubt, the other knew it would be okay. And, for the most part, they'd been right. But for the first time in her life, she wasn't so sure Andrew's words would amount to anything.

"I don't know."

"Well, who can really say what the future might hold? Things look bleak right now, but tomorrow could be your lucky day. Come on, let's get some sleep."

Luck. That word again. Mocha followed Amelia to her room and curled up beside her when she lay across the bed. Pure exhaustion pushed against how wired she felt, despite how much her body screamed for sleep. Her thoughts were swirling as she turned to her side, stroking Mocha while her conversation with Andrew from the day she told him about *The Nutcracker* played in her mind. They'd both been so happy at the thought of him finally getting to see her perform in that show. Later that day she had ordered a Nutcracker ballet ornament she'd found online and sent it to him with a note.

Something to add to your tree and remind you

of all there is to look forward to while you continue your recovery. Can't wait for the performance!

Fresh tears spilled from her eyes. It looked like neither one of them had anything to look forward to. Not anymore.

CHAPTER 2

"I bet Mom is digging around your storage unit for your Christmas decorations," Andrew said on the phone the next morning. Amelia had called him early, as soon as she woke up, knowing he would be up too. They had been early birds their entire lives, always driving their mother crazy with how loud they used to be as kids before the sun fully awakened.

Her mother had popped her head into their phone call to say she was going to grab some coffees for them since she couldn't find any in the kitchen. An hour had gone by and she still hadn't returned.

Amelia laughed. "Well, she'll be down there awhile then. It's not very organized with all the scattered units for these apartments. But the coffee shop is only next door, so you're right, she's fishing for decorations."

"You know her. Christmas lights fix everything!" They both laughed before Amelia let out a yawn through the phone. "Not sleeping well, sis?"

"Not like I usually do, but I was also up late chatting with Lucy."

"She must be really upset…" Her brother had come to know Lucy well over the years of Amelia bringing her home for various holidays since her parents were further away in Florida.

"Very." Amelia turned to her side. "It took at least five minutes for her to stop crying and talk."

"You two are so close. Give her some time. Diana sure cried with Mom before she left to come see you. Diana and I both wish we were with you yesterday for such hard news."

"Actually, it's the other way around. I should be there with *you* right now." Amelia got up from her bed and started rooting around her drawers for a clean sweatshirt. The heat in the building wasn't the greatest and the management had been forever fixing it, so she'd invested in a lot of thick clothing. "How are you feeling today?" She immediately scrunched her nose, knowing how much Andrew had come to despise that question since his diagnosis, not wanting to drag his family down, especially her. Being older than her by six minutes, he took his "big brother" role seriously, always looking out for her and shielding her against everything that would make her sad when they were growing up.

"It's too early for that and I haven't had coffee yet myself."

"Okay, I'll wait an hour then ask again," she teased, putting the phone on speaker and placing it on her dresser while she pulled on her sweatshirt. She picked her phone back up and made her way into the kitchen to feed Mocha.

"The fatigue isn't that bad today and the sun is out so I can't complain. At least Diana already left for work, so that's one less person asking me how I feel." She could hear the playfulness in his tone, but knew he'd rather everyone carry on with their days without worrying so much.

"How's she doing with all this? It's a big change to move back home, even more so for her, I'd imagine."

Mocha yowled at her feet while she opened the can of food.

"She's a trooper. Since she has to juggle teaching and taking care of me, she is relieved to have Mom around me all day." Andrew paused and sighed through the phone. "Have you told the theater yet? I bet Ms. Higgens will be the most devastated. She's the first ballet master of yours that treated the dancers with such care."

Amelia swallowed, remembering the kind words the day before from Ms. Higgens. "I told her yesterday. She's definitely become more than a teacher all these years since I signed with them." After she mixed up Mocha's food, she placed it on the kitchen floor and went to the living room to wait on her mom.

"And you've blown them away with your talent since. You'll have a lot more time on your hands now..." He hesitated. "Okay, I don't want to say it, but I will anyway..."

She could practically hear him laughing through the phone and Amelia's twintuition suddenly knew what he was going to say before he finished.

"No, this doesn't mean I'll run out and get married."

"But it does mean you have zero excuse anymore not to try."

"Andrew!"

"Never know!"

"Just don't get Mom's hopes up with this. She bugs me about it more than you." Amelia rolled her eyes. Dating as a professional dancer had been very difficult with the long hours of practice and travel for performances, plus all the modeling jobs she did as well. Her work had always come first, and boyfriends had struggled to deal with the fact that even when she wasn't at the theater, she'd prioritize extra practice time over spending time with them.

"In all seriousness, you haven't had your final curtain

draw yet. I know you think it's all over, but I told Mom before she left that—"

"Listen," she stopped him. "Even if I could find a company that would take me, it wouldn't be safe. I don't want to do anything to risk making my ankle worse. My dancing days are done."

"Maybe they are, maybe they aren't."

What did that even mean?

"Andrew…" She sat back against the couch. "You make no sense."

Being hired by Northeast Performing Arts had been Amelia's big break. After starring in a few lead roles independently in both Boston and New York, her career took off when she nailed her audition with them. Over the years she'd led them through repeated starring roles, helping the marketing team drive revenue and ticket sales. She'd been a success, by any standard. But that was over.

"I'm your twin brother, you'll catch on eventually."

"Right now I don't understand a word you're saying. The twintuition isn't cutting it." She heard him laughing and her tension broke with a smile. "All that matters to me is you fighting through this and getting better. I want to see you, and—"

"And you will once you figure out your next steps." He finished for her. "No pun intended."

"You're not funny," she poked back, just as the front door opened and her mother came in holding a tray of coffees with a wreath dangling from her arm. "Mom's back. And I can barely see her under the giant wreath she has on her arm."

"Told you. I hope you have a nice day together."

Amelia hung up and stood up to take the coffees. "Let me take those before they drop."

"Sorry to interrupt your conversation and for how long

that took me. I spent forever trying to figure out which storage space was yours down in the basement, and gave up in the end. Whoever is in charge of organizing it needs to redo it. There's no telling which space is whose."

Amelia smiled. "Andrew and I predicted you'd come back dressed in Christmas décor. I'll show you later where everything is that's mine down there."

"How's he doing today?"

"I asked, but we both know how that goes."

Her mother nodded, checking the front door.

Amelia sighed. "I have an over-the-door hanger in the front closet if that's what you're looking for." She opened the closet, found the hanger, and hung it over the door.

Her mother settled the wreath on the hook and stepped back looking pleased. "See now, doesn't that just lift your mood? Since I couldn't find your Christmas boxes, I took a little walk and found this wreath for sale in a small shop near the Green. It's too early in the season to find a fresh one, but there were plenty of decorations on the shelves in the store. The saleswoman told me they'd just finished setting out Christmas stuff only the night before. It's nice to see the city must have followed suit, all dressed in its Christmas best."

Amelia stepped out into the hall to get a better look and nearly laughed when she noticed her neighbor still had a fall wreath on their door. "I've become *that* neighbor."

"What neighbor?"

"The one who puts out Christmas before the trick-or-treaters."

Her mother waved her hand. "Oh, it's okay. Besides, doesn't it make everything feel happier?"

"I love fresh ones." She walked back inside. "They smell so good, but I like how big the red bow is."

"I like that too. It's simple, but it's a start." Her mother closed the door. "So how else did your conversation with

Andrew go? Did he explain his odd request a bit more to you?"

"He did, and…" Amelia followed her to the kitchen where her mother opened the fridge.

"And?"

"It still makes no sense. I don't think it's clicked for him that ballet is over for me."

"Or he's giving you hope for new possibilities." Kimberly bent over and moved a leftover salad box to the side.

Amelia lingered on her mother's words, wishing she knew what was in store for her now. "I guess so."

"No eggs?" Her mother stood up from the fridge.

"I haven't had time to shop. Between hours of practice and physical therapy appointments all summer and fall, I live on takeout salad."

"Just salad?" Her mother eyed her. Amelia's strict diet had always bothered her. "Doesn't surprise me. Well then, let's go out to breakfast. My treat!"

"Let me go get changed." Amelia turned to leave, but her mother gently took her arm.

"It'll make sense soon. Try to have some patience. Your life is just taking one big giant turn for something different."

Amelia tried to appear grateful for her mother's attempt to cheer her up. "Thank you, Mom."

"Now hurry and get changed. Let's have ourselves a day. New Haven is already showing off for Christmas, so let's dive into it. Breakfast, shopping… all of it. I bet the malls are all decorated too!"

When Amelia got to her bedroom, she closed the door and sat on her bed. Her life was taking a turn for sure, and no matter how hard she tried to allow herself to be open to a new direction, dance was still the only thing she saw. Interacting on social media was fun and she certainly appreciated all her followers, not to mention it was still a solid source of income, but it wasn't all she'd wanted to do. And it wasn't dance. She'd never been the perfect ballerina Ms. Ruth had wanted her to be, but ballet was all she knew. The prospect of having to go out into the world and find a new career was terrifying.

～

"WOULD YOU LOOK AT THAT TREE!" HER MOTHER WAVED AT her to follow her onto the Green after they'd eaten breakfast.

Both women stared up in awe as the city workers got the tree set up using a crane.

"A fifty-foot Norway spruce and a real beauty," one of the nearby workers told them as they approached, watching as the crane carefully stood the tree up. "The family who donated it planted it as a baby."

"Wow, must be a big deal for that family to know it's going to light up the city soon," Amelia said.

After watching the tree get positioned to stand tall, the two women continued.

"I just love Christmas trees all lit up. Makes me feel so happy. Let's get you one," Kimberly said.

"Hmm… let me get through Thanksgiving turkey first." Amelia playfully nudged her mom.

"Okay, okay. I'll leave the tree idea alone for now. Let's get to the mall. Retail therapy always helps. I'll drive." Her mother picked up her pace. Crossing the street that led to Amelia's apartment building, her mother pulled out her car keys from her purse. "I bet I can find some new décor for you too. Maybe some new holiday table settings."

Amelia grinned at the joy on her mother's face and followed her to the car. This was the distraction she needed, and if turning her apartment into a Christmas wonderland made her mom happy, then perhaps it would help her too.

Listening to her mom sing along to a popular song on the drive down the highway to the nearby mall began to pull Amelia out of the haze she'd been in since the day before. Maybe she could get a head start on Christmas shopping while they were there.

"I was thinking about getting Diana a new latte machine," Kimberly said, turning the music down. "Hers broke over the summer, and she still hasn't gotten a new one."

"You must have been reading my mind. I was just thinking about gift ideas for everyone since we're going shopping. I want to get Dad something different this year. I think he has enough sweaters by now."

Both women laughed.

After they'd parked and walked in, Amelia's spirits were instantly lifted by the curtains of string lights flowing from the ceiling to highlight the mall's Santaland display that was still being set up. Fluffy blankets of white wrapped around a large sleigh filled with oversized presents in a center arrangement next to Santaland. Holiday music blasted from the speakers, and everyone seemed to have an extra pep to them as they strolled in and out of the stores.

"It looks beautiful in here," Amelia said, turning toward her mother with bright eyes. "It's amazing how fast and early they get the holiday décor up. Something I didn't even realize because I've always been so busy at the theater. I haven't been in a mall in years. I always ordered all my gifts last minute online."

"Then I was right that this shopping trip will lift your mood," her mother said, looking pleased. "Okay, where shall we start?"

"How about we go find that latte machine?"

"Good idea!" Her mother started toward the mall directory, but suddenly stopped short.

Amelia followed her gaze and drew in a sharp inhale

when she saw it. The sign seemed bigger than usual as she stood frozen, unable to look away.

Back by popular demand! Northeast Performing Arts Presents:
The Nutcracker. *Opening performance Friday, December 2.*
Tickets now on sale!

Her mother gently tugged her sleeve as Amelia desperately tried to blink away the sting in her eyes.

"Well, that's a bummer," she said casually, trying not to let it ruin the good day they'd been having.

"Let's walk it off," Kimberly said, pulling at her again.

Amelia's feet felt like bricks. She wanted to walk away, but continued staring at the sign, thinking about how just forty-eight hours ago that sign was her life.

CHAPTER 3

"*P*lease know that this is not the end with us," Sam said as she loosened her grip. "I could hug you for hours. I don't want to say goodbye."

Amelia's mother had left that morning, after spending a few days with her, and Amelia was already feeling lonely. Seeing Sam made saying goodbye all too real.

"I know," Amelia said and looked around the room before sitting down across Sam's desk.

Friday had arrived and it was time to face what she'd been dreading the last few days. She handed Sam the letter Dr. Reed had written that would officially excuse her from her contract. A few of her fellow dancers had begun to trickle into the theater for practice and stopped when they saw her to say their goodbyes.

"We're sure going to miss you, Amelia," one of the dancers said. "You're always there with the best advice when I'm having a rough day and helping me with my posture while en pointe."

"You'll see me again, it's not goodbye. I'll come visit. I'll just need to watch a show or two to double-check you."

Amelia tried to appear positive, but as soon as she said the words she regretted them. It would be very hard to sit in the audience, but she didn't want to leave with her fellow dancers thinking she held any bitterness toward them.

When the door opened again, she had to brace herself when she saw Lucy walk in. Lucy had texted Amelia the night before saying she was back from Florida and would meet her in the office today. Amelia knew seeing her was going to be hard, especially when she saw that her friend's eyes were already red from crying again. It took everything she had not to match her tears, but as she felt them begin to pool in her eyes, she knew there was nothing she could've done to prepare herself to face Lucy.

"I just can't believe it. Who will go next door for manicures with me during our breaks?" Lucy immediately rushed into Amelia's arms the second she stood up.

Amelia pulled back and gave her friend an encouraging smile. "We can still get manicures together. Besides, other people like manicures, not just us," she teased as they both settled into chairs.

"No one else in this group. I've asked." Lucy let out a small laugh, while drying her face with the tissues Sam handed them.

"Hey now, don't hog her. The rest of us want to get in our hugs too!" Ms. Higgens appeared at the doorway, reaching her arms out toward Amelia. The hug was strong and sincere, breaking down all efforts to keep her emotions at bay. She allowed herself to let the tears go.

"I don't even know what to say, Ms. Higgens," Amelia said, struggling to speak between breaths.

"Let's turn those tears into triumph. You've accomplished more leading roles here during these past eight years than any other dancer I've had. You're smart, capable, and maybe the most determined person I've ever met. Whatever you decide to do next, I just know you'll be amazing at it." Ms. Higgens gave her arms a firm squeeze before she let go and leaned on Sam's desk.

Amelia had heard her accomplishments listed off many times, but something inside felt... blank.

"Your success will never be forgotten, and neither will you—by us or any of your many fans," Ms. Higgens said.

The only fan she could see as she looked into Ms. Higgens's eyes was Andrew, who wouldn't have the chance to see the one performance he'd been waiting years to see. *The Nutcracker* was her favorite story as a child and, as her twin, he'd come to love it because it brought *her* so much happiness.

"Thank you," Amelia said, trying to show appreciation. After all, Ms. Higgens was not only known for her motherly instincts and Christmas craze, but when she gave a compliment, everyone knew it was genuine. Her strict-but-fair teachings had served Amelia well as she grew in her career and Ms. Higgens only showed pride in her face rather than tears. It brought the teacher satisfaction to know she'd played a huge part in each of her students' success. The last thing Amelia wanted was to bog down her ballet master with her sadness over Andrew.

"No need to thank me. I should be thanking *you*."

"Your talent has grown this theater," Sam chimed in. "Our ticket sales have increased every year since you started."

"All because of the wonderful team here." Amelia scanned the room one more time, taking in the three special faces. "If you don't mind, there's somewhere I'd like to go see before I leave." She needed to do one more thing before she left.

The older women nodded.

Lucy bent down to grab her purse. "I'm coming too."

"We're all coming," Sam said.

As the four women stood center stage, Amelia could

clearly see the empty chairs in the audience without the bright spotlights, but she could almost hear the cheering and clapping from dozens of past performances. It was as if she were in a time capsule, spinning through each dance and each final bow.

"Goodbye," she whispered.

≈

THE LINE IN THE COFFEE SHOP AN HOUR LATER WAS MUCH longer than Amelia first thought, but when she saw the sign, *Peppermint Mocha is back!* it suddenly made sense. In her mind, the Christmas season had officially begun now that the minty chocolate latte was on the menu, and everyone wanted to get a cup.

As she inched closer to the counter, she noticed that festive garland was strung along the front of the registers, large round ornaments hung from the ceiling above the baristas at different lengths, and string lights glittered along the shelves of coffee mugs and ground coffee for sale. By the time she reached the counter to order, her mouth was watering.

"Hi there! What can I get started for you?" the friendly barista said, her enthusiasm sparking a hint of much-needed Christmas spirit in Amelia.

"A medium peppermint mocha, hot please."

After she paid and spotted a small empty table in the corner, she made her way through the waiting customers and sat down. The speakers were directly above her and she began to hum along to a Christmas classic while waiting for her order. People came in and out, all busy with their days. Then it dawned on her: she wasn't slammed with hours of practice at the theater. This would be the first holiday season in a long time that she was able to actually take it all in. For a moment she wasn't entirely sure how she felt about that—but for now she soaked in the atmosphere, the people, and the décor.

When her order was ready, she smiled in anticipation as she took her first sip. The comforting minty beverage went down with ease. Fun coffee flavors were one of the few indulgences she allowed herself, and they always seemed to make her struggles melt away.

Sipping the last of her latte while responding to some comments on her last post and trying to decide how to break the news to her followers that dancing was now over, she saw the door swing open again and a mother with her young daughter came in. Normally this wouldn't phase her, but the little girl was wearing a bright pink leotard and tights, her tutu sticking out from under her coat. Amelia followed the girl's movements as she twirled behind her mother in line. She stood and threw away her empty cup, and got a little closer to them. As she continued watching the girl practice her spins, visions of her childhood ballet studio crept into her mind.

"Why don't you ever focus, Amelia?" Ms. Ruth's voice crashed through her thoughts. *"Just think of all the money your parents have wasted on these lessons. Aren't you ashamed of not doing better for them?"*

She blinked out of it, and the girl did a giant spin right into her mother, who patiently stayed still. "Nice turn!" Amelia said, smiling at her.

The girl suddenly stopped, backing into her mother. "Thank you," she said shyly.

Amelia looked at the woman. "Hi there, I couldn't help but notice the sweet little ballet dancer you have here."

"Oh, yes, she's always spinning and jumping wherever we go. And this leotard hardly comes off. It'll be her costume tomorrow night for trick-or-treating," the woman replied, looking down at her daughter who was now hiding between her legs. "But whenever someone notices her, she becomes timid. We're still unable to get her on stage for her ballet school's performances, but she loves dancing so much at the practices. It's all she talks about."

When she glanced down at the girl again, Ms. Ruth's voice echoed in Amelia's ear... "*See? Another mistake! No one wants to watch dancers who make too many mistakes!*"

With a quick inhale, Amelia focused on the curious young eyes watching her before answering. "When I was her age, I loved it too. Even when I made so many mistakes that I wasn't sure I would ever surmount them, I never stopped. As of today, I've danced professionally for fourteen years; since I was twenty."

"Did you hear that, Sophia?" The woman looked down at her daughter. "This nice lady is a professional ballerina. Just like you want to be!"

The little girl's eyes were fixed on Amelia as if she were her hero. "You are?" she asked, beaming up at her.

The crushing burden of the news from her doctor that week didn't need to rest on this girl's tiny shoulders. Amelia dropped down a little closer.

"I sure am." Amelia smiled proudly. "Let me see you do another twirl toward your mama."

Her mother had moved forward with the line, and Sophia put her hands up over her head and spun around, making the customers in line chuckle with delight.

"Perfect!" Amelia clapped as others joined her. "Take a bow!"

Sophia stuck one foot forward and bent toward it as more applause erupted, including the baristas'. The young girl's eyes widened as she realized the whole coffee shop was enjoying the show, except this time she didn't run and hide behind her mother.

"Thank you so much for doing that," her mother said while digging in her purse. "Would it be all right to get your email? I would love to stay in contact, especially as I navigate her love for dance." The woman held out a small notebook and pen.

"Absolutely," Amelia said, taking the notebook and scribbling down her email. "If you have any questions about dancing, I'm happy to answer."

"Great! My name is Maddie, by the way," she said, extending her hand.

"I'm Amelia Collins," she said, shaking the woman's hand.

"That rings a bell… Wait…" Maddie studied her for a moment. "Are you the Amelia Collins I saw in the news who suffered a big fall on stage last spring?"

Amelia nodded, trying to keep her composure. "That would be me."

"I knew I recognized you. I've seen your face on ads and social media. I follow a lot of dancer's accounts, as you can imagine with my little ballerina here." Maddie rested her hand on Sophia's shoulder. "Gearing up for another holiday performance?"

Amelia's heart picked up its pace, but she kept her expression neutral. This wouldn't be the only time she'd need to share with strangers that performances were over for her. "Unfortunately, I won't be able to return to the stage because of that injury."

Maddie's eyes widened. "Oh, no, that is heartbreaking. I'm so sorry I brought it up."

"Don't be. It's public knowledge now." Amelia looked past Maddie. "Looks like it's your turn in line."

"Come on, Sophia, let's order you a treat for such a great performance."

"Ok, Mommy!" Sophia spun back toward Amelia and motioned for her to come closer so she could whisper something to her. "I'm going to dance on the big stage just like you one day."

A tingle shot down Amelia's back. *Just like you one day.* The girl's words struck her. Happy images of herself as a little girl dressed in her ballet outfits, just like Sophia, while following her mother around town poured through her mind. How she'd always made her family wait at the dinner table nearly every night because she was still practicing. And how she'd practically stood on her seat to see better when her parents took her to watch her first professional show. No matter what obstacles came along the way or how cruel Ms. Ruth had been growing up—Amelia's love for dance had never slowed.

"I believe it. I can't wait to hear all about you one day."

"Bye!" The girl waved and hopped along behind her mother.

"Bye." Amelia waved back. "And, Sophia?" The girl stopped and waited. "Never ever stop dancing!"

"I won't!"

As Amelia walked out into the cold air, her head was spinning and childhood memories continued to cycle through her thoughts. She had pushed through the challenges as a young girl to keep going and she'd do it again somehow.

Increasing her stride, she quickly headed back to her apartment, feeling hope budding in her heart again. This injury wouldn't crumble her and, as she thought about what her mother told her days ago, she reminded herself again that she didn't need luck—not when she had hard work and determination.

CHAPTER 4

CHRISTMAS EVE, 1894

Joseph O'Shea

"Joseph, darling? Would you mind handing me a nappy?" his wife, Anna, called from the bedside. "I want to get William freshened up before your mother arrives."

Joseph retrieved the cloth and took it to Anna, then stood to watch her carefully change their son and kiss his forehead with gentle love afterward. William was six months old, yet Joseph still admired the motherly instincts Anna had gracefully embraced the moment their baby was born.

"The minced meat tarts smell gorgeous," Joseph said, heading over to check on the fire. "I better head outside to help Michael and find my mother. It's too cold today for her to be out there tending to the chickens."

"Oh, you know your mother. There's no stopping the woman. Even in freshly fallen snow." Anna appeared next to him with William.

A massive storm had blown through the week prior, blanketing the ground with nearly two feet of snow. Anna's parents and brother and his family were due to arrive shortly, and Joseph worried he hadn't cleared enough snow to allow their wagons through. It had taken all the townsmen to roll the snow as flat as they could in preparation for Christmas travel.

"I better go assist with the logs now," Joseph said, glancing down at Anna as she gazed up at him.

Her cheeks glistened against the crackling fire's reflection, making her look more beautiful than the day he'd first seen her. He wanted to reach for her, but a knock on the door grabbed his attention.

"Must be my family," Anna said, turning to settle William into the cradle. "Just in time for my brother's wife to help with Christmas dinner preparation for tomorrow."

"Hopefully," he said, and relief filled him when he opened the door and saw his wife's family had arrived safely. "Welcome!"

Anna came over to greet them. "Father, Mother, so good to see you." She hugged her parents. "I hope Samuel is taking good care of you both." She winked at her older brother.

"Or rather, *I* have a handle on things," her sister-in-law, Marie, playfully answered.

"How are you feeling?" Anna asked, placing her hands on Marie's swollen belly.

"The little one is growing fast. Due in two months' time."

Joseph took everyone's coat and led them in by the fire. "I'll just be outside for a bit, but please make yourselves comfortable."

"I'll assist," Anna's father said. "Not much I can do in the kitchen anyway."

"I'll join you," Samuel said, and both men followed Joseph out.

They spotted Michael still chopping wood by the barn, just as Joseph's mother appeared in front of them carrying a basket.

"Hello there." Ellen greeted them each with a kiss on the cheek. "Great to see you on this fine Christmas Eve morning!"

"Mother, you've been out here awfully long." Joseph looked at her with concern.

"Oh, goodness, stop fussing over me, Joseph. I'm grand. I was changing the bedding in the coop to keep the girls warm. Not much production from the hens lately, so perhaps the fresh wood shavings will warm them enough to give us a better clutch." Ellen smiled at Anna's father and Samuel. "Now if you'll excuse me, gentlemen, I must devote my attention to the women in the kitchen. We have a feast to prepare. And, Joseph"—she looked at him —"come see me when you return inside."

A short while later, with a new stack of logs stored nearby, the men returned to the house and sat by the fire to warm up. Joseph searched for his mother and found her standing over the cooking stove.

"It's just a delight to see how fast this cooker handles the dinner preparations. I'm so happy you had this installed in time for Christmas," Ellen said, admiring the newest addition to the kitchen.

"Yes, it's sure made Anna happy as well."

Joseph watched his mother grab a towel and open the oven to retrieve the fresh loaves. She placed them to the side of the stove, covered them with a towel to cool next to the other loaves, then turned to him.

"Now," she said, throwing a dish towel over her shoulder. "That should be enough bread."

"Looks about right," he said. "Did you want to see me for something?"

40

"Follow me." Ellen led him into her bedroom and opened the top drawer to her dresser, then turned to him holding a folded piece of paper. "Remember when I gave you the coin to present to Anna on your wedding day?"

"Of course," he said. "She still holds it from time to time, especially after we were blessed with William."

Ellen smiled at him. "It has certainly brought abundance to your lives."

"I'm sorry it didn't do the same for you and Father," Joseph said, instantly wishing he hadn't mentioned such a sensitive topic. "Sorry, Mother, I didn't mean to bring him up."

"Nonsense. Here or not, he will always be your father, just as much as Michael has been to you," she said.

Michael had married his mother when he was just a baby, filling in the role as his father all these years.

His mother handed him the paper. "Which is why I needed to give you this."

Joseph unfolded the letter.

"It's from your father," Ellen said. "Go on, have a read first. Then I'll explain."

December 5th, 1869

To my child,

This Christmas, hold the coin you received on your wedding day, and let it remind you that you have all you need to prosper and grow. Christmas is a time to spread joy and good will, and now that you are a parent, I wish you good luck that forever stays. So, my child, *remember to pass the coin down to your own, and watch your heart grow.*

Love,
Father

"Now wait just a moment, December 5th, 1869, was…" Joseph looked up from the letter.

"The day I married your father," Ellen said. "So he must have written it on our wedding day for our future first child. But I didn't know about it until he fell very ill on the ship while crossing over to America. He mentioned a 'letter' shortly before he passed, but I didn't know what he meant until I found it in his luggage."

"Oh, Mother, how terribly hard that must have been to have endured that. You've never talked about his passing in detail like this before."

"I know, but in a funny way it feels good to talk about it. Especially now, giving you this letter. I wish he was here to hand it to you himself, which I believe he had hoped to do the first Christmas you became a parent. But I always wondered why he wrote it, other than because of how much he loved Christmas…" His mother's eyes glistened over in thought. "After all, we weren't quite pregnant with you yet. I had only found out you were on the way a couple weeks after I arrived in America."

"I'm very happy he did write it." Joseph read the words again.

"Me too. I thought about giving it to you years ago, but I wanted to honor what I felt was his intention and wait for this very first Christmas after you became a father. Just know that despite what happened to him, he gave me you… the biggest blessing of my life. The love he and I had has never left my heart, and I couldn't get any luckier than that. Let's light the bayberry candle together, my son, and celebrate all we have."

As his mother lit the bayberry candle, an old New England tradition to seal in another year of health and prosperity, Joseph's heart swelled thinking about his Anna and baby William. He couldn't have asked for more.

"Merry Christmas, Mother," Joseph said, reaching his arms out to her, feeling his father's presence stronger than ever before.

"And the same to you, my dear son."

PRESENT DAY

Amelia startled out of a deep sleep and shot up in bed. The siren outside blared its horn again, pausing directly under her window. Mocha jumped off the bed to hide from the noise. Throwing the covers back, Amelia got up and peeked behind her curtains. A firetruck was slowly making its way through the intersection next to her building, continuing to alert traffic. Red lights spun across her windows; daybreak having barely cut through the early-morning twilight.

Instead of getting back in bed once the firetruck was out of earshot, she headed to the kitchen for some coffee. No use going back to bed now she was fully awake, as was half the city on this Saturday morning. While her coffee brewed, she fed Mocha and got her out yoga mat. Stretching was a habit she'd never give up, even without dance. It helped her feel balanced and strong for the day ahead. After she was loosened up, she went to pour a mug of coffee and sat on the couch. Mocha came too, purring against her.

As more sirens echoed in the distance, she sighed. City

life had perks, like great food choices and entertainment; however, the noise had really started to bother her. Now she wasn't at the studio and distracted, it annoyed her even more. In her younger days, she'd meet her fellow dancers after practice at a bar or for a late-night dinner, barely feeling the early morning alarm the next day. But that fast-paced lifestyle didn't interest her anymore. Even when she was younger, she'd always thought that someday, when her career was over, she'd like to retire out in the countryside somewhere. She loved old farmhouses, partially because they seemed so peaceful and cozy—a nice contrast to her hectic life—and partially because they reminded her of her grandfather, who used to restore them on top of running his building company.

Her family visited her grandparents many summers during her childhood, and she would jump at the opportunity to go to work with him. She remembered walking by his side as he showed her the beautiful workmanship in those old buildings—the time and care that went into the construction of a house built to last, meant to shelter a family for generations. Finding a nice old farmhouse, fixing it up, and enjoying the quiet and calm away from the city had always been her dream for her life someday. She just hadn't expected someday to come quite so soon.

After setting her coffee on the table, she reached for her phone. Ignoring the hundreds of responses to the social media post she'd finally made the night before, announcing her end with Northeast Performing Arts, she opened her browser instead. She'd respond to her followers soon enough, but for now she wanted to check out her favorite site; a little ritual she'd had for years when she needed a pick-me-up and curiosity had her interest.

She went straight to the bookmarked link that showed homes for sale in Litchfield County, Connecticut. She'd driven through the area many times going to and from her parents' home in Massachusetts and loved it more every time she'd passed through. Not all the houses were farmhouses, but plenty were, and it always soothed her to scroll through the available options and think of what her future could look like there.

Just as she was about to leave the website, one of the homes caught her attention. A gorgeous white country farmhouse in a picturesque setting filled the screen when she clicked on it. The black shutters, large front porch, and mature evergreen trees around the front drew her in. Scrolling through the photos, she paused at the large red barn that was part of the property and the fenced pasture area around it. What a dream place to live!

She read through the specs and looked at the interior pictures. The property dated back to the mid-1800s—it could use a facelift, for sure, but she remembered her grandfather's lessons and could see how solid and strong the construction was. It was exactly the sort of farmhouse she'd always wanted.

She was certain it was well beyond what she could afford, especially with the repairs it needed, but she couldn't help but check. Her jaw dropped open when she saw the listing price.

"This must be a mistake," she said out loud. "A house that size, with that much land and a horse barn… It can't be that cheap."

She searched specifically for houses in that area—White Bridge, Connecticut. After comparing the price of other local houses for sale, the price definitely didn't make sense. Back on the listing page, she found the real estate agent's contact information and sent her an email.

Hello, my name is Amelia Collins, and I came across your listing for 12 Maple Ridge Lane. I noticed the price was very low and I'm wondering if that is a mistake? The description just mentioned sold as is. Looking forward to hearing back.

But was she? Moving was such a big step, one she hadn't thought she'd make for several more years. Was she rushing things? What kind of life would she have in a little town like White Bridge? *But then, what kind of life will I have here when I'm not dancing anymore?* Maybe a move was just what she needed—a new beginning in a place where she could explore what else was out there for her.

She opened the recording app on her phone, checked the lighting, and tidied up her hair a bit, then started recording.

"Hi, friends! Thanks so much for all the messages of support. I appreciate you all more than I can say. I also noticed a lot of questions asking me what comes next, and the truth is, I'm not sure. But... a possible first step may have just presented itself." She turned the phone toward her computer to show the listing of the house—she'd edit it before posting to make sure the address was blacked out in case she *did* end up buying it. "Look at this place—isn't it gorgeous? I'm thinking of buying it. I know what you guys are thinking—it's a big change, right? But now seems to be the time for big changes. I want to move forward with my life, not stay stuck in a rut." The more she said, the more certain she felt that she was on to something. "I think I could have a really beautiful fresh start in a place like this."

If she were her mother, she might say something about her luck turning around—but she was *not* her mother. There was no such thing as luck. She worked hard saving her money. Still, if the price really was correct, this might just be a very good thing that had fallen into her lap. Life could be random like that. The important thing was not to let chances slip past.

"I know a lot of you follow me for the behind-the-scenes look at a ballerina's life, and I know you may not want to go on this journey with me. If that's the case, I totally understand, and I wish you all the best. But if you *are* interested in seeing what comes next for me, I hope you'll enjoy the ride with me! I'll be posting all along the way. Take care, friends. I'll talk to you soon!"

She ended the recording. She'd have to clean it up a bit and hold off on posting it for now. She might get an email from the realtor that said the price was a mistake. But if it *was* legit... She'd post the update and see if her online following was willing to join her on a new adventure.

Or was this whole idea absurd? She needed a second opinion. She quickly checked the time and figured it was late enough to make a call.

Lucy picked up, groaning. "I know you must miss me already, but if I'm going to live up to your memory at the theater, I need my sleep."

"All those sirens didn't wake you?" Lucy lived only a short distance away so, surely, she must've heard the commotion.

"Ever hear of sound machines? I'm surprised you don't have one."

"The thought never crossed my mind, but I just came across something and had to call you. Sorry to wake you."

Lucy yawned through the phone. "Okay, let's hear it."

"I'm texting you a link right now. Tell me when you get it."

A few seconds later, Lucy responded, "I got it, but why am I looking at a farmhouse listing..."—she paused—"dated from 1870? It's absolutely gorgeous though, wow!"

"I think I'm going to make an offer."

47

"You're going to what now?" Lucy suddenly sounded much more awake.

"Buy it—if that price is real. Which it's probably not. But if it *is*…"

"You're going to buy a random house out in the country?"

"You know that was always my plan. How many times have I talked about it?"

"A lot," Lucy admitted. "I just always figured I'd be able to talk you out of it when the day came. I mean, why would you want to live out in the middle of nowhere?"

"Just because *you* can't imagine living anywhere but a city doesn't mean I'm the same way," Amelia said.

Lucy sighed. "Yeah, I know. And it *is* pretty. I guess I just don't like the idea of you being so far away. But if this is really what you want, you know I'll support you. Just don't rush into anything, okay? Go look at it and really think it through. And let me go with you to check it out. I'll get Ms. Higgens to give me a day off. When I say it's to help you with something, I'm sure she'll understand."

"But you're in the thick of rehearsals for *The Nutcracker*."

"And I've danced my role about nine different times in my lifetime. It's all good, I promise."

"Okay, you're right. And I could really use your input and company. I already contacted the listing agent to double-check the price."

"Yeah, that is a low listing price. If there was no mistake, the house might be missing a roof and walls for all we know. There's no telling how old those photos are."

"Then I better learn how to make a good fire in one of those massive fireplaces," Amelia joked.

"Am I going to lose you to country life? Are we thinking full-on farm? Horses, cows, all of the above?" Lucy teased and they both laughed.

"I'll let you know what the realtor says when she gets back to me."

After she hung up, Amelia turned on the shower and let the hot water freshen her up, filling her with energy despite the rude awakening she'd had earlier. The more she thought about the house, the more interested she became. After changing into warm leggings and an oversized sweater, the screen on her phone lit up next to her on the bed and she saw she'd received a new email. She opened the app and saw the listing agent's name and quickly opened the message.

Good morning, Amelia,

I just saw your inquiry about 12 Maple Ridge Lane and before my Saturday gets busy with open houses and showings, I wanted to shoot you a quick reply. Yes, that is the correct listing price. The house is being sold as is because it needs a lot of work. The price is also low because the seller is very motivated and factored in all the work needed. But with that said, I can assure you that most of the work needed isn't too major and not an immediate priority. The house has been thoroughly checked, and I can provide letters showing that the wiring is up to date, the plumbing works, the HVAC system is fully functional, and termite control is in place. The roof is old and will need replacing within the next ten years, but I've been assured that it'll get through the next few winters, barring any unexpected disaster. Of course, I'm sure you'll want to hire your own inspectors to verify all this, but I do want to be clear that the house is move-in ready, even if some things might be a little outdated and rundown. Let me know if you have any more questions or want to set up a showing. I have a lot of availability on Monday.

Amelia immediately hit reply and began to type without giving it a second thought.

Yes, I am interested in coming to look at it. Monday works great for me. Just let me know a good time for you.

A spark of joy ignited in her. She'd been drained since the news from Dr. Reed and had felt so lost. As she opened her texts, the new direction her mother reassured her would come was becoming clear as she sent Lucy a message:

Let's go check out that farmhouse. The listing price is correct and the realtor is ready to show!

CHAPTER 5

"*A*melia, look how gorgeous those evergreens are with the snow on them!" Lucy rolled down her window the following Monday and a rush of icy air instantly filled the car. "Slow down, I need to get a picture."

Amelia quickly glanced in her rearview mirror to make sure no one was behind her, then carefully pulled over to the shoulder. "This is a good spot, jump out instead and take it."

Luckily Thanksgiving was still weeks away, so traffic was light on the windy main road to White Bridge. Driving the country roads in the mountains was intimidating, but she'd have to get used to it if she moved. She hoped her little white Kia was up to the challenge. Maybe she should trade it in for an all-wheel SUV.

Lucy got out and began taking pictures from as many angles as she could, and Amelia laughed when her friend kept turning back to look at her with her mouth wide open. This wasn't the first time Amelia had seen such winter beauty, especially having grown up in western Massachusetts, but as a Floridian, it still excited Lucy.

"This just proves how long our hours have been at the

theater," Lucy said, breathless from the cold air and excitement as she got back in the car. It had lightly snowed earlier that morning and the Litchfield hills were postcard perfect, as if they were waiting to show Lucy the frosty magic. "I've been living in Connecticut for almost eight years and I've hardly explored any of the countryside or these mountains. I'm not saying you've converted me from being a city girl, but I will admit that it's breathtaking up here."

"I'm glad you got the day off and get to enjoy this." Amelia slowly maneuvered back onto the road. The GPS informed them they were only fifteen minutes from their destination and both women sat in silence, admiring the landscape as Amelia carefully made her way along the roads. A long, red, covered bridge came into view, and she slowed and peeked at Lucy, who nearly jumped out before the car came to a full stop.

"You can't get more New England than that!" While Lucy walked to as many spots as she could to capture the bridge, Amelia sent the realtor a quick text to say they were close. The woman had said the roads would be windy and, with the recent snowfall, she told Amelia to take her time.

Rolling down her window, Amelia called out to Lucy, "We're going to be late! We can always stop on the way back for round two of pictures!"

Her friend hurried back to the car. When they crossed over the two-lane, concrete, arched bridge, Lucy scrolled on her phone.

"Okay, I had to look it up. This bridge was built a few times, but floods destroyed it. The final construction concluded in 1864," Lucy said, reading off her phone. "Are we going to make it over this thing?"

Amelia smiled. "It's just preparing me for what I'm about to see with this old farmhouse."

A short drive later the GPS informed them that they'd

arrived, but it was a little unclear where. They were on Maple Ridge Lane, but the few homes visible from the road were widely spread apart and no mailbox had number 12 on it.

"Should we call the realtor?" Lucy suggested.

"Good idea." Amelia parked and picked up her phone, noticing a text from the realtor answering her earlier message.

No problem. I'm here, but there is no rush. I forgot to mention to you earlier that the mailbox is directly across from the second driveway on the left, sort of hidden in the bushes.

Amelia looked up and saw that she had to turn around to find the second driveway on the left and, sure enough, surrounded by overgrown weeds, sat an old mailbox with number 12 on it.

"Oh, boy," Lucy said. "This will be interesting."

The long driveway was covered in a couple inches of snow, but because it was flat, Amelia was able to get over it. Large maple trees with old syrup buckets still attached lined the driveway, and she could almost picture how beautiful the red leaves would be in the fall. When they passed the last of the trees, the white farmhouse came into view, and she had to stop the car for a moment to absorb what she was seeing.

"Wow..." Amelia said, her eyes wide with wonder. She immediately pictured herself sitting on the spacious front porch that wrapped around the side with a cup of coffee and Mocha on her lap.

"Wow is right," Lucy said.

"I'm in love already."

Lucy shrugged. "I'm not sure I see it. I mean, I'm definitely glad it matches the pictures—no missing walls or anything. But the entire house needs to be painted. Do you realize how much that alone costs?"

"No, but I'm about to find out." Amelia put the car in drive and parked next to the other car at the end of the drive. "I can't wait to see inside."

"Let's just hope the flooring is in place so we don't fall into the basement. The theater doesn't need both of us out of commission."

Amelia shook her head. "You're too much. Come on, let's go in. And keep an open mind. These old houses are tougher than you think. My grandfather used to work on them, and he always talked about the craftsmanship from that era, how much care they put into building a strong home. I think you'll be surprised at how well it holds up."

A man and woman came out onto the front porch and waved at them.

"You must be Amelia," the woman called with a friendly smile. "I'm Judy, the realtor and this is David, who is acting as the owner's power of attorney. I'm glad you made it. It's quite a drive from New Haven."

"Yes, but a beautiful one. These mountains are amazing," Amelia said, climbing the few steps to meet them on the porch and shaking both their hands.

"Just wait until you see them in the fall foliage," Judy said.

Amelia gestured toward Lucy. "This is my friend, Lucy. She's here to take a look with me."

"Hi there, Lucy, glad you could join us." Judy smiled at Lucy then turned back to Amelia. "Now, before we go in, I just want to warn you that it absolutely needs work. Like many historical homes in this area, the same family has owned this home since it was built in 1870. The current owner, a man named Timothy Allard, is in a hospice facility after a long battle with cancer. David is here to act on his behalf."

David motioned around him. "A property like this requires a lot of maintenance, as you could imagine, and Mr. Allard couldn't keep up with it once he got sick. Plus he is an older man and set in his ways, so he didn't bother with a lot of updates over the years. The kitchen appliances, for example, are pretty old. They still work, but they don't have the digital bells and whistles you might be used to."

"Okay," Amelia said. "My grandfather used to restore old homes. I have some understanding of what goes into it, and I love old buildings like this. I want to see it have a new life again and I am envisioning the potential already. I don't mind a few outdated appliances or features that need restoration, as long as the house itself is solid."

"Great! The place really does have good bones, and the land and home and even the barn…"—Judy pointed across the grass toward the old red barn—"will be spectacular once it's all fixed up. And the price…"

"You can't beat," Amelia filled in.

"No, you certainly can't. I couldn't believe how low it was set for. When you restore it, this property has potential to match the other homes on this street, which are nearly double this asking price. Shall we step out of the cold?" Judy led them inside. "I want to add that the house has been emptied, except for some antique furniture Mr. Allard thought to leave in case the new owners were interested. They sort of complete the look of the home. But if you don't want them, they will be removed."

"I'll let you get to it, Judy," David said. "Ladies, if you don't mind, I'll be in the kitchen catching up on a few phone calls while you tour the home. Let me know if you have any questions that I can help you with." He nodded and walked away.

"Why does Mr. Allard want to sell something that has been in the family so long?" Lucy asked. "Isn't there any other family he could give it to?"

"Very good question," Judy said. "I'm not sure about other family. It's something David hasn't disclosed. I asked, but he's kept mum. Mr. Allard was insistent on selling without any discussion, so I backed off. Ready to take a look?"

Amelia nodded, but she couldn't shake what Judy had just shared. A farmhouse that had been in a family for so long was something she couldn't imagine just giving up, but perhaps there really was no one else to pass it along to once Mr. Allard fell ill.

As she listened to Judy begin the tour, her thoughts quickly shifted away from the owner's decision to sell and toward the timeless beauty that surrounded her. The wide-planked wooden floor felt solid and sturdy as the three women walked into a living area. Dark wooden paneling lined the top edges of the walls, giving the room a classic feel. The space looked and felt warm—and Amelia noted that the HVAC definitely worked. The house also seemed pretty well insulated against drafts.

"Where we're standing in is what they called 'the front room.' It was considered the most formal area in the house and used for important family events and social gatherings."

"Ah, okay. I remember learning about that from my grandfather. I bet lots of weddings took place in here. Would this home be considered a colonial?"

"Yes and no. It's a traditional New England farmhouse, which is why there is that big wraparound porch, which became popular in the 1900s," Judy answered. "I believe the porch was added around that time. But the base design of the home draws on concepts rooted in earlier, traditional colonial design."

On the far end sat a bricked fireplace so large Amelia could almost stand in it. She walked over and ran her hand over the pale green mantle. Most of the paint was still intact.

"All the mantels were custom made in the early twentieth

century," Judy said and pointed to the fireplace. "This was the central fireplace for the other two on this main floor, before the home expanded and a second floor was built with more fireplaces."

"It's so well crafted and designed," Amelia said, imagining all the meals served from the fireplace.

"There's another one in here," Lucy's muffled voice called out from behind a wall. "Except it's a little... caved in."

Amelia found her standing in what appeared to be a dining room. A vintage chandelier was lying on the floor with all the pieces intact.

"What a beautiful lighting piece," Amelia said, looking up at the ceiling where it used to hang.

The realtor flipped through her notes. "It's a brass chandelier dated from around 1940. Not sure how it ended up on the floor though."

The fireplace where Lucy was still standing was indeed crumbled. It didn't seem to present any kind of hazard, but Amelia would need to have an inspector check it.

"Looks like the bricks couldn't hold any longer with this one." Amelia bent down to pick up one of the bricks and white powder dusted all around her before she placed it back down.

"Careful with those, the main chimney that runs all the home's fireplaces is spalling from age and water damage," Judy said, coming over to her. "Which means it'll need replacing. Repairing that is a big expense, but it is one of the few repairs that needs immediate attention so it doesn't start to affect the structural integrity of the home. A lot of the bricks you'll see in the other fireplaces will be decaying from moisture like these, and it would make sense to take care of all of them at the same time, but your inspector will go over the details of that more."

"Oh, boy," Lucy said, glancing at Amelia with a concerned look. "Should we be making a list of all these issues?"

"I'll give you these notes from the owner. Of course, a full inspection will find other things as well." Judy motioned toward the other entranceway of the dining room. "Would you like to head to the kitchen? You'll be pleasantly surprised that there isn't much to do there except updating appliances. It's a good size and fully workable, with a lot of counter space for cooking."

"Well there's some positive news!" Lucy said, while Amelia gave her a slight nudge. "Plenty of room to get creative with those culinary skills of yours."

"Ha-ha." Amelia playfully rolled her eyes. "With a new country kitchen, I'll just have to learn."

The realtor stopped at the doorway and smiled at their banter. "I'm sure this kitchen will inspire you," she said and turned toward it. "Okay, here we are."

The large open room was indeed a surprise. "You were right, it is a good size," Amelia said.

David got up from the table with the phone glued to his ear and walked past them to allow them to look around.

"It was last updated in 1968. Mr. Allard's father had built a small addition, adding this breakfast area and the bay windows, which I think was all very well done. The appliances were last updated in the nineties. This is by far my favorite room in the home. So bright and cheerful. It also features this…" Judy pointed to yet another fireplace that sat adjacent to the bay windows.

"Another fireplace?" Amelia asked, mesmerized by the cozy historic feel it instantly brought her, even if the chimneys weren't usable at the moment. "I love that."

"Me too," Judy said. "Once you restore the chimneys, you can use it in here or just keep it as more of a decorative element. What a feel it gives in here, right?"

Amelia nodded and continued to the rest of the kitchen. The dark wooden beams, like in the other rooms, were still intact across the ceilings, which instantly appealed to her—however, the rest was in need of some modern love. The linoleum flooring had definitely seen better days, and the gingerbread molding on the wooden cabinets would be the first to go. In her mind's eye she could picture the updates perfectly, with lighter cabinets and new appliances, but keeping the farmhouse feel.

"I already have ideas," Amelia said.

"And lots of cooking classes ahead of you," Lucy teased.

The realtor laughed. "This home certainly has a motivating feel to learn something new, doesn't it?" Judy looked at Amelia with hopeful eyes. "I can see the wheels turning in your head from here."

"Oh, they are spinning wildly!" Amelia glanced out the bay windows to a perfect view of the red barn. "I'm torn between picturing what I want it to look like someday and imagining how it looked in the past." The barn stood out against the pristine white backdrop of the snow-covered property, creating a stunning contrast, and she could easily envision horses one day in her view. "And how beautiful those fields would look with horses again."

"From a ballet professional to an equestrian, this girl can do it all," Lucy said.

"You know I'm no equestrian, but if I can learn to cook, I can learn how to take care of a horse," Amelia replied and looked at Judy. "Who knows what I'd do with the barn. I guess I'd figure out something."

"You dance professionally?" Judy asked Amelia, lifting a brow. "That's impressive."

"Used to. I danced for fourteen years, but due to an injury I'll be hanging up my pointe shoes from now on."

"I'm sorry to hear that." The realtor gestured around the

kitchen. "But this home could at least keep you busy and distracted from such a hard change."

"It'll certainly do that all right," Lucy said, examining the room again.

"Lucy is also a professional dancer, so she'll keep the stage life going for me down in New Haven." Amelia smiled at her friend.

"Well, I'm in awe of both of you for your talent. I'll have to look up your next performance, Lucy, and come watch."

Amelia's heart sank knowing that next performance was *The Nutcracker*.

As if Lucy could read her mind, she tugged Amelia's sleeve. "Come on," Lucy said. "Let's go see what kind of repairs you would need to do upstairs."

After thoroughly walking through the four bedrooms and two bathrooms upstairs, which thankfully only needed some cosmetic updates, they walked outside toward the barn. As Amelia got closer, she realized how much bigger it was than it first appeared; the triangular roof standing tall above her once they reached the barn doors.

"These large doors are located on the gable end, which means they're not on the same side, as most New England bank-styled barns, which are built into hills. I heard you mention horses, and this barn is ready to house them again if you wanted to get serious about that." Judy walked over to open the doors. "Want to see inside?"

"Yes, I'd love to," Amelia said. The earthy smell of hay wafted around her, even though the place was completely empty. Amelia peered up at the vaulted ceiling.

"It's about thirty-five feet high, with six built-in stalls on this level and a hayloft above." Judy pointed up to where some old piles of hay were visible.

"The roof is so high. I was expecting a straight hallway down between these stables."

"I believe it was designed to get the wagons in here as well as the animals, which is why there is a lot of wide-open space."

"Makes sense."

"There's a much smaller barn outside and down on the other side of one of the horse paddocks that was actually the original barn before they built this one"—Judy flipped through her papers—"in 1922. But it's large enough for a couple horses. And has a chicken coop."

"Chickens!" Lucy said. "Now we're talking."

"Chickens are actually not a bad idea." Amelia chuckled. "I'll send you a dozen eggs every now and then."

As Lucy and Judy fell into conversation, Amelia looked down the barn, her thoughts pulling her away from them. The history wrapped around her began to unravel as she walked through the space. How many farmers had tended to these stables? Would she really be able to take care of this home? Lost in a whirlwind of curiosity, she turned from the stables and noticed Lucy and Judy watching her. As she stood there on the stunning historical property, the idea of tucking herself away there filled her with excitement. Bringing this place back to life would be hard work, but that had never scared her before. And something about it felt *right* in a way she couldn't quite explain. She just knew this was where she wanted to be.

Walking back to them, she looked directly at the realtor and spoke without a second's doubt. "I'm ready to make an offer."

Lucy's mouth dropped open. "Are you sure?" she asked. "Do you really think you can handle a house and barn?"

"The barn can stay empty, there's no need to fill it," Judy said, gripping the property sheet.

Amelia walked over to the barn door and looked out. The snowy field glistened from the sun's rays, the quiet drawing her in. There was nothing to wake her here, just silence to think about her new future and a house to make her own.

Turning around, she faced both women, already thinking about the video update she wanted to record for her online friends. "Yes. More than sure."

She had no other explanation except that it felt right, and something in her heart knew more was about to unfold in her life. And she couldn't wait to find out what.

CHAPTER 6

"No tree yet, Mom." Amelia put the phone on speaker and placed it on the bathroom counter to fix her hair. "Remember, I don't officially own the house yet. Once I move in, I will make sure to get one."

It was three days before Thanksgiving and in one hour she was due at the lawyer's office to close on the farmhouse. The whirlwind of the past month was at its final step. With a cash sale, everything moved very quickly, and between packing up her apartment—her landlord graciously letting her out of the lease with the purchase of her home—and planning the move, she hadn't been able to slow down once.

While the process had its occasional hard moments with all that was needed for buying a home, everything continued to move forward at a steady pace. Amelia didn't mind because she'd wanted to be in her home and settled by Christmas and felt blessed that she was going to be able to do that. Her grandparents would have been so happy to watch all this happen. It was what they had wanted when they gave her that money: for Amelia to have a home of her own.

When she had woken up that morning, the heaviness in

her chest lifted and she was able to draw in a deep breath for the first time in weeks after anxiously awaiting the appraisal, the final inspection reports, and the bank to prepare for the purchase. Everything was now set for her to sign for the home, and she must have checked to make sure she had the cashier's check in her purse about ten times in the past couple hours.

"Good. What better way to make it your own than to get a tree for it?" her mother said now. "I know... Since you're not coming home for Thanksgiving, let me come down Friday and stay for the weekend. We can finish some more shopping and get the tree together. I want to see this town where you're settling."

Amelia hesitated. Guilt poked at her that she wasn't making her way to her parents' house for Thanksgiving, but with the move planned for Saturday morning, there were so many last-minute things she needed to do.

"I can't wait to show it to you, but..." Her stomach swam with butterflies. "I think I need my first weekend there to settle on my own." She was already overwhelmed with such a big transition, and though her parents always meant well, she wasn't up for hosting them the first weekend the house was hers.

There was a pause before her mother spoke again. "Okay, honey. If that's what you want. You know we're here if you need us, right?"

"I know. I'm fine, Mom, I promise. I have to go, but I love you."

When she hung up, she stared at herself in the mirror, thinking about the shift her life was about to take. It was scary, but it was exciting too. Pulling on her coat, Amelia walked outside. She was doing this, risks and all.

~

"I know I've said this before, but from what the appraisal showed this property to be worth and how low you've purchased it for, this is a great investment," the lawyer said. "Have a look at the latest surveyor reports here. It's actually just under six acres, so a little more than we thought." He handed Amelia the paperwork so she could see where the property lines began and ended.

"Moving from the city to the country is going to be such a change with all this extra space." She studied the surveyor's notes. "But I think it will be a good change."

"Are you ready to sign for your new home?" The lawyer picked up a pen.

Amelia took it and scribbled her name across the line. Placing the pen down and sliding the papers back to the lawyer, she looked at her feet. The day she'd walked onto an empty stage as a young girl to prepare for her very first solo flashed across her mind—how she had looked down at her feet while standing on the blank stage that day, willing them not to let her down. Hours later the stage was transformed into a magical winter scene for the dress rehearsals, the change lifting her confidence to perform.

The lawyer handed her the keys and reached across the table to shake her hand. "Congratulations, Amelia. You are now a homeowner."

"You haven't had your final curtain draw yet," her brother's voice whispered in her mind. New keys in her hand, she smiled. Was this what Andrew had meant? She wasn't sure yet, but she was excited to keep going and find out.

Twelve Maple Ridge Lane… a new blank stage to navigate through the ever-changing choreography of life—all on her own. No stage crew would be there to meet her and make the transformation. This time, it was all up to her.

~

"Maybe we can find somewhere that's serving leftover turkey after the light show." Amelia peeked over at Lucy, holding in her laughter as she slowly switched lanes.

The post-Thanksgiving traffic was in full swing as they made their way to New Haven's famous drive-through light display that Friday evening. They had a tradition of going every year to see all the lit-up Christmas characters, then grabbing a bite to eat. The theater had always given them a few days off for Thanksgiving in the past so it was the only time they could go.

"Stop! It was my first try with cooking a turkey by myself." Lucy crossed her arms in defense. "Your mom's face through the screen still cracks me up." Both women laughed, remembering how they video called her in a panic when they realized the turkey was way overcooked. "I totally misread the cooking times."

"I'm going to hear, 'You two should have just driven up like you always do' until next Thanksgiving," Amelia said, pulling off onto the exit. "At least her suggestions on how to moisten it a bit worked. Somewhat."

Lucy had been a huge help to Amelia, offering to help with the packing in between rehearsals and staying with her for Thanksgiving. With hours of dance practice at the theater every holiday season, flying home for Lucy was never an option, and she'd always spent Thanksgiving with Amelia in Massachusetts anyway. This year they'd tackled the dinner all on their own for the first time, and it had made Amelia grateful for her mother's cooking when they bombed many of the dishes.

"You better start watching all the cooking lessons you can find before moving out to the country where takeout can't save you," Lucy said, turning up the heat in the car. "That was a lot of bird to toss out."

"I couldn't find half my cookware. Most of it is in boxes."

Amelia had spent all morning cleaning up their Thanksgiving disaster and packing the rest of the kitchen.

"Uh-huh… so that's the excuse we're going with?" Lucy teased. "We should have just ordered takeout like I originally suggested."

"Better luck next year."

Lucy chuckled. "Yeah… at your parents' house."

"Or"—Amelia glanced at Lucy—"in my new farmhouse."

"Yes! It will be exciting to host your family there." Lucy smiled at her. "Just leave the turkey to your mom."

"Oh, yes, and just about every side dish." Amelia pulled up to a stoplight and noticed the line of traffic just ahead for the light show. Soft snow began to fall and she turned on the defroster. "Well, isn't this just the most festive setting for tonight? Snow to add a twist to the show."

"Sure is. I don't think it's ever snowed on the nights we've come in the past." Lucy looked out the window. "It'll make tonight more special. Consider this our little celebration for being an official homeowner!"

Amelia smiled at her friend. "A perfect way to celebrate."

"I meant to ask, but I've been so consumed with rehearsals all week, followed by our Thanksgiving cooking nightmare… how did the final inspection report turn out?"

"The roof will need full replacement in the next few years, as expected, but everyone agrees that I still have a little time before I have to commit to that. It was the septic that I was holding my breath for, but it just needs a line repair. Luckily the system was replaced about ten years ago."

"All of that is foreign to me, but if you're happy about it then I am too." Lucy shifted toward her. "How did the conversation with your parents go last night after I left? I know they've been on you pretty hard since they first heard."

Amelia bit her lip. She still felt bad for the way her family had first found out about the house—from her online post rather than straight from her. She just hadn't known how to broach the subject, worried her parents would think she was rushing into such a big commitment... which she pretty much had.

"My father had such a hard time picking out a new TV last year that my mother gave up, and they *still* don't have a new one. He doesn't make decisions very easily, so if I told him I was buying the first house I looked at, he would have tried to stop me. I guess I just didn't want to face that with them, which ultimately backfired because he's spent the last couple weeks doing just that anyway."

"Yeah, but your parents are great. Don't you think they'll come around to it?"

"I'm sure they will... eventually." Amelia fell in line behind the other cars after the light turned. "And last night we finally got to an understanding with each other that this is what I'm going to do, and they would just need to accept that. It's a done deal."

Amelia thought about the conversation and was still a bit surprised by some of the things her parents had said. She'd expected they'd still be worried about her making such a big investment without taking more time to think it over, especially since she was using all the money her grandparents had left her for the purchase of the home, but that wasn't their only concern.

"*I was thinking...*" her mom had said. "*You'll be so on your own out there. No friends, no support network. Nothing to fill your time now without the theater. Won't you get lonely?*"

It was honestly something she hadn't considered. For her entire adult life, she'd been so busy, so focused on her career, on perfecting her craft, that she'd never really had time to get lonely—even though she lived by herself and rarely dated. But out in her new farmhouse, with no hours-long rehearsals or rushed performance schedules or modeling jobs, she'd have time to really sit with herself. Maybe it would be lonely, at least a little, but she thought it would be good for her. The end of her dance career marked a turning point in her life, and she was eager to discover new possibilities about herself outside of being a ballerina. Besides, she still had social media to fill in some of those quiet hours ahead of her. The income she'd earned from her online presence was going to be a huge support while she figured out her next career move.

Lucy chuckled. "Your mother will be first up to help you decorate it once the shock wears off." They moved up with the cars. "The line to get in isn't too bad yet."

"No, it's not," Amelia said, looking ahead at the arched entrance with twinkling lights in the distance. "It's moving pretty steadily, and we made good time despite the traffic on the highway."

"This might be our last light-show hurrah now you're moving to the middle of nowhere."

Amelia grinned. Lucy had been by her side through the entire process of buying the farmhouse, but she didn't hide her feelings about Amelia being farther away. "I'll be less than an hour from you. I think I can swing getting down to New Haven every now and then."

Lucy rested her hand on Amelia's shoulder. "I know I tease you for leaving the city, but I'm proud of you."

"For buying a home?"

"Not just any home, one that will require work to fix up, and buying it all by yourself in a town you don't know anything about." Lucy shifted back against her seat. "I know I couldn't do it."

"I don't know about that—I think you could, if you needed to. Sometimes life leaves you with no choice but to try something new."

"It sure does." They sat in comfortable silence and

watched the snow fall while they waited to reach the entrance. Then Lucy pointed ahead. "It's our turn!"

Amelia switched the radio station to the accompanying audio for the light show and Bing Crosby's classic melody "White Christmas" filled the car. They drove under the entrance, and Amelia briefly rolled down the window to receive their 3D glasses that brought the white and blue snowflakes hanging above them to life.

"The real snow twirling around the lights makes it all so perfect." Amelia slowly moved forward, keeping her distance from the car ahead.

For the next half hour, the women sat in silence, enjoying the enchanted animated figures and holiday scenes. When they reached the end, they parked and got out to walk through Santa's wonderland. The giggling children made it all seem magical as Amelia watched them rush ahead of their parents to go see Santa.

"Look how sweet the kids are," Lucy said, standing by the tented entry while a family passed by.

"It makes the holiday experience better every year."

After walking through and admiring all the animated figures that carried on from the light show, and stopping at the stations filled with vendors selling various handmade items, they came out the other end with two steaming cups of hot cider and walked back to the car.

Turning on the engine, Amelia cranked up the heat and began to reverse. *Moving on*, she thought, mentally saying goodbye to this place. Yes, she'd probably be back again for visits, but it wouldn't be the same. It wouldn't be home anymore. With the keys now in her hand, the move to White Bridge was becoming very real.

CHAPTER 7

ig flakes fell like petals, thick and fast against Amelia's windshield the following morning. It was moving day, and the snow squall couldn't have come at a worse time as she made her way along the winding roads. After pulling over to wait it out, she turned up the heat and noticed the lit-up reindeer and lighted garland draped around the red front door on the home next to her. How beautiful it all looked together. Ideas began to swirl faster than the falling snow, as she created holiday scenes on her new front porch in her mind.

"Now I am turning into my mother," she said out loud, shaking her head with a laugh. It had only been five days since the closing, but she couldn't stop imagining all the possibilities of updating this home.

The clouds began to lighten up, bringing an end to the whiteout conditions. Making her way back onto the road, she glanced in her rearview mirror, wondering if the movers were okay as they tackled the slick roads. Up ahead, Amelia saw the red bridge and knew she was close, but it looked even more enclosed with the amount of snow built up around the entrance from all the snowstorms they'd already had. As she crossed the bridge, panic rose as she realized it most likely wasn't tall enough for the moving truck.

She pulled over again and dialed the number the movers had given her before they left her apartment.

"Hello, Rob's Movers," a man answered loudly above the noise of the truck.

"Hi, this is Amelia Collins."

"Amelia, hi! We were just going to call you. That burst of snow caused a long pause for us, but it looks to be clearing now. We stopped at a coffee shop to wait it out," the mover said. "But we haven't even made our way up the mountain yet."

"I'm glad you found somewhere warm to wait," she said, looking at the detour sign. "The roads aren't too bad, just a little slick as you start going up the hill. But there is a slight issue I wanted to call and warn you about. Have you ever been up this way? There's an old covered bridge that doesn't look like it'll fit the truck."

"We do know about it, and we were already planning on taking route four around it, so we will be a bit behind you."

"I just may go find myself a cup of coffee as well, so take your time and drive safe!"

After hanging up, she carefully turned back onto the road and followed the sign that read: *White Bridge town center, 1 mile.* As she got closer to town, she kept her eyes peeled for a coffee shop and noticed people on the sidewalks dressed in Santa hats and red-and-green holiday attire. She came to a stoplight and watched parents holding on to their children's hands as they walked toward a crowd gathered a couple streets up. As it was the Saturday after Thanksgiving, Christmas activities had most likely begun.

"The snow certainly doesn't slow this town down," she

said to herself, trying to see what everyone was gathered outside for.

Moving again, she saw a coffee shop sign to her left and pulled into the parking lot behind it. Only one spot was left. She parked and turned off the car, still curious about what was attracting all the people in this small town. Opening the door, she heard holiday music in the distance, which only further piqued her interest. She made her way to the sidewalk and around to the front door of the coffee shop where the music was louder. For a moment, she wanted to keep walking to see what was going on, but she was chilled from the cold air and decided to get something warm to drink before she explored.

An adorable wooden sign engraved with *The White Bridge Grind* hung on the front door, and the delightful aroma of freshly brewed coffee teased her senses when she walked in.

"Hi there!" a barista greeted her from behind the counter.

Offering a smile in response and a small wave, Amelia got in line and noticed the smell of pine mingled with the various smells of brew. Directly to her left boasted a beautifully lit Christmas tree with red-and-white baubles and ribbon wrapped around it. Each table had been given an extra touch with a centerpiece of holly and berries, and all the baristas wearing Santa hats made it all the more fun.

At the counter she quickly scanned the choices.

"There are so many wonderful specials to choose from, it was hard to decide," Amelia told the barista. "But I'll try the gingerbread chai tea."

"That's my favorite," the barista said. "Passing through White Bridge?"

"Actually, I am moving here today, so I am brand new." Amelia raised a brow. "I'm impressed you figured it out that quick."

"You'll see real soon that it's not hard to learn who everybody is. That'll be $5.12."

"A big change coming from New Haven." Amelia paid for her tea.

"I bet. Well, welcome to White Bridge! I'm sure I'll see you back here soon. We're the only coffee shop near this area."

"Yes, you will. I need to come back and try the rest of these specials before the season is over," Amelia said. "I saw a crowd out there. Is something happening?"

"Only the annual White Bridge Twelve Days of Christmas town walk. All the businesses participate. It's our little kickoff to the Christmas season celebration. Just follow everyone else if you head down there."

Amelia thanked her and waited for her drink, deciding to take it to go. She pulled her gloves out of her pockets, put them on, and with her tea in hand, headed out to the street. The people weren't bunched together like they were only minutes ago, but were instead walking up and down outside the store windows.

A lady in front of her stopped to take a picture and Amelia followed her line of sight and saw the first display: a structure of twelve drummer boys outside an insurance company with the people who worked there handing out candy to the children. A large sign next to it read: *Twelve Drummers Drumming* from the classic song, "The Twelve Days of Christmas".

Farther down the sidewalk, a flash of a white tutu caught her eye, and she saw a stage set up in front of the town hall with girls giving a ballet performance, surrounded by heat lamps. Along with the tutus, they were dressed in thick red sweaters and red leg warmers. Without even thinking, Amelia drifted closer. The girls were young, but they were putting on a great show, and she could see they had a good teacher—an older lady with gray hair swept up in a bun was in front of the stage directing the dancers. When they finished, Amelia carefully balanced her cup so she could clap along with the rest of the crowd as the children bowed.

A man who appeared to be an emcee stepped onto the stage. "Thanks so much to all our wonderful dancers. And let's have a round of applause for their teacher, the wonderful Ms. Sherry!"

The older woman stepped forward and took a bow as well. After that, the dancers cleared the stage and the man announced that the next act would be a band, starting in twenty minutes. Behind him, people started to set up the instruments.

Amelia wanted to congratulate the teacher, so she turned to head in the direction she saw Ms. Sherry go, but she turned too fast and plowed right into a man she hadn't realized was so close behind her.

"In a hurry?" the man said, holding his own cup out and brushing off the liquid that must have spilled on him.

His dark blond hair shook loose, framing his face in a messy, yet endearing way. Despite his gruff irritation, his hazel eyes pierced into her and they, along with his chiseled features, made Amelia fumble a bit.

"Oh... I... I'm sorry. I wasn't paying attention."

A young girl stood behind him with her hair in a bun and a ribbon tied into it.

Smiling down at her, Amelia bent over. "Hello there, did I accidentally bump you too?"

"No, and it's okay." The little girl noticed the man's annoyance and quickly glanced up at him. "Accidents happen. Right, Daddy?"

The man's daughter immediately offset the scowl on his face. "They sure do, Julia."

"I saw you out there dancing. You did a wonderful job," Amelia said.

Julia's expression brightened. "Thank you! We all worked really hard. Do you like ballet?"

"I could see that. It was a wonderful performance, and yes, I do... I actually danced professionally for a long time."

"Wow, really? Like, on a big stage at a theater? Have you danced in lots of shows? Did people bring you flowers and stuff?"

Amelia's eyes lit up with amusement. "Yes, to all of that! Which is why I was about to go look for your dance teacher."

"Ms. Sherry will love to meet you! She's probably still over by the stage."

"Thank you."

"You know, my mom loved ballet too. She was—"

"Julia, we need to go," the man said.

Amelia moved her attention away from the girl, to the father. Brushing the wave of hair off his face, the man reached down to hold Julia's hand, clearly ready to get moving.

"Sorry to keep you. I hope you have a nice day," Amelia said before he tugged his daughter to follow him.

Julia peeked over her shoulder and gave a small wave, her ribbon blowing behind her.

Carefully weaving through the crowd, Amelia finally spotted the dance teacher still by the stage, as Julia mentioned, busy hugging and congratulating some of her dancers and chatting with their families. Amélia waited nearby until the woman was free to talk and then approached her.

"Ms. Sherry?"

The woman wore a festive outfit—a long red skirt and white jacket—along with bell earrings that jingled as she turned toward Amelia.

"That's what they call me," Ms. Sherry said, flashing a warm smile.

76

Amelia extended her hand. "My name is Amelia... Amelia Collins. I'm a dancer too."

With her mouth agape, Ms. Sherry quietly studied her. "Oh, my, you certainly are! I recognize you from the show-stopping performance you gave two years ago in *A Midsummer Night's Dream*. Oh, and I can't ever forget *Swan Lake*... I think that one was my favorite. I so wish I had been able to attend more of your performances, but running this ballet school has me busy most weekends."

"Totally understandable," Amelia said, her cheeks heating up. No matter how many fans she'd met over the years, it always made her flush when she was recognized.

"And all those stunning ads and commercials I've seen you in." Ms. Sherry looked at her again. "You're more beautiful in person though."

"Thank you for your support. I'm glad you enjoyed those performances."

The woman's face fell. "I just read the announcement from your theater's newsletter that you've had to retire after your injury last spring. I'm so sorry you won't be dancing any longer, but, like me, many others will never forget how amazing you were on stage."

"That means a lot, thank you."

"So, what brings you to White Bridge?"

"I'm moving here." Amelia reminded herself she'd better make her way to the new house soon. "Waiting on the movers as we speak."

"How wonderful! White Bridge is a great community."

Amelia looked past the woman and saw the last of her ballerinas leaving to enjoy the walk with their families. "Looks like your class has left. I'm sorry to keep you from them. I just wanted to introduce myself. Will you be putting on a Christmas performance?"

"We sure will! *The Nutcracker* will be performed Saturday,

December 21 for the White Bridge community at the local high school."

Amelia felt a twinge of disappointment at hearing about another production of *The Nutcracker*, knowing she'd never dance in it again. But then she thought about little Sophia from the coffee shop last month, and how happy she was twirling around her mother. How her eyes had sparkled at learning Amelia was a dancer too. And little Julia today, so excited to talk to someone about dancing.

Without a second thought, the words spilled out. "Need a hand with the dancers?"

Ms. Sherry's face lit up. "So Christmas wishes *do* come true..." she said under her breath as she reached out her arms and placed her hands on Amelia's shoulders. "Come meet the girls. Our next practice is Tuesday at four thirty. The studio is just down here at 89 Main Street."

"I'll be there," Amelia said.

As she watched Ms. Sherry walk off, she pondered over the woman's mention of Christmas wishes, not sure how much value her help would be. She'd never worked with children before, but what better time than now to give it a try.

CHAPTER 8

CHRISTMAS EVE, 1920

William O'Shea

"Villiam? Would you be so kind as to come help me for a moment? I'm upstairs in Sara's nursery," Catherine called down the stairs.

"Of course, dear." William made his way up to his wife, who was still dressed only in her undergarments and bouncing their infant daughter around the room.

"Your mother is still resting," Catherine said, walking over to hand him Sara. "I hate to wake her and, as you can see, I have a ways to go with getting dressed. Could you please hold her for a few minutes? She's rather fussy this evening."

"It would be my pleasure." William took little Sara, comfortably wrapped in a warm blanket, and peered down at her soft brown eyes that matched his. "She is growing so well."

"That she is," Catherine said from behind the room divider.

"And just think, all that worry for nothing. Like I always tell you—"

"Worry never happens," Catherine finished.

She was more than used to the saying by this point. They'd been trying for a second baby for nearly a year and just when Catherine was about to give up, Sara came along. It was a stressful nine months waiting on her arrival, and watching his wife worry every day was hard for William to bear. Looking down, he noticed little Sara was now fast asleep, but he didn't want to point that out to his wife who had been trying to soothe her for most of the afternoon.

"When I gave you the family coin on our wedding day, I knew life would give us challenges, but I also knew it would bless us. Sara is here and she's healthy as can be. How lucky are we?"

"I know and I am incredibly grateful," Catherine said, coming back around the divider dressed in a long, dark green velvet dress. "How do I look?"

"Absolutely stunning." Placing Sara down in the cradle near their bed, he walked over to Catherine, holding her hand as he spun her around.

"Thank you, darling." She giggled as he dipped her back, kissing her cheek like he did on their wedding day. "I better get back in that kitchen to finish the soup and bread rolls. I hope I made enough..." Catherine stared off as she thought about it.

"This is your parents' house, which means there will be more food than any of us can consume. Don't stress."

Catherine's family was one of the most well-off in White Bridge and known to throw quite a gathering every Christmas Eve. There certainly would be plenty of food to go around.

"You know me, it's impossible not to," she said with a

straight face, but quickly softened when William came up behind and cradled her.

"Your potato leek soup will be my favorite there." William lifted his wife's hand, kissing it before the door burst open and their son, James, came wandering in.

"Is it time for the party yet?"

Catherine gazed lovingly at their son. "Almost, sweetheart. Are you washed up?"

"My hands are perfectly clean," James said, holding up both hands to show her.

"I better go check on my mother. It's been hard this holiday season without my father, but I do think being at your parents' dinner party will perk her up." William left the room and made his way downstairs to his mother's door.

He softly knocked. "Mother?"

"Come in," a voice called out.

When he walked in, the curtains were drawn and, with the winter sun nearly set, he could hardly see. He turned on one of the gas lanterns. "There we go, much better. Did you enjoy your nap?"

Looking down at his mother, William tried not to grow too concerned, but it was unlike Anna O'Shea to be in bed before dinner. His father, Joseph, had passed away only a few weeks prior, and his mother was in the deep throes of grief. His parents had been so close and did everything together.

"It was a splendid nap, but I must get up. I didn't mean to sleep this long. Poor Catherine probably prepared everything on her own." Anna sat up, swinging her legs over the side.

William quickly helped her to her feet. "There we are, Mother," he said and began to guide her out of the bedroom. "And don't stress over Catherine. You know her, she got it all prepared. It was no bother to her."

Once in the living room, Anna sat down on one of the chairs. "Could you fetch me a glass of water?"

William went to the kitchen and came back with a glass, and when his mother looked up at him from the chair, his heart pulled at the raw sadness in her eyes.

"Are you feeling up to Christmas Eve dinner at Catherine's parents' house, or would you rather stay home? We're leaving shortly." He bent down in front of her.

"And miss all that delicious food? Are you mad? Of course I'm coming," Anna said.

"Good. That's what I like to hear."

His mother smiled at him, then reached for his face like she had when he was young.

"I know this is hard for you without Father..." He trailed off, not wanting to upset her.

"But it's also a joy. It's a bittersweet mixture of longing and gratefulness. Every time I am with James, I remember how proud Joseph was knowing he was named after his biological father, and how happy that little Sara is here and healthy. A woman can't get any luckier than to be a grandmother who gets to hold another little one in the family."

"Yes, it's been a very fulfilling holiday season, despite losing Father. I'm relieved the children are here to lift your spirits."

His mother stroked his face again. "Me too. The coin is shining through all the darkness. Reminding us that everything will work out in the end."

"Merry Christmas, Mother."

"Merry Christmas, my darling William."

PRESENT DAY

With her cinnamon tea in hand the following Tuesday afternoon, Amelia stood in the front room, staring at the boxes she still needed to unpack. It was amazing how much stuff she'd collected and somehow fit in one small apartment. A bunch of random items, but not enough furniture. She had kept both antique bedframes that had been left in the guest rooms and the hutch in the dining room, but she'd need to buy more. Going from a one-bedroom apartment to a four-bedroom farmhouse meant a lot of empty space to fill. *Like an empty stage preparing for a show*, she reminded herself when the overwhelm of it all began to take over.

It had been a whirlwind two days since she moved in, trying to locate all her belongings. She was glad she'd pushed off her parents coming to see her new home so she could begin to organize everything. They had decided to visit the following weekend, and after experiencing the country's silent contrast to her old city life, she was looking forward to seeing them. The peace and quiet was what she had anticipated, but it would be an adjustment indeed.

Stifling a yawn, she made her way to the kitchen to put her now empty mug into the sink. She'd been up past midnight scrolling through design ideas online and couldn't wait to get started. Glancing at the clock on the stove, she saw it was almost four. She was due to meet Ms. Sherry and her dancers at the studio soon.

After grabbing her purse off the counter, she quickly checked her phone and saw a text from Lucy responding to one she'd sent earlier.

> *Hey! Mocha is doing great! I want to see the house now you're moved in, so save yourself a drive. I can't get there until next Friday because of rehearsal schedule this weekend, so take the time to get more settled!*

Amelia sent a text back, thanking her friend. She'd left Mocha with Lucy so the move didn't make her cat anxious.

Having Mocha back next week would make the house feel more like home and help with the transition—she was used to feeling the cat rub against her legs and cuddle with her on the couch.

The drive to the dance studio in town was quick—she'd have to remember she didn't need to account for New Haven traffic anymore. She drove slowly down Main Street, reading the storefronts' signs and admiring all the holiday lights that lined the windows. Each lamppost had a red bow tied around it, and the insurance agency from the Twelve Days of Christmas walk the weekend before now had a display of lit-up reindeer outside their door. Passing by a lovely little restaurant that had a few outdoor tables in the front for warmer months, she noticed their window was frosted over and a small tree just outside the front door sparkled bright against the setting sun. The quaint town sure knew how to celebrate the holidays.

She finally saw the sign for White Bridge Ballet. After finding a parking spot around the back, she saw another sign on a door that said: *Ballet School Entrance*. The sounds of faint music could be heard just outside the door and when she opened it she saw the young dancers through a large window into the studio where they were warming up, with Ms. Sherry leading the way. Amelia shrugged out of her coat and hung it on a free hook, along with her purse, a knot of worry twisting in her stomach as she pictured herself leading the class. It dawned on her all over again that she'd never done this before, but there was no turning back now. Ms. Sherry was expecting her. She quietly walked to the doorway so as not to disturb the class and watched.

"Okay, ladies, hands on your hips and extend your left leg, point it long..." Ms. Sherry noticed Amelia and motioned her to come in. "Step your feet together. Now the other side." She paused, demonstrating for the class, then walked around to observe their postures. "Let's shuffle both legs back and forth. That's it. Well done, ladies. Chins up high."

Amelia walked behind the girls, a few curious faces turning to see who she was as they continued their warm-up. When her eyes moved down the line, she paused on one familiar face that had lit up when she saw Amelia. Little Julia from the other day waved, and Amelia sent her a big smile and waved back, before pointing to Ms. Sherry. The girl grinned once more and turned her attention back to the teacher.

"Now, girls, let's all take a seat in butterfly while we invite someone special to come to the front with me. Class, this is Amelia Collins, a professional ballerina who just moved to White Bridge! Girls, let's all say hello!"

"Hello, Miss Amelia!" the girls called out in unison.

Amelia walked around to face them, and a sea of young eyes stared up at her. Before her anxiety got the best of her, the girls started asking questions.

"How big are the audiences you've danced for?" one girl asked.

"Very big," Amelia said.

"When did you first get pointe shoes?" another girl chimed in.

"I started practicing with them around age ten, but I didn't perform in them until I was twelve."

"We're going to try pointe shoes next year!" the same girl told her.

"Amelia, this group of girls are my older elementary dancers, and they are just about ready to get en pointe," Ms. Sherry explained.

"How exciting!" Amelia said, smiling at the group.

"Miss Amelia, would you like to lead these ladies through some jumps? It helps to warm them up some more before we start our practice for *The Nutcracker*."

Caught a little off guard, not expecting to participate quite so fast, Amelia's heart picked up its pace. But she knew it would be silly to decline such an easy request.

"Okay, girls, let's all meet in the corner."

In a matter of seconds, the dancers were gathered, ready to spring across the floor. Ms. Sherry began the music, and Amelia demonstrated the first jump. One by one, each dancer leaped across the floor before her. Watching them complete the movements effortlessly lit her up with delight. Maybe she *could* do this.

Ms. Sherry paused the music after they shuffled through the jumps a few times each and walked to the middle of the room.

"Okay, ladies, positions please!"

The girls scrambled and found a spot at the barre.

The teacher waved at Amelia to come next to her. "I like for them to do a couple minutes of practice with balancing as well. I'm sure you have a routine in mind you can do with them?"

Amelia's nerves were on edge once more when the girls all looked at her. Jumps were simple enough, but this would require a little more instruction.

Not wanting to let Ms. Sherry down, she tried to appear confident. "Of course! I'll cue you for the music with my nods."

Amelia gave Ms. Sherry the first nod and the music started again. She faced the girls, slowly pacing up and down the line. "Ready?" she asked.

She saw Ms. Sherry mouth for her to raise her voice. Looking away, she winced in dismay. She should have known that.

"Turn away from the barre!" Amelia instructed louder. "Hands in first with feet together, and let's begin by opening and closing first position."

86

The girls did just that and Amelia began to relax. After a minute of exercising their ankles, the first balancing move popped into her head and she dove in—envisioning herself doing it rather than a classroom of young learners.

"Now turn to the right, hand on the barre!" The girls all followed the instructions and she waited for the beat. "Tendu front! Lift! Hands off in high fifth!"

Some of the girls understood and pointed their left foot forward and lifted, balancing with their arms rounded and held slightly forward above their heads. A few turned to see what the move was, trying to catch up to the ones who got it correct. One girl raised her hand.

"Miss Amelia?" she called out loudly above the music. "Tendu front is pointed foot right?"

Another girl tried to help. "Like this, I think!" She pointed perfectly to the front and lifted her foot, but didn't remember the arms and toppled over. "Sorry, Miss Amelia." The girl frowned.

Ms. Sherry stopped the music. "Everyone, eyes on me!"

The girls all turned toward their teacher, a few more losing their balance, making them giggle.

"Remember, ladies, this is ballet practice, not recess!" Though Ms. Sherry couldn't help but smile a little at their childlike play.

They all stood straight and faced her, and the room quieted.

Amelia's cheeks blazed with embarrassment. "I'm sorry, Ms. Sherry. I didn't explain the way I should have. I'm so used to these moves that I just assumed."

Ms. Sherry waved her hand toward her. "No need to apologize. Working with children takes a bit of practice is all." She turned to face her class. "And we know what practice means, right girls?"

"Yes, Ms. Sherry!"

"Let's try again. Tendu and point your left foot forward, both arms up above your head to high fifth and lift your left foot." Ms. Sherry demonstrated and looked at Amelia. "Always follow up the term with explanation using body parts." Ms. Sherry started the music again. Taking a deep breath she faced the dancers. "Let's start with pointing to the front for the next couple minutes. One, two, three... begin."

This time the girls followed the move in sync. After they completed facing both sides of the barre, the music stopped again.

"All right, ladies, we have our big performance coming up fast. Let's get to it!" Ms. Sherry looked at her. "I'm sure they would love to show you their dances."

"I'd love to watch." Amelia forced a smile, trying not to let Ms. Sherry see the disappointment she felt toward herself. Even though Ms. Sherry had handled her mistake with grace, Amelia suddenly questioned if teaching was the right fit for her.

For the next hour, she watched the girls spin, jump, and practice their routines for *The Nutcracker*. Every now and then, Ms. Sherry peeked over at her as if she wanted to say something, but was too busy with the dancers. Seeing them wave as they glided by with smiles so bright made Amelia uneasy. A part of her wasn't sure she should come back and distract them from the solid routine they had going with their teacher.

"Time for a quick cool down!" Ms. Sherry called out. "And, of course, we need to practice our bows so they're perfect for the big day."

After leading the class through some floor stretches, Ms. Sherry turned to Amelia who was sitting on a chair off to the side.

"Miss Amelia, come on over and let's have a chat." The teacher then looked at her dancers. "Now, we all know Miss

Amelia knows the answer, of course, but let's tell her about the ballet bow and its meaning."

Hands shot up in the air and Ms. Sherry pointed to one girl near the front. "Olivia?"

"To say thank you to everyone for watching!"

"That is certainly true. What else does the ballet bow mean?" Ms. Sherry scanned the room full of raised hands.

Amelia saw Julia shyly raise her hand from the back.

"Julia? Do you know?" Ms. Sherry asked her.

"My mommy always told me it's to show respect."

"And your mom was absolutely right!"

Was? Amelia thought and tried not to noticeably stare at the girl.

"To show respect with a bow is a dancer's way of thanking her teacher and to show her gratitude." Ms. Sherry lifted her hands over her head and slowly dipped down. "And we never want to rush it. Now, your turn, girls. Stand up!"

The class followed her lead and Ms. Sherry clapped.

"Bravo! Class, what do we say to Miss Amelia for joining us today?"

"Thank you, Miss Amelia!" they all said together.

As parents came to pick up their daughters, Ms. Sherry became consumed with conversation and Amelia slipped into another room where the costumes were kept to collect herself before she said her goodbyes. While the girls were cute and fun, and it was sweet to watch them show off their moves to her, she realized that being there and teaching was not something she should do. For her entire life up until this point she had always been the student, and teaching required different skills she didn't naturally have like Ms. Sherry. The last thing she wanted was to ruin their experience as young dancers... just as mean old Ms. Ruth did for her. While she would never be mean, what if she said the wrong thing by accident?

"I'll never get this right!" a girl's voice shouted from behind another door.

Amelia heard the girl groan in frustration again and she couldn't help but peek in to see if she was all right. When she opened the door, a girl a little older than the dancers she'd just watched turned to her in surprise.

"Oh... you're not my dad."

"No, I'm not." Amelia scanned the little room, which had a mirror wall and ballet barre in front of it. "My name is Amelia. I was here watching the class tonight. Was that your class in there?"

"It was my sister, Julia's, class. Mine is on Thursday nights, but I sometimes come and practice by myself back here during hers." The girl looked down to the floor. "Or at least try to."

"I see." Amelia stepped forward. "What's your name?"

"Ava."

"Nice to meet you, Ava," she said as she walked closer.

The girl looked back up at her with inquiring eyes. "So you just came to watch my sister's class for fun?"

"Sort of. I met Ms. Sherry the other day and she had me help out a little tonight, but I'm not sure teaching is my calling."

Ava looked at her with confusion.

Amelia gave a small smile. "I danced professionally for a long time, and Ms. Sherry thought it would be a good idea to work with your sister's class tonight. Turns out, I need a lot more practice learning how to teach."

"Oh..." Ava paused, still watching Amelia and fiddling with something on her arm. "Well, I'm sure you did just fine. Better than I'd ever do. I'll never dance professionally. I'm not good enough. I don't know why Ms. Sherry thought to land me the Sugar Plum Fairy role."

Amelia's stomach dropped, but she ignored it and focused

on Ava, who didn't need to hear about her injury and how that was supposed to be her role this year too.

"I've danced the Sugar Plum Fairy many times. And I know how scary such a big lead role can feel. I was terrified the first year I danced it as a teenager."

"You were?" Ava raised her brows.

"Yup, totally petrified."

Ava went over to her bag and pulled out her phone, tapping something and twisting her arm around again. Amelia saw a white device she didn't notice before attached to her arm.

"Sorry, I have diabetes and I'm checking my levels, which is another hassle right now. Trying to be graceful with this thing stuck to me."

"I'm sorry you have to deal with that," Amelia said and thought about one of her fellow dancers at the theater who also had diabetes. "But you know what? I know a professional ballerina who has diabetes too, and she still gets standing ovations. The audience doesn't see what you see. They will see a wonderful ballerina on stage, not a monitor."

"I hope so," Ava said and put her phone back in her bag. "I've danced in so many performances, but this is the first year everyone's eyes will really be on me. It helps to know you were scared about the Sugar Plum Fairy too. But you went on to become a professional ballerina, so you probably just worried you'd do badly. I really will mess this up."

"Show me what you were just working on."

Ava sighed. "Okay…" She turned to face the mirror. "The timing with the faster spin in the pas de deux at the end with the Prince scares me the most, so I decided to work on the 'Waltz of the Flowers' dance… thinking I'd nail its slower pirouette, but it's really dragging me down tonight too." With her face already contorted in frustration, Ava drew in her breath and tried to maintain control with her spin, but fumbled, losing her grip. "See?"

"Hmm…" Amelia walked over and put her arm around the girl's shoulders. "The first thing I'd like you to try is relaxing your face. Starting a dance with a frown can turn you upside down."

Ava smiled at her in the mirror. "I've never heard that before."

"Well, it's true." Amelia let go of Ava's shoulders and held up her arms in position, extending her leg out wide behind her. "And the key to a slow spin is widening your starting position to help you keep control of your stomach muscles so you can ease around." She leaned forward and did a careful turn, landing with grace.

"Amelia is absolutely spot on." Ms. Sherry came into the room. "Ava, isn't it a wonderful treat to have her here?"

"Yes, ma'am, it is," Ava said.

"Your father is waiting in the front for you." Ms. Sherry paused, her eyes narrowing in thought. "Say, would you like to have Amelia come again to help you?" She turned to Amelia. "Of course I don't want to intrude on all you probably need to do with settling in, but we'd sure be honored to have you."

Amelia's eyes grew wide with surprise. "If you think my being here is helpful. I—"

"Of course it is, don't be silly," Ms. Sherry cut in.

Despite her earlier doubts, Amelia did seem to connect well with Ava, and seeing the girl's eyes light up at the prospect of her giving her private lessons was hard to say no to. "Yes, then I will be here."

"Wonderful! The older girls practice Thursday, same time. And we can have you two back here again."

"See you then, Ava." Amelia smiled at the girl, trying to keep her from noticing how worried she felt. She could hardly lead her sister's class through a basic balance move, but now she would be coaching Ava through the show's leading role.

"Thank you, Miss Amelia. I will see you Thursday." Ava picked up her bag and dashed out the door, looking a lot brighter than when Amelia first came into the room.

Ms. Sherry turned to her. "And of course I will pay you for your time."

"Thank you, this is a nice offer, but…" Amelia drew her brows together. Should she even be paid when she clearly had no teaching skills? "Ms. Sherry, you saw me out there with the class earlier. I made mistakes from the start. I wouldn't mind volunteering my time with Ava instead."

"Nonsense. You are a professional ballerina and will be privately working with one of my students. You will be compensated accordingly." Ms. Sherry walked Amelia to the front door with her arm around her shoulders. "And you saw the girls stumble and then try again. Just like you did perfecting those ballet moves all the years you've danced. You have to find your footing with teaching, and that takes time and practice too."

The street was fully dark and quiet when Amelia stepped outside, her thoughts cycling loudly in her mind. She may not have the footing needed to dance on the stage as the Sugar Plum Fairy anymore, but instead of dwelling on that, she turned her focus on the fact that Ava could. It was comforting knowing Ms. Sherry trusted her enough to work with her student. So that was what she would do. Help Ava dance the best performance she could.

Standing next to her car, she stopped short, her brother's words suddenly jumping into her mind: *You haven't had your final curtain draw yet.* Shaking her head, she laughed to herself, then pulled out her phone to text him.

Your twintuition amazes me and I'm your twin! I just left a dance studio for kids, and I think you were on to something the last time we chatted. Talk soon! XO

After getting in the car, she turned it on, and while it warmed up she clicked on the overhead light and held up her phone. She'd received hundreds of comments and messages from her followers over the last week who were excited about her new journey, which was a huge relief. For years all they'd seen were ads, short clips of performances, and moments behind the scenes of her life as a ballerina. Now a new show was beginning, and she was glad many of them were still around to watch it unfold. After all, without the support of her online community, she wouldn't have been able to move to White Bridge and begin this new life. The sponsorships, paid ads, modeling jobs, commercials... all of it was because of them.

"Hi, everyone! Yes, I am sitting in my car in what appears to be the middle of nowhere, but that's the country for you! I have a little fun news to share... I just left a ballet school for kids and what an experience! I even got to work with the dancers a little, and while I definitely need to sharpen up on my teaching skills, this may become part of my new journey. I'm going to work privately with one dancer in particular who is dancing the Sugar Plum Fairy for the first time, a role I had to say my farewells to for this year's performance at Northeast Performing Arts. So, what do you all think? Me? A teacher? Let me know in the comments!"

Amelia wasn't sure what everything meant as she posted the video, and maybe she was looking for some extra reassurance from her followers, but she was in White Bridge now and there was no turning back.

CHAPTER 9

*W*alking into the studio two days later, Amelia used every ounce of willpower she had to calm her anxiety. *Just do exactly as you did with Ava the other day*, she'd told herself repeatedly on the drive over. She'd spent half of the previous day reflecting on how this all came about. Since she first saw the farmhouse listed for sale, everything had seemed to flow at a speed she could hardly keep up with.

Inside, the studio was full of commotion, and the nervous tension brewing suddenly sent a rush down her spine. The buzz of the dancers instantly took her back to the busy days at the theater. Some dancers were warming up at the ballet barre, some were bent over on the bench lacing up their pointe shoes, and others were going in and out of the dressing room. Ignoring the angst that filled her, she started to look for Ms. Sherry when a draft of cold air blew in from behind her, and Ava and her dad walked in.

"Hi, Ava!" Amelia greeted her with a wide smile, only to receive a worried look back as the girl glanced up at her dad

—the man Amelia had bumped into the other day and who once again looked irritated.

"Hi, Miss Amelia," Ava said in a low voice.

Was she missing something?

"I take it you are her new teacher?" the dad asked.

"I don't think we've officially met. I'm Amelia," she said, holding out her hand.

The man looked at it and gave her a weak shake.

"I haven't replaced Ms. Sherry or anything. I was just asked to work with your daughter privately on her role as Sugar Plum Fairy, which I have danced myself many times." She smiled at him, but his expression stayed even.

"I see," he said, giving Ava a kiss on the head. "Go on and get yourself ready to dance."

Ava walked past her with an apologetic stare mouthing, "*I'm sorry.*"

"Did I do something wrong, sir?"

"My name is Ben."

"It's nice to meet you, Ben. I hope to give Ava a boost of confidence for her big role."

Without acknowledging her position as his daughter's personal instructor, he continued to stare at her with a cross look. "To answer your question, no, you didn't do anything wrong... yet."

Amelia shook her head. "I'm sorry, I don't understand. Are you upset that I'm helping her privately?"

"No, that's a good thing. It was all she talked about the last two nights, and she seems much more excited about the upcoming performance now. She's been nervous about it for weeks."

"Then what's the problem?"

"What you posted the other night on social media. Ava found you online and showed me. She was honored you mentioned her and went off to brag to her friends, but I wasn't so happy about it."

"I didn't mention her name at all. I never would—"

"With the number of followers you have, just keep her off your account. Period."

Ben kept his eyes on her, but she was too stunned to say anything. The last thing she ever wanted to do was upset a dancer's parent, but she already seemed to have accomplished that. Maybe this was a job she'd need to reconsider. Ms. Sherry had clearly worked so hard building such a great little ballet school and Amelia was messing things up.

"I… I'm sorry, Ben. I—" She struggled to maintain eye contact under the intensity of his direct gaze.

"Amelia?" Ms. Sherry came into the front hall from the main classroom and seemed to notice how troubled she was, peeking over at Ben. "Is everything all right?"

"Yes, everything is fine, Ms. Sherry. Ben was just…" She suddenly didn't know what to say and looked at the man.

His face softened. "I think I was a little unfair to Amelia just now. I'm sorry, Ms. Sherry, I don't want to disrupt practice." He turned to Amelia. "Forgive me for coming across so harsh. I tend to get a little overprotective of my girls."

"That is understandable," Amelia said.

Ms. Sherry observed him. "Everything is fine, Ben. No need to worry about a thing. Amelia is fabulous with Ava and will do her good. You'll see."

"Have a good practice." He nodded at them and left.

"So you met Ben Walsh, I see," Ms. Sherry said with concern. "It's not you. Whatever he's grumbling over… It's just how he gets sometimes."

"I posted on social media about privately tutoring a young girl, but I never said her name. I never would—or the name of your studio. I was just excited at the prospect of doing this. I'll delete it."

"Nonsense. I know you would never say her name. And I saw the video too," she said, pausing to put her hand on Amelia's arm. "It's okay. Ben is just… Well, he has been through a lot. He's a great guy under that tough exterior. Now, let's get you back there. Ava's waiting."

When Amelia got to the room, Ava was bent over, adjusting music. The girl popped up and came over to her.

"Amelia! Whatever my dad said, I'm so sorry."

"No need to apologize. He's just being a good dad."

"Are you still going to work with me?" Ava asked with hopeful eyes.

"Of course I am."

"Oh, good." She exhaled. "Ms. Sherry set up music from my dances on a playlist for us to work with this time, as well as some others."

"Great! Let's get you warmed up."

"Let me know if you two need anything," Ms. Sherry said. "I'm going to get the class started now." She dashed off.

Amelia clicked the stereo on to test the sound before settling on a tune for the warm-up. She positioned herself next to Ava to stretch alongside her. She had followed up with Dr. Reed through email about her exact limitations while working with Ava, so she knew what she was allowed to do. Warming up was gentle enough. The important thing was no pointe shoes.

A few minutes in, Amelia was glad to see how smooth their first lesson was going. Being a little older than the dancers in her sister, Julia's, class, Ava moved through the warm-up with little direction and ease.

"The role of the Sugar Plum Fairy is certainly the star of the show and such a wonderful character," Amelia said as she scrolled to find *The Nutcracker*'s soundtrack. She hit pause and turned to Ava.

"I know," Ava said, though her face fell as she looked at the floor.

"Don't worry." Amelia went over and gently prodded her. "We've got this. You will be spectacular out there. Go ahead and lace up."

Ava pulled her pointe shoes from her ballet bag and sat on the floor to begin wrapping her feet. "Miss Amelia, the more I think about this, the more I don't know if I can pull off being the Sugar Plum Fairy. Even the strongest dancers out there, the professionals, have struggled with it. I know you said you were a teenager when you first danced this, but I'm only fourteen."

"Ava." Amelia sat down next to her and put her arm around her. "That's exactly the same age I was. I was so worried I'd ruin the entire show because it's the role that everyone waited for. And to make matters worse, my twin brother, Andrew, was home sick that year with the flu and couldn't be there. He'd always made it for my other performances... and the Sugar Plum Fairy was what he had been looking forward to seeing me dance the most. But you know what? I got on that stage and knew I had to prove to myself that I was chosen for the role for a reason, just as Ms. Sherry chose you for a reason. She believes in you."

"I'm not sure I believe in me." Ava finished lacing up the first shoe and started on the second. "Like, what about the pas de deux dance at the end? I'm terrified about syncing with the Prince if I can't even sync my own turns. And the grand finale multiple pirouette..." She paused, staring at her shoes, then closed her eyes for a moment before continuing. "Ms. Sherry always brings in someone from Hartford College of Dance for the Prince and he's always amazing. Not to mention, the version I chose to do includes the fouetté followed by the pirouette. I'm regretting that choice more and more."

"Well, Ms. Sherry chose the male dancer from the college because she needs strong hands to lift and carry you through the dance," Amelia said and offered her hand to help Ava stand up. "Come on, I have a few tricks up my sleeve to help you remember your timing and to keep everything tight and controlled. It'll all be okay."

Ava took her hand, looking slightly more relaxed. "Thank you, Miss Amelia. Working with you, I feel more hopeful."

Ava stood in front of her with a familiar expression, causing Amelia to pause. Where had she seen it before? And she suddenly remembered… on the sidewalk the other day and in the front hall only moments ago. Ava had her father's eyes and stared at Amelia with that same deep look. This family was holding something painful inside, and it was reflected through their expressions.

"Since we're working privately together, you can call me Amelia. Formalities in ballet often feel rather stiff, don't you agree?"

Ava laughed. "Yes, I do."

"Ready to get started?"

STILL WINDING DOWN FROM THE FIRST LESSON WITH AVA, Amelia realized she'd been standing in front of the nearly empty fridge for a couple minutes just staring at it. While the lesson had gone well, there were some areas she needed counsel on. For one, she'd never worked with a teenage girl on anything, never mind helping one with a dance performance. She was used to encouraging her fellow adult ballerinas at the theater, but the mindset of a fourteen-year-old had her fumbling her words a few times as she tried to direct Ava through the obstacles.

During one of their water breaks, she'd texted Ms. Higgens asking for suggestions on fostering a teenager's emotions and growth. Amelia's old ballet master understood her in a way Ms. Sherry couldn't yet, and Amelia felt more comfortable confiding in her. She had already updated Ms. Higgens the day before on this new experience, and she'd told Amelia she was there for any bumps in the road—so Amelia was asking for her first unknown: a teenager's mood.

She turned to the cabinet and found some organic soup she'd brought from the apartment.

"This will have to do," she said to herself. Her mind was so busy thinking about Ava that her appetite was low anyway, but she made a mental note to go to the grocery store in the morning. "Now a pot to heat it up."

After rummaging through a few of the kitchen boxes, she found what she needed. Scrolling through her phone while she waited for the soup to heat up, she thought about Ava some more. Never having taught ballet before, Amelia knew she really needed to give herself a break. Outside of working through Ava's up and down emotions, she was easily able to spot the problem areas in terms of her skills, and she had been right—her timing needed some help. Overall, Ava *was* a strong dancer, so Amelia was determined to learn how to do her job better to help the girl improve.

After pouring the soup into a bowl, she grabbed a piece of whole wheat bread and sat down to eat. Aimlessly scrolling while she ate, she came across a few videos on her phone about teaching ballet.

Soon a message from Ms. Higgens popped up.

Amelia, even the greatest ballet teachers in the world have their very first lesson. And I don't care who you are, none of us do it 100% right. You think I became the ballet master I am today without trial and error? Like I told you yesterday, I have taught my fair share of teenagers and they are not easy. In order to foster her growth, it will take repetition. Which is pretty much the same idea when you're perfecting a dance, yes? We practice it over and over. Reiterate to young Ava that she needs to put her chin up, try again, and focus on the journey rather than the destination, just like professionals have to do. And that improvement is not instant. It's a gradual process. Remind her it was that way for you, even if you have to tell her the same story many times. Let me know how the next one goes. XO

Ms. Higgens's message felt as if she was there giving Amelia a big hug. It was exactly what she had needed to read. When she finished her soup, she went upstairs for a shower. After turning on the water, she glanced around her new bathroom. It was a fairly large size for such an old home, but she remembered the realtor explaining that the entire bedroom was expanded and updated with the bathroom in the 1950s. Eventually, she'd need to add this room to the list of updates. Pulling up her long brown hair, she sighed. *One day at a time.*

After her shower she ventured into the living room, feeling clean and cozy in her pajamas. The house was so silent she could practically hear her own heartbeat. It was in the stillness of the evening that the country quiet really hit her. While she didn't miss the sirens from the city waking her up, she did feel a little lonely in such a big home all by herself. Once Mocha arrived, it would help having her purring next to her. Amelia chuckled, thinking how panicked her cat would be seeing all the extra space, although she would have fun finding new places to hide.

She picked up her phone, found her brother's number, and called to check in.

"Hey, sis," he answered, sounding tired.

"Oh, no, did I wake you?"

"No. Diana just went to bed and I'm downstairs watching an old western that somehow interested me. How's the farm?"

"It's not much of a farm without any animals."

"What do you mean? You have Mocha. She'll be a perfect asset for rounding up the cows once you get them."

"There will be no cows. And I won't be letting Mocha outside once she gets here. She's never been outside. She'd get lost in the woods."

"Mocha is one mighty kitty, you'd be surprised. How have the first few days been?"

"Rather quiet."

"Well, what did you expect moving out to the middle of nowhere? Maybe you should get yourself a rooster to stir things up."

Amelia grinned. "Not happening. But I feel a few chickens poking around would complete the scene."

"And give you free eggs. Should I get you a guide to gardening 101? Off-grid style?"

"I'm not lost in the Appalachian Mountains, Andrew, I'm in Connecticut. There is an actual town here with people and everything."

"Cool. So do you make the population kick up to above fifty now?"

"Something like that." She shook her head, but was loving the conversation. Andrew always knew how to make her laugh.

"I saw your post about the dance studio. Who thought it would be a good idea to let you loose around kids?"

"The town's dance teacher," she said laughing. "I have absolutely no idea what I'm doing or where it's all going, but gosh are those little dancers adorable."

"You know Diana is here if you need any pointers for working with kids. Have you taught a class yet?"

"Actually, I was assigned a really special job. Which is what made me think of the conversation we had after I saw the doctor. Speaking of, when is your next appointment with yours?"

Andrew sighed through the phone. "Tomorrow. But I don't want to talk about me. I want to hear more about this new job."

It was too late to press him, but she at least always asked. "Let's put it this way, the Sugar Plum Fairy role isn't finished with me. It's just not me dancing as her. I'm privately helping a girl named Ava who is dancing it in a couple weeks."

"Wow… that must be tough. Of all roles to work with her on. What crappy timing."

"It is… but maybe it isn't. We'll see what happens. I just started and Ava is sweet. I can't let her down. She seems so relieved that I'm helping her. But I think you had a hunch about all this before I even got here though."

"Don't I always with you? But I'll be curious to see how things go. Either way, I'm not worried for you. Something good is brewing with all this."

"You mean teaching Ava?"

"That and you buying the house. I just sense a big change happening and not just you becoming a farmer."

"Andrew! Well, if I do become a farmer, then you and Diana can come on over with your gardening gloves."

"Diana? Gardening? Now you're just being silly. I can see *you* out there before she would ever step foot near a raised bed."

She smiled. "Thanks for chatting with me, bro. You better turn that movie off and go to bed. You need your rest."

"Story of my life."

Amelia put her phone next to her and curled up against

the couch cushion, feeling a lot more settled. Near or far, her twin brother always made things better. Her mind was too busy thinking about all the changes he'd mentioned to notice the silence that returned once she'd hung up. Despite what had been lost, she was anxious to get her new life in White Bridge on the right track—whatever that meant.

CHAPTER 10

The tiny market in town was nothing short of adorable with its frosty holiday magic displayed in the front windows and the hot chocolate and cookie station right inside as Amelia entered, greeting her like a warm embrace.

It was Friday morning and hardly anyone was there, so she was able to zip through her shopping. The staff was friendly, and the store had all her favorite essentials despite being so small, so it was a successful trip. After putting her groceries away, she was ready to brew some coffee and get back to unpacking. Heading to the kitchen, she stopped short at the empty counters. Which box did she put the coffee maker in? Digging through the three boxes next to the table, she practically jumped with joy when she found it and held it up as if it were a prized possession. She had luckily packed the coffee right next to it and after setting the machine on the counter, she clicked it on and sat down to wait.

Her plan was to tackle more boxes and finish getting her clothes put away before she was due to be at the studio later for their first rehearsal on the high-school stage. Ms. Sherry had planned on holding Friday and Saturday rehearsals for the next two weekends until the opening night. The pile of clothes Amelia had unboxed the night before sat in her bedroom on her chair. Fresh mug in hand, she took a long sip and allowed the hot brew to awaken her while she climbed the stairs. Finding some holiday tunes on her phone, she turned up the volume, took another big swig, and got to it.

After an hour of hanging and sorting what she wanted to keep and give away, the pile on her chair was almost gone. Cringing at the other boxes filled with more clothes, she figured there was no time like the present to keep going. She picked up the box on top to move it closer to her closet, pausing when she saw the box under it, which was labeled "dance costumes/shoes." Her heart picked up speed. She wasn't ready to face this box yet. That part of her life had closed, so they could just stay in there.

She grabbed the box and made her way to the stairs to the attic. For an old farmhouse, it had quite an impressive walk-up staircase to an attic she could stand up in. She had gone up during her first tour of the house with the realtor and remembered all the space. She got the box up the short flight of stairs and placed it on the floor before pushing it to the corner. A string for a ceiling light tickled her face and she pulled it so she could see better. Some other bins and boxes were stored in the corner, and she curiously walked over to the first one. Inside were dusty plates, mugs, and cookware, and she guessed them to be old by the rust that had gathered under the pots. Moving the box behind her so she could toss the contents, she opened the next box and noticed it was clothing. She groaned to herself. *Not more clothing.* But she gasped when she pulled out the first article: a long red silk gown woven with gold threads.

"Amazing," Amelia said out loud, holding it up to her as if she were planning to try it on.

The dust from it stung her eyes, so she carefully folded it back up and placed it inside the box again. She'd need to figure out what to do with the vintage attire, but for now she kept the box in its location. A couple of others were filled with old and mostly broken toys and some long-stemmed candles that had seen better days, so she moved them next to the kitchenware box to also throw away. Turning back around, she'd spotted a dark brown chest tucked away in the corner. The one light was not nearly bright enough to see it fully, so Amelia quickly ran down to retrieve her phone, that was still blasting Christmas music, and went back upstairs, shining her phone's flashlight toward the chest.

Reaching down, she tried to open it, but it was locked, so she moved it out from the wall to see if a key was anywhere close by. When she pointed the light behind it, she saw a small felt string pouch. She picked it up and brushed off the cobwebs as best she could, feeling something hard inside. When she opened it, her jaw dropped at what appeared to be a bronze British coin. Holding it up close to her phone, she barely made out *1860* engraved in it. Two small pieces of folded paper were also inside the bag, and she opened the first one, squinting to read the faded words.

Pass this coin along for generations to come. May it always bring our family good luck. —Ellen O'Shea

She opened the next one.

December 5th, 1869

To my child,

This Christmas, hold the coin you received on your wedding day, and let it remind you that you have all you need to prosper and grow. Christmas is a time to spread joy and good will, and now that you are a parent, I wish you good luck that forever stays. So, my child, remember to pass the coin down to your own, and watch your heart grow.

Love,
Father

Interesting. After tucking both the coin and the notes safely back in the pouch, Amelia turned off the light and took it with her downstairs. Sitting on the edge of her bed, she held the bag and tried to think of what to do with it. Did it hold value for this Ellen O'Shea? As she repeated the name in her mind, she felt more drawn to it. Was she a visitor to the farmhouse? Or did she live here?

The year 1869 suddenly struck her, as she realized it was only the year before the house was built. Putting aside all she still had to unpack, her interest in the coin deepened. Anything to distract her from going through all her clothes; but this coin had her attention and based off the notes, it seemed like an important coin, anyway. The town may have more information for her, so that was where she decided to go. Maybe they had interest in the vintage clothes too? She'd hate to keep them stuffed away in the attic.

Once downstairs, she put the bag inside her purse, grabbed her coat, and went outside. The crisp December air was refreshing after being in the dusty attic, and the sunlight dancing off the snow-covered fields in the backyard caught her eye as she walked to her car. Gratitude filled her when she took a moment to look at the picturesque scenery. This peaceful view was all hers now and with the craziness of moving, she really hadn't taken the time to soak it in yet.

A wreath, she thought when she turned back to her car, catching a glimpse of the bare front door. The one her mother bought a few weeks back was lying on top of one of the boxes in the hallway. A few touches of holiday cheer would make the farmhouse feel more like home. Her parents were due to visit the following weekend, so she made a mental note to find a tree soon—especially for her mom.

The town hall was easy to find. When Amelia parked and got out of her car, she immediately heard a faint chorus of people singing.

"Christmas carolers?" she mumbled out loud.

When she got to the sidewalk, sure enough, she saw a group dressed in traditional, old-fashioned Christmas outfits stop in front of a hardware store, singing "Joy to the World." The staff opened the door to listen, and Amelia wanted to as well, but she had an old coin to figure out.

Inside the front entrance of the town hall, stairs wrapped in garland stretched up three floors. A large painted mural covered the walls leading up. It portrayed pictures of historical homes in checkered squares and, without looking at the directory, she walked up the first flight, slowly looking at each house, stopping at one she instantly recognized. It had the large porch, white exterior, and black shutters with the same maple trees that lined her driveway. At the top of the first flight of stairs, the mural's title in large black letters read: *Historical Homes of White Bridge*. It reminded her that she needed to get onto finding a solid contractor as soon as possible, one who understood how to remodel historical homes.

Another directory was on the second level, but she didn't see a historian listed, so she made her way to the clerk's office. A bell rang when she opened the door, and two women sitting at their desks looked up as she approached the counter.

"Hi there," one lady said, standing up to greet her.

"Hello. My name is Amelia Collins and I just moved into the farmhouse on Maple Ridge Lane," Amelia said. She paused when the other woman stood up with a wide smile.

"So you're the one who took it on," the second lady said, coming to stand next to the other clerk.

"I sure am," Amelia said and shook both their hands. "Nice to meet you both."

"We're just delighted to have you here in White Bridge and to pour some much-needed love into that farmhouse. It's one of the town's most beloved historical homes," the first lady said.

"I can see why. It's a gorgeous house. Which brings me to my first question. I'd like to know if the town has names of contractors who can help with remodeling it. One who understands older homes. I know historical remodels present extra complexities."

"Oh, we absolutely do. We have a couple men who head that up here in town. I'll contact Chris Murphy, the head of the historical society and co-owner of his construction company, M&W Remodeling. He's overseen many projects in town with older homes. It's their specialty. Let me see if he's here or in his other office. I'll be right back." The first clerk dashed off to her desk and picked up her phone.

"How courteous of her to make that call," Amelia said.

"That's White Bridge for you! And I hear you bought the house all by yourself?" the second lady asked.

Amelia grinned. Small-town talk already.

"Yes, I did. It's a lot of work for just me, but I am thrilled to get started." She reached into her purse and pulled out the small bag she found behind the chest. "The other reason I'm here is I'm hoping to find someone in town, perhaps a historian. If Chris is also the head of the historical society, maybe he can point me to the right person." She opened the bag, pulled out the coin, and handed it to the lady. "I need help with what I just found in the attic."

"Wow, look at this," the clerk took the coin and leaned over for a better look. "That's an old one for sure."

"Would Chris be the right person to ask about it?"

"No, Chris just volunteers his time to help lead and manage. A small town means a crossover in jobs. But we do have a town historian who works out of our museum in White Bridge's oldest neighborhood," the clerk said.

That explained not seeing them listed on the directory. Amelia thought about the vintage clothes she'd found. Maybe the museum would take them.

The first clerk hung up the phone and came back to the counter, holding a yellow sticky note. "Is that a Queen Victoria penny?" she asked, squinting to get a better look.

"I don't know, but that looks to be about right," Amelia said, holding the bag open for the coin when the clerk handed it back. "I was just telling your co-worker that I was hoping to find someone who could help me figure it out because it looks valuable and special. She mentioned a historian who works in the old museum?"

"Wait," the first clerk said. "I believe the historian is here in the basement looking for something they need to prepare for an event after the holidays with the middle school. Let me find out for you." She went back to her desk and picked up her phone to make another call.

"Was the coin all that was in the bag?" the second clerk asked.

"No, I also found two notes. One from a lady named Ellen O'Shea."

"Wow, it's like you moved into a little mystery."

"Starting to look like that," Amelia said.

"Okay, it's your lucky day," the first woman said, jotting something else on the sticky note. "Chris is a hard one to get ahold of and I happened to catch him in between jobs. He said he'll call his business partner to see if next Thursday at ten works for him and hopefully for you too. He's leaving the office now for the rest of the day, but he said to call and let his secretary know if that day and time works for you and to leave your number with her. Here're his contact details and the historian's, whose name is Tom. One of the administrative assistants is going down to the basement to see if he's still there, since no one is answering the phone. So it will be just a minute to wait. Hopefully he can meet with you while he's here."

"Wonderful! Thank you for your help with all that." Amelia put the sticky note in her purse. "Say, that mural along the stairwell is impressive."

"Yes, it's rather new actually. An artist who traveled through White Bridge a couple years ago was so impressed with our historical homes, he offered to gift us that mural. Did you find your house?"

"Yes, I did. It was easy to spot with the maple trees," Amelia said, hearing the phone ring on one of the desks. The first clerk went to answer it, and Amelia glanced at the clock on the wall. She still had plenty of time to meet with Tom before her lesson with Ava.

"Okay, he's still here," she said coming back. "Again, his name is Tom and he said he'll meet you up here in a minute.

Why don't you have a seat in the private room we have just back here." The clerk motioned for her to follow.

Amelia took a seat and put the small bag on the table, then pulled out her phone and looked up Queen Victoria pennies. There were a lot of articles with information, depending on the year the coin was from. After she clicked on one and got lost in the details, a small knock on the door pulled her out of the article and an older man with wisdom streaks of graying hair walked in.

"I'm Tom," he said, extending his hand to her.

"Hi, Tom, my name is Amelia Collins," she said as he gave her hand a firm shake. "Thank you for taking time out of your busy day to meet with me."

"I heard there's an old coin involved. How could I not come up to meet you?" Tom winked at her as he leaned back in his chair. "But it's truly no problem. I needed a break from the basement anyway. All that dust was getting to me."

Amelia thought back to her stuffy attic. "I know what you mean. So I bought the farmhouse on Maple Ridge Lane and I was in the attic this morning when I found this." She pushed the pouch toward him.

Tom sat up and took the bag, pulling out the notes and the coin. For a moment, all he did was hold it up close, flipping it around and around as he studied it. He pulled off the readers hanging on his sweater, put them on, and brought the coin closer.

"No way," he mumbled to himself, before looking up at her. "You said you found this in the attic?"

"Yes, it was kind of lost behind an old chest. It looked valuable and I wanted to figure out what kind of coin it is and possibly who I can return it to," Amelia explained, watching him squint at the coin some more.

"Would you mind if I took this back to my office and

viewed it under my microscope? I'm also going to show it to a buddy of mine who is a numismatist—he studies coins. I need to make sure I can confirm what I'm seeing." Tom placed the coin down and read one of the notes. "Ellen O'Shea…" he trailed off in thought.

"You'll have to explain what you think you're seeing. Like in Coin 101 because I don't know anything about them. All I gathered was that it was a British coin," Amelia said.

The man chuckled. "Sorry, I was just taken aback. Coins are not my area of specialty, but I do know quite a lot. From my knowledge, this looks to be a very rare coin, if I'm correct with what I see." Tom flipped the coin over and handed it to her. "Try to look at the date on the back."

Amelia held the coin closer and saw the same date she'd seen earlier. "It says 1860."

Tom nodded. "Yes, but from what I can tell, that was stamped over another date, which is 1859."

Amelia narrowed her eyes, trying to see it. "You know… it does look like it's reprinted on top of a previous date, but it's so hard to tell. Is that uncommon?"

"Very. It would be an extremely rare and valuable British penny. Worth thousands."

"Wow," Amelia said with a low whistle. "Then my hunch was correct that this is a special coin. Belonging to Ellen O'Shea, who I assume is most likely no longer with us."

"No, she's not," Tom said, shaking his head. "She was the original owner of your home."

Amelia stared at him, wide-eyed. "I can't believe I found this coin. And of course you can take it. Let me leave you with my number." She pulled out a small notepad she always kept in her purse, scribbled down her cell number, and handed the page to Tom. "I'd like to return the coin to its rightful owners. When I first looked at the date, I recalled that the realtor told me the same family owned the house until I bought it. So the last owner must be connected to Ellen O'Shea, correct?"

"Yes, and that would be Timothy Allard you're referring to." Tom paused, looking directly at her. "He passed away about a week ago."

"Oh, no, I'm sorry to hear that. I knew he was sick." Amelia lowered her eyes toward the coin in Tom's hand. "Was he really the last of that family?"

Tom fiddled with the coin. "No... he wasn't. But it will be tricky to track her."

"Track who?"

"His sister. She..." Tom stopped, stilling the coin in his hand as he looked at it. "Let me do a little digging for you and confirm the facts on this coin. And I think I can get ahold of his sister too. Like I said, she's a little hard to find, so I can't promise anything. I'll give you a call as soon as I have some information."

"That sounds like a plan. Thank you for your help with this." Amelia stood and Tom followed her lead, escorting her out the door and into the hallway.

When Amelia walked back into the cold December air, her mind was going in circles from her meeting with Tom. Sitting in her car, she considered everything she'd just learned before driving home. She pulled out the sticky note and called M&W Remodeling to confirm with the secretary that the following Thursday worked for her and left her number. Then she turned her mind to Mr. Allard's sister. She couldn't stop thinking about her. She wanted to return this coin to the right family, but—even though it wasn't any of her business—it was difficult not to wonder why the sister was hard to track down. Or why she didn't take the house when her brother got sick. Perhaps she was estranged from him, but it was such an old and valuable property in her family to just let go.

Amelia didn't have answers yet, but she was looking forward to figuring it all out.

CHAPTER 11

*T*he dancers filled the first few rows of the high-school auditorium, ready to get up on the stage. Ms. Sherry told everyone to take a seat so she could go over a few things before they got started. It was the first stage Amelia had been to since she'd said goodbye to her own in New Haven. With a heavy heart, she placed her bags on a table behind the curtain and slowly walked out to the center. Many of the girls in the first row quieted, watching her. One by one, the rest stopped talking, too, observing the moment.

"Dance for us, Amelia!" one of the girls called out.

Amelia smiled at her. "I wish I could." She walked to the edge of the stage and sat down. "The reason I'm not on the stage anymore is because of an injury. I realize now I didn't share that before."

"My mom told me about it," another girl said.

"Me too," the girl next to her added.

"It's something we should have talked about before now," Ms. Sherry said, walking out behind Amelia. "Girls, as you know, Miss Amelia retired from dance, but for those of you who may not have heard, she hurt herself during a perfor-

118

mance earlier this year that caused her to end her career sooner than expected."

The dancers sat still, some seeming sad to be hearing this news and looking down—making the energy in the space feel stifling. Not a good place to begin their practice.

"Hey now, let's not get down about that!" Amelia rose to her feet and flashed them a beaming smile. "We have *The Nutcracker* to get ready for!"

"Yes, we do, ladies! Eyes on me!" Ms. Sherry waited until they were all looking at her. "Now, listen up, I have a few formalities to discuss before we get started on rehearsal."

As Ms. Sherry started updating the students, Amelia realized she'd left her spiced chocolate latte in her car. After retrieving it, she saw Julia and Ava getting out of their dad's car.

Ava rushed past her. "Am I in trouble? Did they start?"

"No!" Amelia called out. "They only just started the announcements!"

"That's still late to Ms. Sherry!" Julia said and followed her sister, hoisting her ballet bag as she tried to keep up with Ava.

Ben came up next to her and they watched the girls hustle inside.

"Sorry about that. Got caught in the office with a client."

Amelia shrugged. "It happens. I'll tell Ms. Sherry." She started to head back inside. "We'll see you after."

"Wait…" He gently touched her shoulder. "Do you have a minute?"

"Sure." Amelia braced herself—the weight of his thoughts was etched on his face.

"I just want to say… I really do appreciate how hard you're working with Ava. She seems to feel better about the dances she will be doing. But…" He stuck his hands in the pockets of his coat, moving his eyes toward the darkening sky. "You see, my wife… She's… I don't know how to tell you this—"

"Ben, it's okay…" She held up her hand to stop him. "You don't have to tell me anything you aren't comfortable saying." By this point, she had already pieced together that something had happened to his late wife, since she hadn't met her yet and she remembered Julia referred to her in past tense that first day she came to the studio, but that was so personal, and she didn't want him to feel obligated to tell her. "Besides, I think already know," she gently added.

When he looked at her again, for the first time Amelia saw beyond the hard edges. Ben shifted in his stance; letting his guard down was clearly not easy for him. She kept her gaze on him, and he loosened his tough exterior further, revealing a man and father trying his hardest to overcome a difficult past as best he could.

"Losing their mother has impacted Ava the most, being she's the oldest. She's always…" —he let out a long sigh—"tried to fill in as mom in a way for Julia. But for the past few years of doing that, it's taken a toll on her. She's put this pressure on herself that I can't seem to shake off her, and it plays out in everything she does, including dance. I just wanted you to know so your time together is smoother. I'm sure you've seen the frustration."

"I have." She thought about her text to Ms. Higgens that first night working with Ava. "But I'll continue to do my best to work through it with her and be the best mentor I can."

Neither of them moved, gazes locked, the only light coming from the building behind them. Ben's eyes were like dark pools against the reflection, deep with a story that was just waiting to be heard. Amelia swallowed, taking a step back.

"I better get back in there. But, Ben…?" She gave him an encouraging smile. "Thank you for sharing this with me."

His eyes, now relaxed from getting what he'd wanted to say off his chest, moved up and down her face. "Thank you for listening..." A small smile tugged at the corners of his mouth. "And for being there for Ava. It means a lot."

She sensed his lingering stare while she walked away, but she didn't look back. They had been talking about Ava, yet when she got to the door all she could think about was him. The boundaries between them seemed blurred now, leaving her enthralled by the man she'd just seen underneath his protective barrier.

WHEN AMELIA STEPPED OUTSIDE THE NEXT MORNING TO RUN an errand at the hardware store, a sharp gust of wind greeted her. The new layer of freshly fallen snow glistened in the yard and she slid her sunglasses on before getting into her car. Besides the rehearsal that afternoon at the high school, she had the weekend cleared and the only thing she wanted to do was finish unpacking the last of the boxes. And keep her mind off Ben.

Ms. Sherry had asked her to observe Ava at yesterday's rehearsal so she could work with her today on whatever she'd noticed needed some extra time. Since she didn't have to instruct, she was left with her thoughts, which had made it difficult to concentrate—especially as she watched Ben's daughter perform. Everything he told her about Ava made a lot of sense and this new understanding should make it easier to work with her, but it felt the opposite for Amelia. What if she made it worse?

Stick to ballet... She willed herself out of the worry. Pulling out some notes she'd scribbled down yesterday, she checked them over and added a few things she had missed. Scanning the list one last time, she had a good idea of which moves to work on today with Ava.

She turned up the music in her car and admired the scenery with the snow adorning the trees along the windy roads. The hardware store was next to the town hall and she wanted to go there to ask about a snowblower and shovels. One of her neighbors had knocked on the door a couple days prior and mentioned having both on hand, and she agreed that was a good idea, especially since she'd already come to learn the person who had been plowing her driveway was often unreliable.

Her dashboard notified her of an incoming call and she smiled when she saw it was Sam.

"Hey there, stranger," Amelia answered, slowing behind a snowplow.

"Amelia! It's so good to hear your voice. Ms. Higgens and I are both in the office and wanted to check in on you out there in… White Bridge, is it?"

"Yes, that's where I've landed, and it's good to hear your voice. I'm hanging in. It's a whole new world up here."

"I bet," Sam said.

"If you're going to own a country farmhouse, you better have it decorated to the hills for Christmas when I come visit," Ms. Higgens chimed in.

"Then you better make that visit next Christmas, Ms. Higgens, because I'm meeting with a contractor next week to start some big remodel work. I doubt I'll be able to get every room decorated to your liking since walls might be covered in tarps for painting soon."

"Then it sounds like that farmhouse has your hands full," Ms. Higgens said.

"I'm still unpacking and besides the notes from the inspection and those updates, I'm still figuring out what other work I'm going to be doing to it. It'll definitely keep my hands tied up. But you are both welcome to come here any time."

"I might just do that. A little drive to the country sounds like a nice break. Lucy is keeping us informed down here, but we wanted to hear your voice as well," Sam said. "We really miss you, Amelia."

"I miss you all too. Once I get my life in order up here, I will come visit."

"We are training a few new recruits, and it's just not the same without you," Ms. Higgens said. "They have big pointe shoes to fill."

"That really means a lot to hear, but I know you will whip up some amazing new dancers, Ms. Higgens. Your teaching skills are the best there is." Amelia paused, pulling up to a stoplight. "Speaking of teaching… your advice was so helpful. Thank you again for that."

"You never cease to amaze me," Sam said. "After years of dancing and an injury that ended it all, you turn around and give back. Ms. Higgens filled me in about your text to her the other day and that young dancer you're privately coaching."

"I don't know what I'm doing though. I've never taught before."

"You don't have to know, it's in you," Sam said. "I watched you mentor your fellow dancers here at the theater for years."

"Mentoring an adult is one thing, but a teenager? Totally different experience," Amelia said.

"How has it been going with Miss Ava?" Ms. Higgens asked.

"It's getting better. It's not her dancing I worry about, it's more her confidence. I'm able to give her repetitive encouragement like you told me, but sometimes she really gets down on herself over the smallest mistake. Like in this past Thursday's practice we were running through her part in the promenade she'll be doing with the Prince, who will be played by a young man from Hartford College of Dance. I filled in the role of the Prince and she transitioned a little too quick into the glide en pointe around me. When I stopped the music, she burst into tears. Something is gripping her."

"Have you spoken to her parents about this?" Sam asked.

Amelia thought about her conversation with Ben the night before. "It's just her father at home and, actually, last night, I was able to get a little out of him. Ben is rather…" Amelia paused to think, and also moved forward when the light turned green. "Hard to talk to."

"Ah, well, remember you're brand new there. It takes time to build rapport both with your dance students and the parents. Keep trying with him," Ms. Higgens said.

"She's right, Amelia, these things don't just happen overnight," Sam agreed.

"I just want to help her through whatever is holding her back. She's a strong dancer," Amelia said.

"You will. Especially after having some pretty amazing teachers yourself," Ms. Higgens said, playfully coughing through the phone. "I won't name any names… but in all seriousness you are the perfect person to lead that young dancer."

"Like I said, you are the best there is Ms. Higgens. I'm not sure I can ever replicate your teaching skills," Amelia said, swallowing against the image of Ms. Ruth's nasty glare in her mind.

I hope I can provide the guidance Ava needs. They didn't need to hear about her fears. Or how she spent the whole week stuttering over her instructions during their practices because she was terrified to say the wrong thing. Her insecurities had been coming out strong since being at Ms. Sherry's studio, but Ava now depended on her, and Amelia would be there no matter what.

"You'll do just fine. We'll let you go to get on with your Saturday. The studio here will be filled with dancers any minute," Sam said.

"Thank you for calling. Give everyone my love." When she hung up, she cruised down Main Street until she spotted the hardware store.

It's in you.

Sam's words simmered down the extra anxiety that always came when Amelia thought of Ms. Ruth. The harsh memories of that mean old teacher who still haunted her came in bits and pieces, but the impact of everything she still remembered felt as if it was happening in real time now that she was the teacher. Like when Ava tumbled during a warm-up exercise that same day as the promenade scene, and the look on the girl's face had made it seem as if she was going to give up right then and there. Her words had stuck with Amelia for days now—running through her mind all over again.

"And Ms. Sherry still wants *me* to dance the Sugar Plum Fairy? I just fell over doing ankle strengthening. What's wrong with me, Amelia?" she had asked, struggling to hold back her tears.

Amelia had immediately gone to her, holding her in a tight hug. "Nothing. Absolutely nothing is wrong with you." She sat with Ava for a few minutes on the floor, telling her to take deep breaths, just as she did the same—her past creeping up on her.

"I can do it right, Ms. Ruth! Let me try again!" Amelia had said one day when she stayed after class to prove she could do the jeté just as the teacher had instructed. The other students were gone, and it was just them.

"You should have been able to get it right in class! Your mistakes are for your private practice time. By the time you're in

front of me, I expect perfection. If you can't deliver that, then stop wasting my time."

Amelia had squeezed her eyes shut above Ava's head. If it wasn't for the knock on the door from Ms. Sherry right then, letting them know the young man had arrived to practice with them, Amelia was fairly certain Ava would have called her dad to come pick her up.

Thinking back to that moment as she parked her car, it felt good to be holding Ava through the same worries she herself had as a novice dancer. After only a couple days of working with her, Amelia saw a part of her younger self surfacing through Ava, but she didn't know how to maneuver through the bad memories teaching had triggered in her.

All she knew was that she had to get Ava through their one goal: to dance as best she could as the Sugar Plum Fairy.

AFTER PICKING UP A SHOVEL AND PLACING AN ORDER AT THE hardware store for a snowblower to be delivered to the farmhouse, Amelia stood in the long line at the only deli in town. Once she reached the front, she placed her order for a honey-roasted turkey spinach wrap and caught Ben out of the corner of her eye standing up from a table with Julia and Ava. Unable to move from her spot in line while they finished putting her wrap together, she waved at him and managed to catch his attention. Ben gave her a slight nod, but didn't approach her. Then Julia caught sight of her and waved, casting her a big smile, and causing Ava to turn toward her too.

"Hi, Ms. Amelia!" Julia called.

"Hi, girls!" Amelia waved back. "See you both this afternoon for rehearsal!"

She flashed a smile toward Ben, who hesitated, but held up his hand when he saw his girls were watching him. *What is his deal?* Amelia arrived at the cash register to pay. *Didn't we make some progress last night?*

"He's always like that," a female voice said behind her.

When Amelia turned, she saw it was one of the clerks from the town hall. The woman's holiday earrings jingled when she smiled.

"So it's not just me?" Amelia asked, pulling her credit card from the machine. "Thank you," she said to the cashier and stepped aside so the clerk could pay for her food.

"No, not at all. My name is Sandy, by the way. I don't think we properly met the other day when you came to the town hall." Sandy extended her hand out and when Amelia shook it, the woman nodded toward the door, just as Ben and the girls left. "He hardly smiles at anyone since his wife passed, but he did do that 'look back' thing men do when you turned around."

"A what?" Amelia chuckled.

"You know, when you want to sneak another glance at the person. He totally did that. And you did get a wave from him." Sandy finished paying for her food and they stepped out of the line together.

"I'm teaching his older daughter privately at the dance studio. He's just trying to be polite, I think."

"I know I'm giving him a hard time, but he's a good guy," Sandy said.

Amelia remembered Ms. Sherry saying the same thing.

"He's just not one to easily get warm and fuzzy with. But, boy, does he love his girls. I've witnessed some amazing dad moments with him. So hard to do all on your own, but he's doing it well."

Amelia nodded.

"It was just..." Sandy continued, "so tragic when this town lost her."

"I'm sure it was. I'm sorry he had to go through that. His girls are both wonderful, so from what I can see, he's doing a great job."

"I agree." Sandy smiled. "Well, good luck with your search on that coin. If anyone can figure it out and get it back into the right hands, it's Tom. I got an update myself about it just yesterday. He's still waiting to hear back from the farmhouse's previous owner's sister."

"Yes, he told me he was reaching out to her. He also said she's tough to get ahold of. Why is that?"

They walked to the door of the deli and paused outside.

"Even though I grew up here, I still don't know the full details of what happened with the O'Shea family. Well, of course the name changed throughout the generations, but Ellen O'Shea was the original owner of your house. Anyway, everyone just knows more or less of the same—something happened to Timothy's sister when she was a teenager. There are rumors that have flown around here and there, and I don't like to invest in any one in particular, but I do know the town is happy you are in that house. It'll be a home again."

"Glad to hear everyone feels that way."

They parted, and Amelia thought about what the clerk had told her. She sure hoped she didn't let White Bridge down with her restorations.

Amelia got back to her car and noticed the time on the dashboard, which told her it was 1:30 p.m. She needed to get home, eat her sandwich, and get ready to meet with Ava at rehearsal.

The midafternoon sun had helped melt some of the snow for the drive back, and Amelia turned up a Christmas song as she drove. Thinking about her conversation with Sandy again, Amelia was grateful she'd run into her. It helped her understand a little more of the history behind the family that owned her house for six generations. *May it always bring our family good luck.* Ellen's note came to mind, and Amelia honed in on the word *luck*—not her favorite topic, but something suddenly occurred to her. Thinking about the young dancers as they prepared for their holiday performance and what gifting a nutcracker meant, a smile slowly spread across her face. She had the perfect story to share with them. She'd wait until regular practice next Tuesday to do it, since rehearsals at the high school would be busy, but it would be a great way for all the dancers to get to know her and build some more rapport with them—just as Sam said.

"Okay," Amelia said out loud, trying not to cringe. "Let's spread some lucky holiday cheer."

CHAPTER 12

$\mathcal{T}$uesday afternoon came fast after Amelia spent the rest of the weekend sorting through boxes. She didn't get through them all, but she got a lot done and was now able to locate most of her things—except the rest of her cold-weather dance clothes. She needed more to stay warm now the outside temperature kept dipping as the December days crept closer to Christmas. When she'd left the studio the night before, her legs were still ice-cold when she got home.

When she finally found the box she was searching for in her bedroom, she pulled out leg warmers, her thicker tights, and a long-sleeved leotard before dashing down the stairs. Pushing aside a few boxes in the front room, she spotted her Christmas box and ripped it open. Her holiday décor once felt like enough, but now seemed scarce for her large farmhouse. Quickly rummaging through, she spotted what she needed, her nutcracker, grabbed it, and ran out the door.

Turning onto Main Street with minutes to spare before she was expected at the studio, her growling stomach and the array of sparkling Christmas lights made her change direction and pull into the coffee shop. Unpacking had absorbed most of her attention all day and she had skipped over lunch. She hopped out of her car and ducked in to see what she could quickly find to eat.

Stepping into line behind a man wearing a beanie hat, Amelia squinted to read the specials listed ahead of her, but she had to shift herself around him to try to see better. Losing her balance, she stumbled against the man's back. A little girl stepped out from in front of him, and she instantly recognized Julia and Ben when he turned around in surprise. Taking a step back, she held her breath, but instead of aggravation, he gave her a small smile.

Progress!

"Bumping into you two again, quite literally," Amelia said.

"Pretty clumsy for a ballerina," Ben teased, keeping his amber eyes on her, stripping away another layer of his armor.

His vulnerability struck her.

"She's awfully pretty, isn't she, Daddy?" Julia's little voice broke their stare.

Amelia looked down at the young face beaming up at her. "Why, thank you, Julia. I have to say, you're quite beautiful too." Amelia smiled at her. "And I am really enjoying working with your sister and getting to know you both."

"So where did you used to dance?" Ben asked as they all moved up in the line, making it much easier for her to see the specials. Noticing her staring at the board, he moved aside and placed his hand on the small of her back, urging her to come forward so she could see better.

"I..." Amelia tripped over her words as she tried to answer, his hand still sitting gently on her back. She caught herself staring at him again instead of the specials. His natural charisma intrigued her. Was this really the same man who practically growled at her on the sidewalk that first day she met him? She managed to answer his question.

"I danced professionally in New Haven for years before moving here."

"I see," he said, dropping his hand and approaching the counter. When he turned to order, Julia stepped a little closer.

"My class is going to the studio in a little bit to do a final fitting for our costumes," Julia said. "Are you going to be there to help Ava?"

"Yes," Amelia answered. "Your sister is working hard on her role." She glanced around. "Is she with you?"

"Ava's in the car," Ben said as he paid for his order and took Julia's hand. "Come on, we better get you girls to the studio."

When he took a step forward, Amelia found herself inches from his face before he moved past her. A subtle fresh scent of his aftershave carried over to her as she watched them retrieve their order from the other side of the counter.

His eyes flickered toward her. "See you in a bit," he said.

She drew in a breath. *Okay, Amelia, he's Ava and Julia's father, get it together.* She blew the air back out, but the warning was already forgotten when he grinned at her before exiting the coffee shop. His former demeanor had overshadowed his good looks, which were now nearly impossible to ignore.

The studio was packed with dancers when Amelia arrived a few minutes later. The hot vanilla latte and cranberry-pear buttered biscuit—a splurge she hardly ever allowed herself— gave her a much-needed boost of energy. Keeping fit as a professional ballerina had been a challenge all those years, but now that she wasn't dancing anymore, she realized how many holiday treats she had missed out on.

Carrying the bag with the nutcracker in one hand and her half-drunk cup of coffee in the other, she walked toward Ms. Sherry's office and found her on the phone. When the woman waved her in, she put her bag and coffee on an empty table and shook off her coat.

"I will email everyone tomorrow by midmorning to make the call. The storm looks to be a toss-up with how much snow is expected, so I will wait and see before I cancel." Ms. Sherry smiled at her from over the phone. "Okay, sounds good, Mrs. Roberts. See you after practice." When she hung up, she rolled her eyes. "That's phone call number five about Thursday's storm. All my parents know I send out an email to let them know if I'm closing the studio, but there's always dozens of calls anyway."

"Storm?" Amelia asked.

"Oh, yes, nothing major, but according to the latest forecast it's going to be enough to most likely close down the studio. But the freshly fallen snow will be perfect for this weekend's kickoff with the Holiday Express Train. It's always such a big affair around here with Santa and Mrs. Claus on the train, and a bonfire and music to enjoy while everyone waits to board. Better grab some tickets before they're all sold out. You can buy them right off the town's website."

"Wow! That sounds like so much fun." It was something her parents would also enjoy when they came to visit that weekend. She'd get tickets online later. A thought suddenly occurred to her. "I've been so busy settling in and practicing with Ava, that I totally forgot to mention my parents are coming this weekend. Would it be all right to miss rehearsal this Saturday?"

"Absolutely. You enjoy your time with your parents."

"Thank you." Amelia noticed how Ms. Sherry watched her, evidently something crossing her mind. "Everything okay?"

"Everything is good with me, but I was just wondering about you. How are things with Ava? From what I can see, her dancing is already stronger than it was only two weeks ago. You really are good with her, Amelia." Ms. Sherry leaned onto her desk.

"I'm relieved you are seeing an improvement," Amelia said. "But do you really think I have a knack for it? I've never been properly taught how to teach dance."

"Neither have I," Ms. Sherry said.

That caught Amelia by surprise. "You haven't? You're so perfect in the way you teach those girls. I'm far from that."

"You can't perfect teaching right away. In fact, it's never perfect. It took me years to get my teacher's feet planted solid on the floor before I was comfortable in there. Amelia..." She hesitated, then looked her straight in the eye before continuing. "This performance will be my last with the girls. I'm retiring at the end of the year."

"You are? Who will replace you?"

"Well..." Ms. Sherry stood and came around to sit in the chair right next to Amelia. "I was hoping you would."

Amelia sat back. "Ms. Sherry, I—"

"Before you object, just know I've been searching months for the right teacher. I was so worried I wouldn't find one and even thought about staying on. That is, until you showed up. You are the exact woman for this job. I just *know* it." Ms. Sherry held up her hand. "And you don't have to answer me right now. Please..." She picked up Amelia's hand, giving it a squeeze. "Just think about it, will you?"

Amelia didn't know where to begin with how she felt about the question. Coaching Ava had been one thing, but taking over the entire studio? Like Ms. Higgens, Ms. Sherry was someone hard to replace.

"Okay..." Amelia finally answered. "I'll think about it."

"Good!" Ms. Sherry looked down at her bag. "Is that a nutcracker sticking out the top of that?"

"Yes, it is." Amelia opened her bag to show the older

woman. "I have something I'd love to share with your dancers."

"That's beautiful and looks to be specially made."

"It was. My mother and brother found it at a Christmas fair when I first got the role of Clara in *The Nutcracker* as a young girl. It's been with me ever since."

Ms. Sherry picked it up. "It's a nice big one too."

"I think it'll look lovely above one of my fireplaces this year. I've never had a fireplace before and now I have three! I'm going to need to do some shopping to fill that house with holiday cheer." Amelia took the nutcracker back from her. "Anyway, I'd like to tell the dancers the story of the nutcracker, particularly about what it means to gift them."

"That sounds wonderful." Ms. Sherry clapped her hands together. "The girls would love it. Let me gather them up. Both classes are in the back for dress fitting, so they can pause for a short while."

"It won't take long. I just remember hearing this story when I was young and I loved it. And afterward, I'll hit it with Ava. Sound good?"

"Sounds great. Let's go."

Amelia picked up her nutcracker and followed Ms. Sherry. After they brought all the dancers together in the studio and got them all sitting, Amelia pulled up a stool that was in the front of the room and placed the nutcracker on top.

"Hello, ladies!" Amelia greeted the dancers with a wide smile.

"Hi, Ms. Amelia!" the girls responded in a chorus.

"I have had so much fun helping you get ready for *The Nutcracker* and working with our Sugar Plum Fairy." Amelia smiled at Ava. "And I thought I'd share a little story. I know you all must know *The Nutcracker* story itself, but there's more." Amelia pointed to her nutcracker on the stool. "And I brought mine today to show you. This was gifted to me by my mother and brother the very first year I was granted the role of Clara when I was nine years old. Where's our Clara?"

A girl from the middle of the group raised her hand. "Here I am, Ms. Amelia," the girl said.

"Hmm… Jocelyn, right?"

"Right!"

"Would you please come up here, Jocelyn, and pass the nutcracker around? Be very careful with him, he's special to me." Amelia handed Jocelyn the nutcracker and continued. "When I was young, I had a substitute dancer teacher for a week when my regular teacher was sick with the flu. The other dancers and I adored this substitute teacher, and she shared with us what I am about to share with you. I've never forgotten it."

"Ms. Amelia?" one girl raised her hand.

Ms. Sherry stepped forward. "Girls, please introduce yourselves before you ask questions. Ms. Amelia is still learning names."

"I'm Kara, and I wanted to know if you have danced all the parts in *The Nutcracker*?"

Amelia shook her head. "Not *all* the parts. I never got to be the Mouse King, although I think I would have done a fabulous job." The girls giggled and she turned to Jocelyn, who was passing the nutcracker around. "Jocelyn, you know how Fritz is not so happy in the beginning of the first act?"

Jocelyn nodded. "He's jealous that I received the nutcracker as a gift from our uncle."

"Right! Well, if I were Fritz, I'd also be a little upset I didn't receive one of these nutcrackers as well because getting one is quite an honor. It means something unique. Does anyone know what it means to be gifted a nutcracker?"

Letting the dancers quietly think for a moment, Amelia looked at all the curious young faces and became overcome with a sense of contentment. Storytelling with children had a magical way of bonding and connecting, just as she'd hoped to do. But as she looked at the little sets of eyes watching her, she thought about what she was about to share, and tears burned in her own eyes. The day she'd first heard this story as a little girl was the last time she'd ever felt lucky and blessed inside. After that she was plagued by an unyielding standard of excellence—nitpicking every flaw in her movements and every mistake she'd ever made—taking up Ms. Ruth's harsh criticisms, which quickly drowned out the joy she'd always felt from dance.

How could she even begin to unwind from that? Or be able to lead these girls as their new head teacher with that mindset? She didn't have an answer, but in a room full of young dancers with hearts still full of hope, she suddenly wanted nothing more than to make each one of them feel that same bliss this story had temporarily brought her.

"When you are gifted a nutcracker, it is said that they represent strength and power, and will watch over your family, keeping evil spirits and danger away, and bringing you luck for your future."

"Wow!" Ms. Sherry chimed in. "I feel safer now with mine watching over me at my house. Who here owns a nutcracker?"

A couple of hands shot up.

"That is great to see," Amelia said. "So if you are going to gift one of these nutcrackers or receive one as a gift, just remember: they bring luck to the family, and will protect the home and you as you continue your journey as dancers. You can look at them and always remember how special you are while they watch over you." She swallowed back the tears. "And, do you know what reminded me of this story?"

The girls perked up, sitting as tall as they could to listen.

"I found an old coin in the farmhouse I bought here in

White Bridge. A coin that traveled all the way from Europe from when the house was built in 1870."

The dancers' eyes all widened.

"How much is the coin worth?" one girl blurted out before quickly glancing at Ms. Sherry. "My name is Theresa."

"Well, that's a great question, Theresa. I'm waiting to hear from a man in town who is looking into all that for me. He's also trying to track down who to give this coin to because there was a note inside the bag that made me realize how special the coin is. The note said: 'May it always bring our family good luck.'" Amelia took the nutcracker back from Jocelyn after everyone had had a chance to look at him. "Just like these nutcrackers do. Which is why I wanted you all to know this before you dance the performance. Who knows, maybe a nutcracker will be gifted to you this year. For now, I'll let you all borrow mine. I think I'll leave him here while you practice for a little while."

Ms. Sherry began to clap, and the dancers all did as well. "Thank you, Ms. Amelia, that was a wonderful story. Girls, what do you say to her for taking the time to share this with you?"

"Thank you, Ms. Amelia," they said in unison again.

"You're all welcome! Better get back to the costume fittings." Amelia scanned the room until she spotted her. "Ready, Ava?"

"Ready!" Ava stood up, waving at her friends before walking over.

"How much practice time did you get with those exercises I had you do from last weekend's rehearsals?"

"A *lot*," Ava said.

Amelia laughed at her animated expression.

"My dad and sister are just about ready to lock me out of my bedroom. It's the only place I can focus without disruption from the TV or Julia bouncing around me."

Amelia laughed again, remembering herself many years ago doing the exact same thing. At the time it hadn't seemed a big deal, but now she was viewing it through a new lens as an adult, she wasn't so sure. Ava had the same drive she'd had, but that wasn't always a good thing.

"Did you take time for anything else?" she asked.

"Like?"

"Friends, schoolwork, other hobbies… eating?"

"Of course I ate, Amelia." Ava giggled.

"Just checking. You're only fourteen. There's a lot more in life to do than just dancing." Amelia couldn't believe the sudden protective words she'd just spoken. There was once a time when she wouldn't have been caught dead saying such a thing.

"Well, in order to achieve what you have in dance, I'll be locked in my room for many more hours."

They reached their rehearsal room and Amelia flicked on the lights, thinking about what Ava had just said, and it didn't sit right with her—but with the performance less than two weeks away they couldn't waste too much time chatting. She would save that conversation for another day.

"Lace up and I'll put on some music for a quick warm-up, and then we will begin."

After Ava got her pointe shoes on, Amelia got her stretched and warmed up with some calf raises.

"Okay, good. Feel warmed up and ready?"

"Yes."

"We're just going to focus tonight on those fouettés. On my cue, but let's start from the demi-plié to the passé instead of the tendu. I want you to focus on sinking back and making sure those hips are neutral before you rise. Then we will spin." She walked over to the music.

Ava followed directions and, on cue, she began… but toppled.

Amelia quickly intervened, pausing the music when she saw frustration begin to brew across Ava's face. "It's all right, shake it off and we'll begin again."

She started the music again, and Ava spun twice this time before losing her balance.

"What is wrong with me tonight!?" Ava shouted.

"Ava, take a breath. It's all in the pause before you shift from one move to the next. And, remember, I told Ms. Sherry we're not doing fast pirouettes. We are toning down these fouettés. The Sugar Plum Fairy is delicate in her movements, which will slow this down."

"What if I fall on stage?"

"Then you simply get back up. The show must always go on." Amelia walked over and put her arm around Ava.

Tears spilled out of the girl's eyes and she sat down, burrowing her face in her hands. "I can't have that happen."

"Ava…" Amelia sat down next to her. "Tell me what's going on."

Face soaked with falling tears, she looked up at her. "I just want to make my sister and dad proud."

"They already are proud of you."

"No, you don't understand."

"Help me understand."

"My mom danced the Sugar Plum Fairy…" Ava began, and Amelia could feel her shoulders draw up as she tried to slow her breathing. "When she was my age. It was the same night she met my dad. I just…" She sniffed, wiping her eyes. "I want to make this special for him."

Everything suddenly made sense. This was more than just dancing the lead role. It held a special meaning for her—just as it did for Amelia. She decided to tell her more about Andrew.

"Ava, can I share something with you?"

The girl looked up at her and Amelia reminded Ava about

what she had told her the first night they'd met about how her brother missed her dance as the Sugar Plum Fairy growing up. How it was supposed to be her role at the theater this year before she found out she couldn't dance anymore… which meant he would never see her dance the role, and how much that disappointed her.

When she was done, Ava was quietly staring at her with a concerned expression.

"And now you have to watch me dance something that is special to you too. I'm sorry, Amelia…" Ava looked down at her feet.

"You have nothing to apologize for," Amelia said and lifted Ava's face to meet hers. "I promise. You know why?"

"Why?"

"Because working with you is giving me back everything that was taken from me."

Ava perked up. "Really?"

"Really," Amelia said, thinking of the nutcracker story she'd shared with the dancers earlier. She gave the girl an encouraging smile. "It's bringing me happiness, Ava. How lucky am I?"

Ava smiled at her. "You mean that?"

"More than ever. Now come on, we've got this."

They stood back up and Amelia clicked the music on again. The melody flowed from the speakers, and Ava began with a determination Amelia had never seen. Relief settled over her as she watched the girl glide through the movements. This unexpected road was becoming a beacon of hope —something she had thought was lost. Maybe luck *was* truly on her side.

~

THREE HOURS LATER, AMELIA FLOPPED ONTO HER COUCH. OUT of habit she looked for Mocha who always joined her. She really missed her. Lucy was coming that Friday morning before her own rehearsals, and Amelia's parents were expected to arrive shortly after. She couldn't wait to show them the new home.

Bending over to rub her feet, she laughed, realizing how today's practice with Ava was showing her how out of shape she already felt having not danced around the clock the last few weeks. But her tired muscles didn't bother her one bit as she thought about the look of excitement Ava wore as she showed Ms. Sherry all they had accomplished tonight. After their conversation, something had shifted in Ava, and she went through the moves with ease and grace, not beating herself up so badly when she slipped up. Amelia could see the trust in the girl's eyes as she corrected her and guided her.

When Ben picked up his girls, he curiously eyed Amelia as Ava ran to him with enthusiasm.

"Thank you," he'd said to her just before they left.

"Wow." Ms. Sherry had come up next to her. "I'm impressed. Ben really seems to be relaxing around you. What a treat to see."

Ava wasn't the only one who had left class feeling more hopeful. Amelia felt the same, and for the first time she was starting to understand not just *what* to teach when working with young dancers but *how* to. She remembered Sam's advice—*"It takes time to build rapport"*—and she smiled to herself at how far she and Ava had come together.

Her phone lit up with an incoming call from an unknown number. Normally she ignored those calls, but something made her answer.

"Hello?" Amelia said.

"Amelia?" a male voice said.

She recognized the voice. "Ben?"

"Yes, it's me."

Surprised, she sat up. "Hi there."

"Sorry to bother you. I hope it's all right that Ms. Sherry shared your number with me."

"It's quite all right." Panic suddenly hit her. "Are the girls okay?"

"Yes, they are, but… I'm not." Something in his voice had changed since earlier and it didn't sound good. "I understand you shared a story today about a doll offering protection and luck?"

"Yes…" Amelia was a little taken back. "It was just some of the history about the nutcracker doll. I thought the girls would like to hear more about it since they will be performing in the ballet."

"I get why you shared the story, but I really don't want my girls' heads filled with tales about being lucky."

Amelia stayed silent, racking her brain for an appropriate response. "I certainly didn't mean—"

"I know you didn't," Ben cut in, and she heard him sigh through the phone. "I don't mean to sound so harsh again, but we've been anything but lucky in this house for years now. Ever since… Well, ever since it became just me raising them all on my own."

"I understand," Amelia said, even though she hadn't meant her story's message as he took it. Her big step forward with him now felt like two giant steps backward. "I'm really sorry, Ben."

"Look…" He paused. "I'm probably just overreacting. But it was hard to listen to the girls talk about how things might get luckier for us if we buy one of those nutcrackers, and I just don't want them disappointed again if it doesn't."

Amelia closed her eyes, thinking about everything Ava had shared during their practice that evening. It was all becoming clearer. Like his oldest daughter was for him, Ben was worried about disappointing Ava and Julia—trying to avoid any accidental triggers or painful memories.

"I'll talk to them if you want. It was just a story, but now I understand how deeply it could impact them."

He grew quiet for a moment. "No, you don't need to do that," he slowly said. "I'm the one who is sorry. I know you didn't mean any harm by it. I guess I just needed to vent."

You and Ava both. She kept the words to herself, not wanting to upset him further. There would hopefully be another time to share what his daughter had expressed to her, but only if Ava needed her to. Amelia wanted them both to feel comfortable coming to her.

"I'm here anytime you need to do that," she said and was surprised how much she meant it. She felt as if she was balancing both of their deepest emotions, but instead of feeling burdened, she embraced it. "You're a good father, Ben. You're just trying to look out for them in a difficult situation. I'll be more careful with my words from now on."

"Thank you, Amelia. Really… Thank you. Ava was a different person tonight."

"That's great to hear."

"Have a good rest of your night."

Amelia placed the phone down, feeling fatigue wash over her, and she got up to head to bed. The moment her head hit the pillow, her eyelids drooped shut, and she drifted fast asleep.

CHAPTER 13

CHRISTMAS EVE, 1946

James O'Shea

"Just one more page left in this chapter," Susan called out to her husband, James. Hardly able to put the book down after she finished, she placed her copy of *The Greatest Gift* on the side table beside her chair.

James appeared in the doorway glancing at the fireplace. "I best cut some more logs to keep the fire going this evening. The air is like ice it's so cold. Must be snow coming. Are you enjoying the book?" James asked, giving his wife a tender look and holding his arms out to her. It had been a very hard six months, and he'd hoped reading uplifting stories of hope and redemption would help her move forward since the passing of one of their twin babies, Edward. Born premature, their son died within weeks of his birth. Their other twin, a girl they named Brenda, held on, miraculously surviving the low odds the doctors placed on her.

"Philip Van Doren Stern sure rewrote it well. I really like

the added Christmas theme to this version. We must find some time to sneak off to the cinema to watch *It's a Wonderful Life*. I'd like to see how closely the film resembles the book." Susan stood and stepped into his embrace.

"I heard in the latest headlines the movie isn't doing so well, but we could always judge that for ourselves. It would be nice to get out on the town with my beautiful bride." James held her tight, hoping to provide a brief respite from her sorrow. They'd married right after his discharge from the military after World War II, only a year prior, and Susan became pregnant with their twins right after their wedding. It still felt as if they were newlyweds.

A soft cry echoed down the stairs from the nursery on the second floor.

"I'm delighted Brenda took such a good nap," Susan said, looking over her shoulder at the stairwell.

James followed her stare, catching sight of the new bubble lights that shone brightly from their tree. "She's just preparing for Christmas Eve celebrations," he said, turning toward Susan again and giving her hand a kiss before she pulled away.

Susan smiled as James caught her eye. Brenda's cries grew louder.

"You are such a distraction," she teased him. "I better tend to her. She's surely hungry. Could you please tell your mother I'll be right in to finish helping her with dinner preparation as soon as I settle the baby and change? I'm looking forward to wearing my new red dress for candlelight Mass tonight."

"She told me to tell you to take your time reading and with Brenda. Rest is what you need, dear." James looked at her with concern. "Brenda is still not sleeping through the night, and between that and tending to the house and everything you are feeling, Mother is just as worried as I am."

"Darling…" Susan sighed. "Keeping busy is how I cope. I've noticed that many days you are also at the factory longer."

James nodded. She was right, keeping busy helped him too. Some days the grief was so heavy on him that seeing his wife's sadness was something he couldn't bear. Staying late at work helped him get through those harder days. But Christmas felt like a fresh beginning with the New Year around the corner. Susan was starting to come around, as best as a mother could under such circumstances, and his new promotion at the factory promised them more for their future.

"Remember last December when you returned home from the war?" Susan said, her eyes looking away dreamily. "I met you in New York City and we danced together at that jazz club, thrilled to finally have the war behind us and be getting married?"

"How could I forget? It's one of my most favorite nights with you," James said, closing his eyes.

"Well, after we get home from Mass and Brenda is down for the night, save a dance for me. Right here next to the fireplace. Let's celebrate the season together with hope for an easier year. I love you, James," Susan said, enticing him with a playful stare before dashing up the stairs to fetch their baby.

James watched her walk away, falling in love with her all over again. He turned to the cabinet bar, picked up the decanter and a glass, and poured a drink. The spicy kick going down was quickly tempered by the bourbon's silky texture. After placing the empty glass on a table, he noticed the bag with the coin on the mantel. How did it get there? Susan must have taken it out of the drawer where they kept it. Perhaps in an effort to find solace against her sadness. How strong his beloved wife was against all the pain and mourning over losing Edward. She had fallen into motherhood with Brenda with ease despite the loss, and he couldn't be more thankful for that this holiday season. He smiled at the bag—feeling a hint of the coin's luck still holding strong for their family.

The new year ahead looked positive for the O'Shea family.

∾

PRESENT DAY

Spending all day Wednesday unpacking, Amelia finally ripped open the last box in the front room early Thursday morning, and was relieved to see it was only extra blankets and a few breakable picture frames she'd stuck in between them. She was finally nearing the end of all her boxes. It had amazed her how much stuff she had in one small apartment.

After she put the blankets away, leaving out the thick cream wool throw and folding it over the top of the couch, she stood back and looked around at her progress. Just as she'd told Ms. Higgens in their last conversation, she only had enough holiday decorations to set up around her living room, kitchen, and the front room. Next year, after the remodeling work was complete, she'd have more time to fill the house from top to bottom, but with what little she had, it was already making the farmhouse feel like home.

On the coffee table next to her sat a large glass bowl holding dark-green-and-gold baubles, and now that she'd found her favorite wool blanket she couldn't wait to curl up on her couch later. Green, white, and gold were her favorite colors to spread about during Christmas, and she was looking forward to getting a tree up in the corner, with its twinkling lights set to complete the living room. The fireplace mantel sufficed for now, sparkling with lit greenery with copper eucalyptus woven in between.

Her tall, white-lacquered nutcrackers looked much better standing in the large hearth versus where they used to stand near the small electric heater in her apartment. Running her hand over the top of one, she thought about her special nutcracker that she'd left at the ballet studio. Ben's words swam through her thoughts. *"It was hard to listen to the girls talk about how things might get luckier for us if we buy one of those nutcrackers."* But what she'd first thought were steps backward now seemed like necessary steps toward progress, as he'd seemed to let go of his defenses for a moment and shared his heart.

Heading for the kitchen, she picked up the last decorations she had—three faux-frosted pine wreaths with the same green and gold baubles from the coffee table—and hung them on her big country kitchen windows using green plaid ribbon. Now done, she retrieved her empty mug from the living room and filled it with coffee to take upstairs while she got ready for her meeting with the contractors. She was proud of the unpacking she'd accomplished just in time for her parents and Lucy to visit. Maybe after the meeting she'd go get herself a tree before she went to the studio.

Before heading upstairs, she picked up her phone from the kitchen table and quickly recorded all the decorations she'd put out for her followers who were asking to see more inside videos of the farmhouse. She captioned the video *First farmhouse Christmas!* and uploaded it to her socials before scanning through a handful of comments from her previous post. A few people wanted to know the same thing… Was she finding time to date now? Her cheeks heated at the image of Ben's face that immediately came to mind as she tried to suppress the sudden surge in her pulse. The man was attractive, for sure, but did he look at her the same way?

Taking a large swig of coffee, she brushed off the thought and made her way upstairs to her bathroom. She had a meeting to get to. Glancing at her reflection in the mirror with her hair a mess and no makeup, she made a face. She'd spent more time unpacking than she had wanted, so there wasn't time for a full shower. *Time to rally.*

After splashing her face with cold water, she changed into jeans and an oversized black sweater, pulled out her makeup bag, and went to work. Freshened up with a little blush and mascara, she already looked like a new person. Holding a few bobby pins in her mouth, she quickly styled her long brown hair into a loose French braid down the side, a style she'd perfected during her years dancing. The ballet bun took a lot more effort to do for every practice, so braids had become her go-to hairstyle. A final check in the mirror and she was satisfied, feeling a little more put together. Glancing at the time on her phone, she realized the meeting was in fifteen minutes. She went downstairs, pulled on her thick coat and a hat, and hurried off.

Outside, the penetrating cold air seemed to blow right through her heavy winter coat. Even her car protested when she got in, taking an extra second when she turned the ignition. Giving it a minute to warm up, she pulled out her phone to connect her GPS to her car and plugged in the address the contractor's receptionist had given her. At the same time, a text from Lucy came through on her screen.

> Hey! Can't wait to see you tomorrow! Neither can Mocha! I think she's getting sick of me.

Amelia sent a response.

> I can't wait to see Mocha! Maybe we can grab a quick coffee while you're here?

She turned up the defrost and rubbed her icy hands together before another text came through.

> Yes to coffee! I have the morning off and due at the studio by four, so I'll be there around noon. See you tomorrow!

A short drive later, Amelia's GPS prompted her that she had arrived. She saw a small stand-alone building on the side of the road with a sign at the entrance reading: *M&W Remodeling*. Underneath were the words: *Preserving the Past, Constructing Your Future*. She felt excitement build within her. That was exactly what she intended—to make sure this farmhouse held on to its history during the remodel. There was a little pressure being the first one to buy it outside of the original family, but she couldn't wait to take something that held so much history and make it her own.

A secretary was sat at a desk when Amelia walked in and the older woman hardly lifted an eye toward her when she approached.

"Hello…" Amelia began, stopping when the lady kept typing on her computer. "My name is Amelia, and—"

"They will be right out," the disgruntled woman said.

Guess not everyone has small-town charm.

Finally, the woman looked up, giving her a small, forced smile. "Have a seat. There's coffee over on the counter, and water."

"Okay, thank you." Amelia bypassed the beverage counter and sat down, deciding to scroll through country-styled New England farmhouse décor while she waited.

Minutes later, with her nose in her phone and drooling over the custom-built hutches she'd found on one designer's blog, someone cleared their throat above her. Startled, she looked up and saw a man not too much older than her, wearing a dark blue workwear vest that said "M&W Remodeling" on the side and casual jeans with heavy steel-toed work boots. Unlike his secretary, his smile was friendly.

"Wasn't sure if I should disturb you," the man said. "Amelia, right? I'm Chris." He stuck out his hand as she stood up to shake it.

"Sorry, I didn't hear you walk over. I was absorbed in design blogs." She shook his hand. "Yes, I'm Amelia. Nice to meet you, Chris."

"I don't blame you. Buying a beauty like you just did up on Maple Ridge will draw you into every possible design out there. It's a gorgeous home, isn't it?" Chris led her down a hallway.

"Yes, it is. I knew I wanted to buy it the second I saw the listing online."

"Then this home was meant for you. We're happy you're considering us for the job. My partner would be handling your remodel, but I wanted to join you for the first meeting."

"Sounds like a plan," Amelia said.

He paused outside an office door. "We're meeting in my partner's office because he has more space. Our regular meeting room never heats up properly and it's a cold one out there, especially with the snow coming in this afternoon."

"That's what I hear. But the snow just makes it all the more magical on a property like mine," Amelia said.

Chris knocked and opened the door. "Ready for the meeting?" he asked a man sitting with his back turned, typing on a laptop. "Our ten o'clock appointment is here."

When Chris stepped aside to allow Amelia into the room, she nearly dropped her phone.

Ben Walsh swiveled in his chair and locked eyes with her.

CHAPTER 14

*C*hris seemed to encourage the awkward silence as he glanced back and forth between Amelia and Ben, before finally gesturing for her to have a seat. "My partner has lost his manners it seems. Sit anywhere you'd like. Are you sure you don't want something to drink? I must say, for a construction site the coffee we have isn't bad. My wife makes sure our secretary buys from the coffee shop in town when she stocks the pantry." Chris nodded toward the door. "I'd be happy to get you a cup."

"Well, then I must have some," Amelia said, sitting down. What was one more cup at this point? "Just a little cream and one sugar, please. Thank you."

"Refill?" Chris held out his hand toward Ben's mug.

"Yes, thank you." Ben handed him the mug, but his eyes stayed on Amelia.

When Chris walked out, she looked at Ben and shrugged. "Looks like you can't get rid of me, can you?"

Ben's mouth twitched in response. "Looks like it."

"Is that the beginnings of a smile I see?"

A grin broke out across his face. "I must say, there's something about you that fascinates me, Miss Amelia."

"After last night's phone call, I'm not sure if that's a good thing or a bad thing," she said and shifted in her chair, hoping he didn't take her teasing the wrong way.

This time Ben laughed, the unfamiliar sound hooking her as she watched his sandy hair fall back over his face after he ran his hand through it. There was no denying that Ben Walsh was handsome.

"Definitely a good thing," he said, his stare holding her still.

"Well then I hope I can continue to intrigue you, and that you can continue to trust me with your daughter," she said, trembling against his steady gaze.

Letting out a sigh, he leaned onto his desk, looking down at his hands. "Amelia, after I hung up from our call last night, Ava talked to me for at least an hour about how much you helped her at the studio. Being the Sugar Plum Fairy… is just so…" He trailed off, playing with a piece of paper on the table. "Well, it's just not easy, and for reasons that have nothing to do with ballet."

I already know, she thought. But she didn't want to interrupt what he was trying to get out, and she wanted to stay on the right track with him and not poke into his personal life too far—especially for Ava's sake.

"I felt really bad about how intense I came across on the phone. I'm sorry again," Ben said.

Amelia crossed her legs when his eyes found hers once more, the green-and-gold specks piercing into her. Despite her valiant efforts to maintain boundaries between them, she found herself powerlessly drawn to him.

"Ben, I—"

"Three coffees hot off a freshly brewed pot." Chris waltzed back into the room and placed a tray down, handing each of them their mugs. He settled into an empty seat and took a sip. "There, now we're ready to start." Looking between them, he seemed a bit perplexed. "You two look like you're deep in discussion already. Did I miss something important?"

"Nope, we were just discussing the upcoming ballet performance my girls are in," Ben answered Chris but kept his focus on her. "Amelia is helping Ava privately with her lead role in the show. She used to be a professional ballerina."

"That's wonderful. I bet Ava is really enjoying herself," Chris said.

It took an extra beat for Amelia to break herself from those sunlit boughs in Ben's eyes. Wishing she'd had a few more minutes alone with him, she picked up her mug and glanced at Chris. "I'm enjoying it as well," she said. "And I'm excited to hear your ideas about the house and what you know. As you could probably guess, it's just me living there, so I'll need a lot of direction with this."

Ben adjusted his position at the mention of her being alone, but she kept her attention on Chris and the reason she was there.

"The first thing we need to do if you decide to go ahead with using our services is submit an application to the town so we can properly evaluate the home, since it's in one of our historical districts. We're both pretty familiar with the property, but it's been a while since I've been inside the farmhouse, so we'll need to complete those formalities with the town and then tell them what we're going to be doing to it and what needs updating," Ben explained.

"But our biggest goal with M&W Remodeling is maintaining the original character of the house, while adding some modern touches that match your style," Chris said.

"I'll be the one doing the evaluation." Ben watched her, as if to see what she thought about that.

"That all sounds great." She gave him a reassuring smile and his face brightened. Or maybe it was all in her head.

"It's my favorite part of the job," Ben continued. "I always make sure to get the big stuff out of the way that will cost you the most. These old homes can gather expense pretty fast, so I will do my best to give you the most accurate estimate I can, with fifteen to twenty percent added on."

"An add-on?" Amelia swallowed.

"We always add that extra percentage for unexpected fixes that almost always pop up once the remodel starts," Chris quickly explained.

Amelia glanced between both men, trying to stay composed. Despite feeling excited for this, it was rather overwhelming listening to them lay down how it would work when she would be the only one footing the bill.

"I'm going to type all this up for you," Ben said, opening his laptop. "I can already see the classic homeowner hesitation building on your face."

"I feel like I'm opening Pandora's box with this and have no idea what is about to come out," Amelia said, watching Ben click open a new document and begin typing. "Thank you for taking notes for me. My mind is all over the place with ideas and questions."

"Well, let's hear some of them," Chris said.

For the next hour, the three of them went over all angles of remodeling a home like their past clients with similar homes and what they did to them; examples of unexpected costs, rules, and regulations with historical homes; and how they could sometimes cut expenses on bigger items, like windows, that didn't always need replacing. Ben typed up the first steps for her to take home and then showed her pictures and testimonies of completed jobs.

"This house we did in the town next to us last summer has a wide-open porch, just like yours, with the Victorian-style columns. It looks original from the style, yet that porch is brand new. Porches are my favorite part of old homes and I always keep the style historically accurate, but sturdy enough to last another hundred years with the right materials." Ben sat back, looking pleased as he admired his work on the screen.

Amelia was impressed. "Mind if I poke around your website?" she asked. Ben handed her his laptop. "You do wonderful work by the looks of it and from the testimonies of all those happy clients." She scrolled through the review page. "And you certainly know your historical homes. Let's go ahead and schedule that evaluation, and I'll get the application in tomorrow morning at the town clerk's office."

"Great. It'll take the town a day or two to process it, so let's set up a tentative date for next Tuesday morning. Okay?" Ben asked, pulling out his phone and typing.

"Sounds good to me," Amelia said, entering the appointment in her calendar.

"And here." Ben turned his chair and opened one of the drawers on his desk. "We keep some copies of the application forms. That way you can just drop it off in town tomorrow."

"Perfect, thanks." Amelia took the pages. "Say, do you guys know where a good place is to get a Christmas tree? Not too far, since the weather isn't looking great for the afternoon."

"Do you have all-wheel drive?" Chris asked.

"No, I declined the all-wheel drive add-on when I bought my car since I was living in New Haven at the time and didn't need it. Maybe I'll save tree shopping for another day."

"Nonsense," Chris said. "What better day to get your tree than today? Decorating it with snow falling outside is the way to go. Ben was just telling me before you came that his girls' school is closing early because of the incoming weather, and he was going to take them to the tree farm to get their tree today too. He also has a truck. Ben, why don't you escort our new White Bridge neighbor and client here and help her get a tree?"

"Oh, no, you don't need to do that," Amelia quickly said when she noticed hesitation on Ben's face. "I could always get a fake one at the store since it's just me. You go and have a good time with Ava and Julia."

"Fake? White Bridge has one of the most popular tree farms in the area. I couldn't sleep well tonight knowing you went out and got a fake tree," Chris said, the grin on his face telling her he was oblivious to Ben's reaction. "Go on, Ben, show her a White Bridge staple for Christmas—Miller Tree Farm. Besides, Amelia will probably need help cutting it down, so you should be there anyway."

A small smile spread across Ben's face. "Okay, you're right, Chris." He turned to Amelia. "Plus I'd never hear the end of it if Mrs. Miller found out I didn't bring you, and you ended up with a fake tree."

"Oh, definitely. She would personally come find you to share a few choice words." Chris chuckled and looked at Amelia. "Mrs. Miller's grandfather started planting Christmas trees on that farm in the 1800s. They have been officially selling Christmas trees for decades now. It's a real good time to get a tree there, especially with all the treats she bakes for her customers."

"I don't want to leave a bad impression on Mrs. Miller then," Amelia said. "Will the girls mind if I tag along?"

"Not at all. They haven't stopped talking about you since you showed up that first day for Julia's class." Ben's smile faded a bit, something evidently had crossed his mind, but he seemed to shake it off just as fast. "Let's get your car back home. I'll follow you, then we can pick up the girls and head out there."

The dynamic between them was changing and while he

was most likely just being polite—he was so hard to read—Amelia found herself looking forward to spending time with the Walshes.

"Sounds like a plan."

Amelia followed the men out of the office, the crisp air seeming to whisper snow as the gray clouds released the first few flakes. As someone who once cringed each time winter weather hit—since she'd have to trudge through the cold, muddy slush to get to the studio for ballet practice—it was strange to realize that snow now brought her a thrill. The blanket of white only enhanced the Christmas magic she'd felt around White Bridge since she'd arrived. Rather than having been churned with dirt by city traffic, the snow gleamed against her surroundings.

Cutting down a Christmas tree seemed fitting now she was living there, yet her mind wasn't on the Miller Tree Farm as she pulled out onto the road. She glanced into her rearview mirror at Ben's truck, which closely followed her. His somber gaze through the reflection was alluring no matter how hard it was to decipher his complex moods.

"Miss Amelia!" Julia jumped into the back of the truck. "I didn't know you'd be here."

Amelia turned and smiled at her. "I didn't either. How was school?"

"Long." Julia rolled her eyes and buckled her seat belt.

"How is that when you got out early?" Ben peered at his daughter in the rearview mirror.

"It's always long," Julia said. "So how'd you end up in Daddy's truck?"

"Your dad and I had a meeting about my house. He's going to help remodel it, and he told me he was going to take you girls out to get your tree. I need one too, so I tagged along. Is that all right with you?"

Amelia nearly laughed at Julia's face as she squealed with delight.

"Of course, it is! Daddy, are we really getting our tree now?"

"Sure are, J-Bear."

"Daddy always calls me that." Julia giggled. "You can, too, if you want."

"I'll leave that one for your dad." Amelia looked over at Ben who seemed relaxed as he pulled into the middle school to pick up Ava.

"When Julia was a baby, her big brown eyes matched her mother's and looked like pools of chocolate," Ben explained, stopping behind a car in the pick-up line. "And unlike Ava, who was always more independent and couldn't wait to crawl and move away from us—Julia was my brown-eyed cuddly bear."

"Oh, Daddy, I'm still your cuddly bear," Julia said. "Especially now Ava is always cranky."

Ben chuckled. "That's to be expected at fourteen."

Ava approached the truck once they got to the front of the school and hesitated when she saw Amelia in the passenger seat.

"Hi, Ava," Ben said, turning around when she opened the back door.

"We're going to get our tree and Miss Amelia is getting hers with us too!" Julia blurted, barely giving Ava time to get all the way in.

"I see that," Ava said. "Hi, Amelia."

"Hi, Ava." Amelia twisted in her seat to face her. "Is it all right if I go with you all?"

The falter in her face relaxed. "Yes. I don't mind at all. I was just surprised to see you in my seat. I've only ever seen you in the ballet studio."

"And getting coffee! She and Daddy both love coffee," Julia added.

Ben laughed.

Ava's response sat with Amelia as they drove away from the school and through the windy roads to the farm. Remembering what Ben had said the night before on the phone about how Ava had been trying to overly compensate for their mother's absence, Amelia feared she had over-stepped from the way Ava had said "my seat" just then. She hoped she hadn't upset her.

They rode in silence with only the low sound of music from the speakers. Every now and then Amelia heard the girls quietly bickering in the back, and when she turned around she was always met with Ava's rolled eyes.

"The joys of being an older sister," she told Amelia.

"I'm not a big sister, but my twin brother, who I told you about the other day, annoyed me a lot growing up, he was always wrecking my dolls."

"You have a twin?" Julia asked. "That's so cool!"

Amelia smiled, but her thoughts went to her brother and the illness he fought every day. How she wished she could go back to the days he chased her around the house or jumped out to scare her from every corner—driving their mother crazy. Amelia understood the girls' mother wasn't with them anymore, and she didn't know what had happened to her yet, but she could gather it was a hard story for the three of them to tell.

Ben turned at a large wooden sign with an evergreen painted on it that read *Miller Tree Farm* and Julia cheered, snapping Amelia back to the present.

Flurries were circling around them when they got out. The parking lot was a field and quite a number of cars were there for the middle of a Thursday afternoon. Amelia heard a notification come through on her phone. It was a text from Ms. Sherry.

> Just a quick update that the studio is closing for the evening due to the snow. Could you make it tomorrow afternoon for a quick makeup practice with Ava after she gets out of school? How about 3 p.m.? Her father already confirmed earlier it was fine with him.

She sent a quick reply.

> I'll be there.

"I just got a text from Ms. Sherry to say she decided to close the studio with the snow coming in. Ava, you and I are on for practice tomorrow to make up for today."

"Okay," Ava said.

Looking ahead, Amelia saw smoke coming up from a cabin that sat in front of a hill of evergreen trees.

"I bet they have the firepit going for s'mores!" Julia's excitement radiated onto the rest of them and despite the near silence in the car after Ava got in, everyone perked up in response.

"Looks like the rest of the town had the same snow-day idea to come get a tree," Amelia said.

"It's like this almost every day here once Thanksgiving passes." Ben opened the toolbox in the back of his truck and pulled out a larger coat.

"Come on, Amelia, Mrs. Miller has the absolute best hot chocolate," Ava said.

Amelia breathed out a huge sigh of relief seeing Ava's face brighten as she looked at the cabin with them. The last thing she wanted was to ruin a special outing for the girls or get in the way.

"Why not? Sounds delicious. I haven't had it in years."

Julia's mouth dropped. "What! *Years?*"

"I was always so busy in the Christmases before now, preparing for holiday performances, that I missed out on all the hot chocolate," she told her, realizing she shouldn't have let that slip out. Her overly strict ballerina diet was not something the two young dancers needed to follow her footsteps in. She quickly changed the subject. "But I've danced the hot chocolate role many times in *The Nutcracker.*"

"Rebecca is doing amazing with that chocolate scene," Ava said. "Her fouettés are perfect..." Her face fell.

Amelia gave her shoulder a pat. "No one is perfect in dance." Just as soon as the words came out, an understanding dawned on her: Ava's deep-seated desire to master her skills in dance mirrored that of Amelia's own as a young dancer. It was interesting to now view that pressure as an outsider looking in.

"Come on, Ava, I'll race you." Julia tugged her big sister's arm and Ava cheered up at her little sister's sudden playfulness.

"Ready, set... *go!*" Ben called out and the girls dashed off.

He instantly chased after them and when the three reached the barn, Amelia watched him scoop up Julia and pretend to go after Ava like a monster. The teenager who had rolled her eyes only moments ago was now full of laughter, playing along with her dad and sister with such happiness.

It was a beautiful moment to witness and to see Ben effortlessly switch gears into his role as a father, showing her the true depths of his character. His on-and-off, guarded body language told one story, but he was something entirely different here with his girls. A rush went through her as she thought about the farmhouse renovation. She hoped she got to work alongside this Ben. He had her mesmerized.

CHAPTER 15

"Girls, I need to take our tree back before I cut Amelia's. I'm not about to carry two trees down this hill." Ben picked up the bottom of the trunk and began to trudge down the slope.

After about a half hour searching for their trees, a fresh layer of snow now blanketed the ground and was the fluffy kind you could shape and play in. Amelia knew she would regret it—she wasn't wearing the proper clothes—but she lay in the snow and moved her arms and legs up and down.

"Snow angels!"

Julia joined her, but when Amelia sat up, Ava was quietly staring at them.

"Want to make one with us?" Amelia offered a smile, but it was as if Ava was in a trance. "Ava? Are you all right?" An alarm sounded from nearby. "Is that your blood sugar monitor?"

Suddenly, Ava dropped to her knees. "I'm feeling a little dizzy."

"Ava!" Julia jumped up and ran to her sister's side. "Let me check your phone." She searched the snow around them and found the bag where Ava must have dropped it before she felt dizzy.

Amelia quickly joined them, putting her arm around Ava. "Here, lean into me."

"I... I wasn't feeling so great after I raced Julia when we got here, but I didn't want to ruin the afternoon." Tears pooled in Ava's eyes.

"It'll be okay, I'm right here." Amelia tightened her grip.

"Her blood sugar dropped. I'll go get Daddy." Julia handed Amelia the phone and went down the hill as fast as she could given the slippery snow.

Amelia looked at the screen, ignoring how fast her heart hammered, and saw the flashing that Julia had seen. She didn't want to mess up anything so she just held on to it and focused on helping Ava breathe slowly and deeply. When she saw a figure racing through the trees, alongside another man and Julia, relief poured through her.

"Ava!" Ben called as he approached them. He crouched next to them, and Amelia moved to the side and let him take Ava. "Let me see the phone." He took it from her and studied it for a few seconds, then looked up at the man who came to assist. "Can you hand me her bag next to your feet?" He quickly gave it to him and Ben pulled out a container. "Here, Ava, take these three glucose tabs."

"Let's get her back down to the cabin," the man said and helped Ben lift Ava.

"Ava, sweetheart, when did you start feeling bad?" Ben asked her.

"When we got here," she barely mumbled.

"Like I've said a million times before, you can't wait to tell me."

Amelia felt Julia's hand slip into hers as they followed the men and Ava carefully down the hill. When she looked over, she saw a tear fall down Julia's face and paused, turning the girl toward her. "It'll be okay, Julia, your daddy has it under control."

"I know." Julia kept her eyes on her sister and didn't say anything else. Amelia just wanted to get her to the cabin where it was warm.

Once they were there, Amelia was quick to order their hot chocolates, hoping to distract Julia and cheer her up while Ben got Ava's blood sugar stabilized in the privacy of the office. She handed Julia her hot chocolate and the girl blinked up at her with those big brown eyes Ben had talked about and said, "I bet this will taste extra good for you since it's been so long since you had one."

Amelia took a sip. The warm, smooth, and velvety chocolate melted in her mouth, and she looked at Julia. "Mmm... even better." She took another drink. "Wow, that's good."

Julia's eyes sparkled with satisfaction. "Told you!" They sat down at a table. "I know you said you've been too busy dancing for hot chocolate, but didn't you eat and drink anything when you were a ballerina? My daddy always makes sure I have a good snack with protein before I go to dance practice. Looks like you didn't learn that."

Her mouth twitched at Julia's freewheeling choice of words. "Of course I ate and drank, just not enough I suppose. And your daddy is absolutely correct. I just..." She paused for a minute, considering what to say. Looking back now, it was evident she had been extremely fixated on maintaining a polished image both on stage and off, with modeling and her social media presence. That had been the wrong approach and one she did not want Julia to fall victim to. "I didn't listen to my own mom about protein and I should have."

"Uh-oh... I bet that made your mom mad."

Amelia laughed, thinking about all the faces she had received from her mother over the years when she'd been so picky with her food. "Oh, yes, very mad."

"Ms. Sherry always has extra snacks too. She says a good dancer is a well-fed one. I bet she'd have been mad at you, too, if she was your teacher growing up."

Amelia froze against a fragment of her past that suddenly burst forth, startling her with its vividness. Ms. Ruth had been the opposite, always quick to scold Amelia about her diet, saying she lacked discipline, that she'd never succeed as a dancer if she didn't have self-control. More unattainable perfection.

"Miss Amelia?" Julia asked. "Are you okay?"

She could still hear Ms. Ruth whispering in her ear but shook it off and smiled at Julia.

"Yes." Amelia leaned closer to the girl, lowering her voice. "How about we sneak another one before your dad comes out of the office."

"I like that idea!" Julia said in a loud whisper.

A little while later, the two of them were settled with their second hot chocolates in hand, still waiting on Ben and Ava. Julia was also enjoying some s'mores she'd been given by the man who had helped Ben with Ava.

The man extended his hand. "I know we didn't get a chance to formally meet up there on the hill," he said. "Rick Miller."

"Hi, Rick, I'm Amelia Collins."

"New to White Bridge?"

"Brand new. Bought the farmhouse up on Maple Ridge."

Rick nodded. "That's what I heard from Ben. He's looking forward to starting that job. The house has needed some TLC for years now. It's a gorgeous home." Bending down, he reached over and tousled Julia's hair. "How're the s'mores? Brady saw your sister not feeling well and rushed to make those for you."

With a mouthful of melted marshmallows and chocolate, Julia mumbled, "Good."

"How is Ava? Have you been back there?" Amelia asked, looking over her shoulder toward the office.

"Ava is just fine. Ben has her feeling much better," Rick said, watching Julia finish off her treat, licking the extra chocolate off her fingers. He looked back at Amelia. "My son Brady is always glued to the s'mores station out there. He'd be happy to make you one too. Would you like a s'more?"

"No, I'm..." she started but then saw Julia eye her. "Actually, I'd love one."

"Julia, why don't you go out there and tell Brady to whip up a few more." Rick pointed toward the door.

The girl raced off.

Amelia held up her cup. "This is delicious, by the way. What's your secret?"

"It's my great-grandmother's recipe. Even I haven't had the privilege to know what it is yet. My wife's eager to get it someday soon."

"Don't blame her there. Do you and your wife run the tree farm?"

"Yes, and my mom is still around, too, baking all the sweets for the kids every season. Brownies, just about every Christmas cookie recipe there is, cakes... Even at seventy-one years old, she hasn't slowed down on that job. When my dad passed away a few years back, she said it's this farm that gets her by. I hope you come back for your tree soon."

The office door opened, and Ben and Ava came out. Amelia was happy to see the color had returned to Ava's face.

"Thank you, Rick. I will. I'm not worried, the season is far from over. I'm just glad to see Ava is okay."

Rick walked away, patting Ben on the shoulder and making his way back outside to his customers.

Amelia stood up and went to put her arm around Ava's shoulders. "Feeling better?"

"Yes, but still a bit tired."

"Brady gave me four more s'mores!" Julia came back inside, holding up a napkin with the gooey treats. "One for each of us! Here, Amelia." She handed Amelia one and everyone waited.

"Well, down it goes..." Amelia took a bite, a little of the marshmallow falling onto her chin. "I could get used to these," she said between bites.

Julia giggled.

"Let's take the rest of those with us and get Ava home, then I'll drop you off, Amelia." Ben gave her an apologetic look. "Sorry we didn't get your tree."

"Daddy, why doesn't Amelia come help us decorate ours?" Julia turned to Amelia. "We always order pizza while we decorate."

Could she even remember the last time she'd had pizza? Greasy, carby, delicious pizza... It sounded so good, but she didn't want to overstay her welcome. "Oh, I don't know..." Amelia hesitated when she looked at Julia's pleading eyes.

"Come on," Ben said. "You didn't get your tree, so the least I can do is feed you dinner."

Amelia noticed Ava staring at her quietly. It was difficult to read her expression.

"Maybe I'll just have one quick slice and then you all can get to your decorating." She kept her eyes on Ava.

"You can have two if you'd like." A smile spread on Ava's face. "And my dad will definitely need your help with the lights since I'm just going to be watching."

"Or three!" Julia chimed in and they all laughed, making their way out to the parking lot.

"Lights and pizza it is!" Amelia said once they got to the truck and Ben helped Ava in.

The slight breeze swirled the snowflakes in a graceful dance as they tumbled and twirled to the ground. Chris had been right before, the snow was making the perfect background for tree decorating. This time the ride was livelier as Julia talked about what she wanted that year for Christmas and sang along to various holiday tunes on the radio. Ava stayed quiet next to her, only laughing when her sister belted out the chorus to "Jingle Bell Rock."

"She seems like a patient older sister," Amelia said to Ben, leaning in a bit so she didn't interrupt the girl's singing.

"She has her moments, just like any other teenager. But like I said last night, ever since my wife passed, she's picked up a lot of responsibility with Julia and has done a great job. But she's only fourteen, and I want her to focus on being that."

"I'm so sorry you lost her," Amelia quietly said, turning to see if the girls were listening, but they were still in their own world filled with presents and holiday excitement.

Ben didn't answer and kept his eyes on the road, slowly making his way through the snow. Amelia didn't mind. Just telling her as much as he had the past couple days was probably hard enough.

THEY LIVED IN THE MOST ADORABLE COTTAGE. IT WAS SMALL, yet beautifully updated, which didn't surprise Amelia. After Ben got the tree inside and into its stand, she helped him string the lights around it. Just as she was about to sit and enjoy the twinkling glow while Ben went to the basement to get the ornament boxes, Julia grabbed her hand.

"I want to show you my room," Julia said, tugging.

The first thing Julia showed her was the handcrafted bunkbed with a desk that fit perfectly underneath.

"My daddy built that bed for me up high so there would be more room when Ava was in here with me. We used to share a room for a long time until Daddy made the loft taller and wider and gave her a bedroom up there. We don't have a second floor, so that was the only option," Julia explained.

"Pizza is here!" Ben announced from the front door.

"Coming!" Julia called over her shoulder. "I'm starving, let's go eat."

"Even after all those s'mores and hot chocolate?"

"I'm a growing girl," Julia said, rubbing her belly.

Amelia grinned. "That you are."

She followed Julia back into the living room and saw Ava sitting up on the couch after taking a quick nap.

"Wait, Dad, did you—" Ava started to say.

"Order a few extra slices of sausage, peppers, and pepperoni for you? Sure did." Ben placed the large box and a smaller box down on the table next to paper plates, waters, and napkins. "Ava is the only one who likes peppers on hers, but I realized I didn't even ask if you did. The larger one is half cheese and half pepperoni. Is that all right?" He looked at Amelia.

"Perfectly fine by me. You all dig in, and I'll find a slice once you have yours." Amelia picked up one of the waters and took a sip.

The fire Ben had started was blazing and Christmas music played from speakers in the other room. It was the coziest scene, making her miss her parents and Andrew.

"How'd you like the tour? Didn't take long, I bet. Not much to see," Ben said, pulling a slice out for Julia before handing Ava her special order and making a quick check of her monitor.

"Well, I only made it to Julia's room, but there is a lot to see. Everything is remodeled and crafted so nicely. I'm assuming this is all your work?" she asked Ben, glancing around the room at the custom bookshelves and up at the painted planked ceiling with beams that ran across and then down to the rich wooden floors that looked freshly redone.

"Yes, everything in this home was rebuilt or updated by me, despite it being so small."

"For the space you have, you've made it feel shiny and new and roomy with all the creative storage. Gives me a good example of what's to come for my own house."

Ben smiled. "Thank you. I can't wait to get my hands on that house of yours. By the time the evaluation comes, I will probably have a hundred new ideas." He took a bite of his pizza and pushed the box toward her so she could get some. "I've done a lot of work to get this house ready for the market. Hoping to sell it by the spring, so I can move these girls into something a bit larger."

"And with a backyard so we can get a dog! Right now, our backyard is a tiny patch of grass that runs up against a river," Julia explained with a little string of cheese falling from her lips.

Ben handed her a napkin and smiled. "Yes, we hope to get a dog. The girls have been begging me for years now."

"A dog would be fun," Amelia said. "I had a Doberman growing up. He was a big dog, but so gentle and fun to play with. How long have you been in this house?"

"This was the first home my wife and I bought together. We originally had plans to upgrade to something bigger, so it's well past time to do that."

Ava loudly closed her box and plopped it on the coffee table. "Think we can decorate tomorrow, Dad? I'm still feeling a little tired from before. I'd like to go read for a bit and then go to sleep."

Before Julia could protest, Ben held up his hand to silence her, giving her a warning look. "Of course, Ava. Are you feeling better?"

"Yes, but I will be even better after a good night's rest."

"Go on and get yourself ready for bed. I'll come up later and check your monitor one more time before you go to sleep." Ben glanced at Julia who was clearly disappointed. "Don't worry J-Bear, the tree isn't going anywhere. Besides, it's always better to let the branches settle a bit overnight before we put the decorations on. You know this. Ava will feel stronger tomorrow and have more energy to help."

Julia sighed and stood up. "Okay," she relented. "Mind if I go play in my room?"

"Not at all. Could you take yours and Ava's plates to the kitchen?"

Julia collected the plates and left. Ben immediately turned to Amelia. "The joys of parenting. Never know how things will go."

Amelia finished chewing her pizza and wiped her mouth. "The pizza was a sure success. Thank you for having me for dinner."

"Sorry about Ava. Sometimes when her blood sugar is off, she can get a little cranky. But I don't blame her, it's a difficult thing to handle every day."

"Please don't apologize. She's been a brave sport all afternoon, even when she didn't feel well."

"That's been the theme around here for the past few years. We lost her mom right before the Christmas season, too, so this time of year brings back a lot more memories for Ava versus Julia, who was only five at the time." Ben picked up his water.

Watching him take a long sip, Amelia's mind raced ahead of her as her voice posed the question before she could stop it. "How did you lose her?"

The reflection from the fire made the inner gold of his eyes radiate, while his shoulders slumped a bit.

"I'm sorry. I shouldn't have asked that."

"No… it's really okay. I don't mind." Putting his water down, he closed his eyes for a moment before he began. "Let me start with explaining Ava. We first noticed the weight loss in her and the need for something to drink more than normal…" He watched the flames flicker for a moment.

"Are you sure you want to talk about this?" Amelia reached over and placed her hand on his shoulder.

"Yes…" Ben looked from the fireplace back at her. "It actually feels… rather nice to talk about it. I don't do it very often because ever since I lost Molly my focus has been the girls. It's like I went into autopilot—wanting to keep things in control as much as possible. Selling this house is bittersweet, but I'm ready to create something new for them in a different home."

"You are a wonderful dad. In the little time I've spent watching you with them, I've been so impressed."

Something changed in his face with her compliment. "That means a lot to me. All I want is to raise them with as much happiness as possible, given what's happened." He looked at her, and the pain from his past spoke volumes through his eyes—the story that she knew was there the first time she looked at them.

"The night we finally got Ava's diagnosis was the night I lost Molly. Ava was at ballet, and Ms. Sherry called to tell me she had collapsed in the studio."

Amelia watched him stand up and poke the fire, which told her he needed a few seconds to gather his words.

"I was at my office, about ready to leave to pick up the girls at the studio and meet Molly at a restaurant for dinner. It had been a hard couple months for Molly at work. She was a nurse in our local nursing home. The flu had hit the staff bad that year and she was working more shifts to help out. When she got the call that Ava was taken by ambulance, she was at the end of working a double shift. The exhaustion and panic and the slippery roads from a cold blast we had that afternoon didn't make for easy driving and she lost control of her car."

Amelia quickly figured out the ending and jumped in so he didn't have to say it. "I couldn't even imagine witnessing your wife and daughter in the hospital all at once."

"Even the emergency room doctors were at a loss for words, having them both there." Sitting down on the couch again, he leaned back. "It's been three years since that night and while it's become easier in some ways, in others it's not. I just want things to be… stable and for our days to run smoothly. But they often don't. Like when Ava hit her teen years and I had no clue how to help her with all the changes she was experiencing or how to do that ballet bun. I still can't get it right."

Amelia smiled. "I think I can cover that one for you if you'd like."

"I'm out of the bathroom now, Julia!" Ava's voice trailed in from somewhere in the house.

"Okay!" Julia called back from her room, followed by footsteps and the slam of the bathroom door.

Ben smiled. "I love hearing them go back and forth, whether it's an argument or they're getting along… either way it's great to see them together. I was alone growing up, no siblings, so I'm happy they have each other."

Amelia almost told him about Andrew, but could see on his face there was more he wanted to say. "Me too," was all she said instead.

"I was adopted right after I was born," he explained, looking a little more relaxed with the change of topic. "My parents couldn't have children of their own, and they didn't adopt again, so it was just me."

"Did you grow up in Connecticut?"

"Yes, a few towns away from here, the same as Molly. She and I were high-school sweethearts. I was also born in Connecticut, but the state keeps my original birth records sealed, so that's about all I know."

"And your parents never shared anything with you about your birth parents?"

Ben considered the question before answering. "I was twelve years old when they told me I was adopted, and they told me a little about them at first. That they were both teenagers at the time of my birth and weren't prepared to take care of a baby. Once I grew up, I got more curious."

"Which I would imagine is natural for a lot of adopted kids... to want to know more about where they came from."

"It wasn't until well after I graduated college that I finally asked them if they could get in contact with my birth parents. Unfortunately, my mom couldn't get ahold of my birth father or his family, and she said my birth mother had passed away."

"Ava!" Julia came out of the bathroom and crossed through the living room toward Ava's loft. "You left your phone in the bathroom!"

"It's getting late, I should probably get you home." Ben stood up. "I'll let Ava know she has to keep an ear out for Julia until I get back."

A few minutes later, they rode in silence once again, but it didn't feel strange or as if they had to fill in every second with conversation. Ben hummed to a familiar song on the radio and when he pulled into Amelia's driveway, her dark house felt so empty after such a lively afternoon and evening. Knowing he was going home to his small cottage, her large farmhouse, just for her, suddenly felt massive... and lonely again.

"Well, this was quite a day," Amelia said, turning toward him when he parked. "I really did have a great time, despite the lack of a tree for me."

Ben didn't answer at first, looking at his hands that were still on the steering wheel. "That is a relief, considering all that happened. Thank you for being there for Julia when Ava got dizzy up on that hill."

"I know we just met and I'm now one of your clients, but the girls already mean a lot to me. Helping Ava with her part as the Sugar Plum Fairy has been a joy to me so far." More than she even realized it would be. "So I'm here for you with whatever you need, including that ballet bun." They both laughed. "And I'm looking forward to starting the farmhouse remodel."

"Me too." He glanced at her. "I'm glad I got this chance to spend time with you, and… thank you for letting me share my story. It just sort of fell out of me."

"Then you needed to share it. I'm happy I was there so you could." Amelia opened the truck door. "Don't forget about the makeup practice tomorrow at the studio."

"See you then."

Ben flashed her a smile, igniting all her senses at once. She'd wanted to get through that wall and, after today, it felt as if she was standing clear on the other side.

CHAPTER 16

CHRISTMAS EVE, 1969

Brenda O'Shea-Allard

*B*renda couldn't believe it. Shivering, she went to the hallway, turned up the dial on the thermostat, and tightened her robe before going back to the kitchen. With snow already piled up outside and the next storm due to arrive in a couple days, she was grateful for the new gas-fired central heating system her husband, David, had installed the summer before—along with the new bay windows in the kitchen. The Maple Ridge farmhouse had gone through many updates over the past five years since it was handed down to them on their wedding day, but the new heating and surprise she'd just found in the kitchen topped them all. Running her fingers over the handle, Brenda pulled open the door, mesmerized by all the compartments of her new under-counter, front-loading dishwasher.

"Your dream kitchen is starting to come together," a low voice said behind her, and she straightened to see David standing in the doorway with his newspaper. "It was quite a long night getting this installed while you slept." He sat down at the kitchen table with a straight face and opened the paper.

"Who helped you?" Brenda looked wide-eyed at her husband. He was certainly handy enough around the farm with all the changes they had made, but installing a dish-washer wasn't one of his skills.

"Mr. Burke's son happens to be a plumber now, so he lent me a hand," David said, scanning through the headlines. "Now you have your hands full with the new baby and our son, hopefully this will make your days with them a bit easier."

"Anything helps. And washing dishes all day does take up a lot of time."

David read the paper for a minute. "Woodstock is still the talk of the news." He peeked over the top of the paper. "Coffee?"

Brenda stood motionless, still processing what he'd done for her with the dishwasher.

"Brenda?" David pressed.

"Hmm…" Brenda blinked, glancing at her husband, who was staring at her with an annoyed expression. "Did you ask me something?"

"I asked if there was any coffee made."

"Yes, sorry." Turning around, she got two mugs, poured coffee in both, and sat down across from him at the table. "I'll put on breakfast in just a moment."

Bringing the mug to his lips, David took a sip and put his attention back on the newspaper. "I assume your parents will be joining us tonight for dinner. Or will it just be Christmas dinner tomorrow?"

"I'm not sure yet. They said they would call this morning to let us know their final plans."

"Mommy?" Their son Timothy interrupted and came into the kitchen, rubbing his eyes.

"Good morning, sweetie." Brenda put down her coffee and opened her arms for her boy. Timothy climbed onto her lap, leaning his head on her shoulder, and she inhaled the fruity notes from his bath the night before.

"Baby Lisa is making those grunting noises from her crib again," Timothy said, looking up at her with his sweet blue eyes.

"Thank you for telling me. For being only three, you sure do help me so much." Brenda kissed the top of his head and moved him into the seat as she got up. "Would you like some milk while I give Lisa hers?" Timothy nodded and she reached for his favorite Mickey Mouse cup in the cabinet and filled it with milk.

Trying to ignore the fact that her husband hardly took notice of their son, Brenda retreated upstairs, sliding her hand up the railing—the same one that held so many fond memories of her as a child going up and down the same stairs. When she reached the nursery, Lisa was wide awake, quietly chewing on her fingers. Since birth, her baby girl had been easy and calm, unlike Timothy who had challenged her with colic during his first few months.

Picking her up, Brenda kissed her soft cheek and took her to the changing table. "Good morning, little one," she said, staring into the same blue eyes as her son's. Reaching over, she picked up a diaper from the bin close by and took a breath against the rise of emotions that suddenly came.

Her husband's closed-off demeanor had been that way for weeks, ever since they got the most shocking news in the mail—a draft card. Vietnam was still holding strong, and the possibility of her husband being called to serve was a very real and terrifying prospect. It was the first lottery drawing

LINDSAY GIBSON

since World War II, and thousands of men across the country were most likely feeling the same worry they were. David had quietly meandered around the house ever since he got the card, distracted and distraught. Spoiling her with Christmas gifts, like the dishwasher and new rollers for her hair, the last couple days must have been his way of meeting her needs since he feared he wouldn't make it back from Vietnam if called.

Picking little Lisa back up, she decided to nurse her in the chair by her own bed as it had the best view of the fields. When she got to her room, she sat down and got her baby comfortable against her. Before she gazed out the window, the small bag she'd kept on her dresser by her jewelry box caught her attention and the sadness that surfaced only moments ago began to wash down her cheeks. Shifting Lisa so the tears didn't hit her face while she nursed, Brenda quickly wiped them with the back of her hand and willed herself to calm down. The old coin inside that bag had been a staple in her family for a century now and with the reality of what their family was about to face with the war—the coin's luck was needed now more than ever.

Attuned to her mommy's sadness, Lisa continued to nurse but reached her little hand up across Brenda's neck. She smiled down at her baby, holding her tiny hand in hers. The encouragement her father, James, had given her the day before lingered in her thoughts. *"Brenda, darling, I'm still here. World War II didn't defeat me. David will make it through too."*

Looking at the bag again, she remembered David's excited face on their wedding day when he handed it to her. Closing her eyes, she sat with that beautiful memory, savoring it in her mind. Rubbing her thumb over Lisa's hand, mentally grasping the coin from that day as if it were now her lifeline—a pillar of strength.

"Don't fail us now."

PRESENT DAY

Elaborate patterns of icy crystals lined the windows and glittered through the late-morning sunlight. Amelia hardly ever slept in, but clearly she had needed it. She shielded her face when she opened her eyes, thinking she should order thick curtains as soon as possible. Walking over, she noticed ice buildup at the bottom of the windows.

"That can't be good," she said out loud and made a mental note to point it out to Ben during the evaluation. The inspectors had mentioned the windows were a bit dated but had said they didn't need immediate replacing yet.

She went to the bathroom and turned on the shower, then went back to her room to wait for the water to heat up. With Ben on her mind, she sat at the edge of her bed thinking about last night's tree and pizza adventure. Something had been building between them since he had called her, upset, the other night. Steam from the bathroom started to pour into the room and she shook off the smile that had become glued to her face. *Okay, Amelia, don't get ahead of yourself.* But something about the shift definitely had her attention.

She opened her dresser and pulled out some clothes to change into after her shower and heard her phone buzz from the bedside table. It was a text from Lucy.

On my way! I'll be there in about forty-five minutes. Mocha has been yowling nonstop since last night. I think she's officially all done with me. Ha!

Laughing, Amelia typed a quick response.

That sounds about right. Mocha sure gets moody. But she probably feels abandoned by me. See you soon!

Amelia couldn't wait to see her fur baby. It was quite an adjustment getting used to all the quiet space, and having Mocha to keep her company would make it feel cozier. She was thankful Lucy had taken care of her as long as she had. Going from their small apartment in New Haven to a farmhouse with two floors would have really made her anxious. Since the living room was the most complete, she would set up Mocha's bed and toys there where she could shut the doors until her cat got used to the bigger space.

Stepping inside the bathroom, she felt her cold bare feet tingle as they regained feeling inside the warm fog. When she'd finished her shower and turned off the water, a thump from outside made her jolt in surprise. The last time she'd checked in with her brother, he'd warned her that there would be more animals around, even black bears. Maybe one had moseyed onto her porch. Wrapping her towel around her body, she feared her heart would pound through her chest as she slowly walked over to the window to see if she could spot any animal tracks in the snow.

The sun's glare was too bright to see anything, so she went to get dressed, pulling on a long sweater and thick leggings. Suddenly the sound of a truck turning on echoed outside. *What in the world?* Looking out the window again, she made out Ben's truck heading back down the driveway. He must have tried to knock. Dashing down the stairs, she opened the front door to see if he'd see her and turn back around, and nearly collided with a mounted Christmas tree right outside her door. Stepping on the porch beside it, she looked up. The tree must have been a good foot taller than her. An envelope with her name on it sat in its branches.

Amelia,

I didn't want to knock in case you were still sleeping. I felt bad we didn't get your tree yesterday. Rick Miller cut this one down for you, and I went to pick it up early this morning. I hope it's the right size. Wasn't sure how tall your ceilings were. We can exchange for another one if it doesn't fit.

Tomorrow is White Bridge's Holiday Express Train celebration, in case nobody told you about it yet. Santa and Mrs. Claus will be on board, and there's food and a bonfire. It's always a good time.

Ben

Was that an invite? Either way, she already had purchased tickets and was looking forward to experiencing it and now perhaps seeing Ben there too... Her dripping wet hair felt like an ice helmet outside, so she tucked the letter under arm, mounted the screen door open, and lifted the tree to see how heavy it was. It wasn't so hard to lift, so she picked it up and brought it just inside the door. Even though she'd already planned on having it in the living room, she paused with her hands on her hips, and debated where else she could put it. She'd never had so many options before. Sitting by the lights was her favorite part about the holidays, so she stuck with her original plan and dragged it into the corner of the living room.

After running back upstairs, she towel-dried her hair

and ran a comb through it, applied a little makeup and grabbed her phone. Her followers would love this! She had received a lot of messages in the past week with tips and design ideas for an old farmhouse and she'd even written some of them down. Her audience seemed to be enjoying her new life, but many still asked her what her plans were now for work... and she really didn't have any yet. The Christmas tree set-up would have to hold over their curiosity.

Back in the living room, she searched for a place to prop her phone and settled on the fireplace mantel. She hit record with an excited smile. "Hi, everyone! I wanted to show you all what was delivered to my house this morning..." She picked up the phone and pointed it toward her tree. "Isn't it beautiful! I will update you when it's all decorated!" When she hit the post button, she laughed, knowing what a lot of people would ask... *Who* delivered it? Sometimes it was fun to keep them guessing.

She scrolled through her phone and found her mom's name and sent her a text.

> Hey, Mom! Looking forward to seeing you and Dad this afternoon. Take a look at my latest post. You will be especially pleased!

After watering the tree's base, she stood back and admired its natural beauty. Even without lights and decorations, it was lovely. The smell of fresh pine wafted under her nose, and the tree was just tall enough to leave a couple inches between its top and the ceiling—a perfect size.

The sound of a car crunching over the packed snow in her driveway caught her attention and she hurried to put her boots on before going outside. Lucy was just getting out when Amelia hurried down the steps.

"Mocha!" Amelia opened the back seat.

"It's so good to see you, too, Amelia," Lucy said, standing behind her as she jokingly hugged herself.

"Oh, yes, you too," Amelia said over her shoulder before picking up a yowling Mocha in her crate. "I know, girl, you're mad. You hate the car and the cold and it's all those things up here in our new home."

Lucy went around to the passenger side and picked up the bag with Mocha's bedding and toys with one hand and grabbed the handle to the covered litter box with the other. "I know you just moved in, but pulling into the driveway this time felt different. Not so..." She pushed the door shut with her body.

"Overwhelming?" Amelia held Mocha's crate in both arms, the cat's cries only growing louder.

"Yes, exactly. For some reason when we first came to see this place, the property felt bigger."

Amelia placed the crate down and propped open the front door, allowing Lucy in ahead of her, before putting the crate in the living room. "I'm going to put her bed and toys in here. Can you put her litter box in the bathroom over there?" Amelia pointed across the room.

Lucy put down the bag, took the litter box to the bathroom, and met Amelia back in the living room. Amelia took the bag and pulled out everything, placing Mocha's bed by the couch.

"And I know what you mean. There's still a lot of room everywhere, but it's really starting to feel like home, especially now my tree is here." Amelia shut the doors to the living room, a definite perk of an old home, instead of wide entryways between rooms, and bent down to let Mocha out.

"I see that. What a big tree. Must be at least seven feet. How did you haul that thing over here from wherever you got it?" Lucy walked over and touched the branches.

"I didn't." Amelia sat crisscrossed on the floor, willing

Mocha to come out by shaking one of her toys. "It showed up at my doorstep."

Her cat refused to move.

"They deliver Christmas trees here? That's handy, especially when you live alone." Lucy sat on the couch and looked down at the crate. "Well, for someone who wouldn't stop yelling at me the entire drive up here, she's now quiet as a mouse and won't even come out."

"She's nervous. Maybe some food will entice her." Amelia stood up and opened the bag Lucy brought, got out Mocha's dry food, and shook some out in her bowl. "And, no, they don't deliver trees here, just mine."

Lucy's brows scrunched together. "Just you? Then this is one friendly town toward their newbies." Her friend eyed her for a moment and Amelia grinned. "Wait... *who* delivered it?"

"His name is Ben and—"

"A gentleman is already making personal deliveries to you?" Lucy sat back. "Okay, spill."

Amelia rolled her eyes. "It's not like that. He's the father of one of the ballet students in the little school here in town."

"Does he happen to be the father of the student you are helping privately?" Lucy waggled her brow. "And if he is... have you had some private time with him too?"

"Lucy!" Amelia chuckled. "It's not like that. He's just being nice because I'm helping his daughter."

"Uh-huh..." Lucy stared her down. She knew Amelia so well. Hours and hours practicing at the theater made it very hard to get anything by her. "Then why's your face look like a tomato it's so red?"

"Cause you're making a big deal out of nothing." Mocha finally popped her face out of the crate and Amelia scratched her ear. "See? Mommy is here. Come on now, your food and toys are here too."

Purring, Mocha came all the way out and rubbed against Amelia's knee.

"I guess she's forgiven you for leaving her for over two weeks."

"Gosh, has it been that long?" She rubbed her cat's back. "I'm sorry, girl. I've just been busy getting everything settled in our new home."

Lucy looked around. "This room looks to be all unpacked. But I saw a few leftover boxes in the front room by the door. After I get through the performances; I can come back and help you really get this place organized if you want."

"I've had time to do it, but with all the remodel work that's heading my way, I wasn't sure I should unpack everything and get my stuff in the way. Those boxes are dining-room stuff, which I will keep in there for now."

"Until that fireplace isn't crumbling and the light fixture is re-installed in the ceiling."

"Yes, exactly." Amelia eyed her friend, knowing how Lucy was about to react. "And Ben's coming to do the evaluation on Tuesday, so I'll know more then about what needs to be done."

"Ben again?" Lucy smiled. "Okay, I need to meet this hunk."

Amelia tossed one of Mocha's toys at her. The cat herself was now perched on the back of the couch, gazing out from her new lookout spot.

"Hunk? I never told you what he looks like."

"You don't have to. Your face, that's still burning red, says it all." Lucy stood up. "Come on, let's go get some coffee and food in town before I head back to rehearsals."

"Sounds like a good idea. Do you mind if we make a quick stop at the town hall? I need to drop off an application so the town can approve the evaluation, and I don't want to forget.

Plus, my parents should be here a little after lunch, and I won't have time then."

"Yeah, no problem."

Amelia scooped up Mocha and took her to the bathroom to show her the litter box and let her sniff around. "There you go, that's your new bathroom." Mocha quickly ran back to the living room. "Poor thing will be so confused for a while."

"I'll drive," Lucy offered, and Amelia opened the closet for her coat. "Coffee, food, and the town hall. Let's go."

CHAPTER 17

"*A*melia!" a male voiced called from across the street, and when she turned around, Ben was jogging toward her.

"Well, aren't you just the popular one here already? Personal tree delivery and already being recognized in town." Lucy nudged her.

Leaning over, Amelia whispered, "That's Ben."

"Oh…" Lucy said, pulling off her sunglasses to get a better look.

Amelia lowered her voice even more. "Please don't embarrass me." Looking directly at him, she threw up her hand. "Hi, Ben."

Ben noticed Lucy silently staring and stuck out his hand. "Ben Walsh."

"I'm Lucy. Nice to meet you," Lucy said, moving her eyes up and down, shaking his hand. "I'm Amelia's best friend and favorite fellow dancer at her ballet theater. Well, it *was* her ballet theater before she moved up here and met you—"

"What she means is," Amelia cut in as her cheeks began to

heat up. *So much for not embarrassing me.* "We danced together in New Haven for many years and are now good friends."

The corners of Ben's mouth lifted while glancing between the two women. "I see… Well, Lucy, it's nice to meet you too." He turned to Amelia. "How'd the tree work out?"

The amused expression on his face threw her off guard. "The tree?"

"Yes, Amelia. The beautiful tree I saw in your living room only an hour ago." Lucy rolled her eyes at Ben. "Maybe I need to buy her another coffee." They had spent an hour talking in the coffee shop about farmhouse decorations, studio gossip, and dance rehearsals for both Lucy and Amelia's student.

"The tree… yes! Sorry, I was thinking about my parents coming to town right after the makeup practice with Ava and got a bit distracted." Amelia bit her lip against the lie. There was no reason to be so nervous, but she kept her eyes off him in an attempt to steady herself.

"That's nice your parents are coming to visit," he said.

"I'm looking forward to it. And I was going to call you today to thank you for the tree, but I'm happy I get to do it now in person. I can't believe you took the time to bring that over this morning. That's so nice of you." She finally drew her eyes up to meet his.

Ben shoved his hands in his jacket vest, appearing just as uneasy as she felt.

"Well, this is awkward," Lucy chimed in. "I hate to break up this chat, but I have to get back to New Haven."

"Okay," Amelia said and shrugged at Ben. "She's my ride and I need to change before I head to the studio. But it was—"

"I can give you a ride home," Ben quickly offered. "That way Lucy can just jump onto the main road back to New Haven from here instead of driving you back up the hill."

"That's very kind of you, Ben Walsh," Lucy said, widening

her eyes at Amelia while he waited on an answer. "It is much easier to get on the road from here, you're right."

"You sure?" Amelia asked him.

"I'm heading back to the office, but I'm in no hurry."

"And don't worry, she got the application all done and we dropped it off before we had coffee. You'll be set to go for the evaluation." Lucy winked at Amelia who almost shoved her off the sidewalk.

Ben laughed. "Why, thank you for the update, Lucy. Will you be the point of contact for Amelia during the construction?"

"Just keeping you up to speed. I know you must be excited to get going on it. The house will be stunning, I'm sure, once you're done." Lucy leaned in and hugged Amelia, stopping just beside her face. "Are you kidding me?" Her friend breathed into her ear so low, she hardly heard her.

"Drive safe!" Amelia straightened up, practically pushing her toward her car. "Text me when you get there."

Amelia rubbed her hands together when they got into Ben's truck. "It's the type of weather today that hurts to breathe it's so cold."

"Yes, it is." Ben blasted the heat and shook his hair, which looked a little wet. "Probably should have dried my hair all the way before coming out here."

Amelia giggled as he wiped out a few pieces of frost. "Your hair turned to ice."

"Now it'll melt all over me before I get to the office." He reached behind him to get a towel from the back seat, the fresh scent of his morning shower rushing by her. "I keep this here to dry the seats with the girls dragging snow in and out. An Arctic blast is pushing through tonight. Make sure to dress in many layers if you come out tomorrow night for the train ride." He glanced at her as he ran the towel over his hair. "I assume you got my note too?"

"I did, and I still need to talk to my parents, but I think they'd love to come. Especially my mom who is a huge Christmas fan. Besides, Ms. Sherry also told me about the event, and I already have tickets, so they can't say no."

"She'll definitely love the Holiday Express then."

He tossed the towel to the back seat and reversed his truck, casting his arm behind her headrest, making her skin prickle. Her phone sent her a notification and she reached into her purse to see if it was her parents. It was Lucy sending her a text.

> Just wow! A rugged, good-looking country boy who has EYES ON YOU!

Nearly snorting with laughter, she put her phone down before he noticed. "Yes, I'm sure she will. White Bridge sure knows how to do Christmas," Amelia said, looking out the window at the winter-white scenery and the homes adorned with the classic charm of New England's traditional ivy and holly. She thought about Lucy's text. Did Ben have his eyes on her? She wasn't sure, but she realized for the first time in many years that she was curious to find out.

"Just look at this place, Steve!" Amelia heard her mother's voice boom from all the way inside the kitchen where she was cleaning up before they arrived. After getting back from practice with Ava, she had rushed to put a few leftover dirty dishes into the dishwasher, and now hurried to the front door.

"Mom! Dad!" Amelia waved from the doorway.

"You've really outdone yourself here, Amelia," her dad said, turning to look out toward the barn.

Her mother was quickly coming up the porch steps with

her arms extended. "I've missed you so much!" Kimberly gave her a big hug.

"It's only been a month, Mom," Amelia teased.

"Has it?" Her mother shook her head. "Feels longer. Well, it doesn't matter. I'm just happy to be here and see this magnificent farmhouse." Her mother turned around. "Come on, Steve! Let's empty the car now while the sun is still out. The scenery isn't going anywhere."

"I don't blame him. The views are what sold me the first time I saw them too."

"We'll lose him out there if we don't watch him." Her mom shook her head toward her husband before looking around the porch. "I've got a trunk full of holiday decorations because I knew you wouldn't have enough to fill this house. And I was right, just look at how big this porch alone is."

Amelia chuckled. "I figured you would." Looking past her mom, she saw her dad was now pulling bags from the back seat. "Let me help you!" She called out and stepped into her boots by the door.

"There's a whole lot of Christmas back there," he said, placing two small suitcases on the driveway then gesturing toward the trunk. "I have no idea why your mom packed so much for only two nights. She said we needed a lot of warm clothes."

"It's supposed to reach negative digits overnight, so I'm glad she did. How was the drive?"

"Longer than anticipated because we had to stop to buy all that Christmas stuff." Her father playfully rolled his eyes at his wife.

"I'm sure it'll add an extra boost of holiday magic." Amelia smiled at her mom, who was still on the porch.

Her dad reached for her and pulled her into his arms. His familiar scent took her back to her childhood.

"It's so good to see you, kiddo." Leaning back, he studied her. "You don't look like a farmer yet, especially in those city boots."

They both looked down at her leather boots and laughed.

"Let's give it until your second visit. I'm sure my attire will adjust by then." Amelia took one of the bags. "Come on in. It's so cold out here. I'll come get the Christmas stuff in a bit."

The living room was empty, and her mother was nowhere in sight when they walked inside.

"Mom?"

"Back here!" her mother's voice echoed from the kitchen. "There are so many more cabinets than I imagined!"

"I know, it's pretty impressive!" Amelia called back. She looked at her dad. "Let's get these bags upstairs."

"You sure it's okay for your mom and me to stay here? You only had the one bed in New Haven. We won't be offended if you need us to get a hotel room nearby."

"It's absolutely okay. There were a few pieces of antique furniture included in the sale. One being a queen-size bed frame and mattress in one of the bedrooms. I already had plenty of extra bedding for it too. I put my space heater in there for added warmth because my bedroom's heat works great."

"It feels surprisingly warm for such an old house. I hope that means it's insulated fairly well."

"Yes, that's what the inspector said. The windows aren't new, but the heating in general is not bad."

Her dad walked up the stairs behind her and they put the suitcases in the guest room—just as Mocha ran in with them.

"What a view from up here." He walked over to the window and Mocha followed, perching herself on the small windowsill. "I can understand now why you bought this place. I just worry about you here alone in such a big house."

Amelia gestured toward her cat. "I'm not alone, I have Mocha." Her dad shook his head and she grinned. "Okay, yes, I know what you mean. It's been an adjustment, but I really don't mind being alone, especially out here in the quiet." She joined him at the window and looked out at the fields blanketed in winter. A red cardinal landed in a large oak tree just below them, its crimson plumage standing out sharply against the snowy backdrop.

"Do you see the cardinal on that branch?" Her dad pointed out the window. "It looks like a Christmas card."

"I sure do. It's all so magical living in this house."

They went and sat on the bed, while Mocha stayed watching out the window.

"Life was so busy in New Haven I never had a spare moment to notice what was around me like I have here. Now I'm unpacked and feeling a little more settled, it'll be amazing to just be with nature. White Bridge is a lovely town. I can't wait to show you."

"We can't wait to see. And your mom and I are here to support and help you with this remodel in any way we can. Just let us know." He patted her on the shoulder. "I'm proud of you."

"For buying this house?"

"Yes, but not just that."

Amelia recognized the look on his face. It was the same one he gave her when she got her first solo performance at twelve years old and when she got her first contract to dance professional ballet—the look of a proud father.

"For facing what happened to you and then taking charge," he continued. "I know retiring from your dance career in the way you had to was devastating and shocking."

Amelia nodded. "I'm still reeling from it."

"I bet you are. Mom and I are too, and so is your brother. But here you are now. In this brand-new town and home.

And buying this on your own shows"—he looked away and she noticed his wet, reddened eyes—"well, it just shows off what you've accomplished with all those lead roles in so many performances and growing that social media presence. Not to mention the modeling jobs that had you missing holidays while you traveled. Proud doesn't even cover how I feel right now."

Leaning into him, she hugged her dad tight. "That means so much. Thank you."

"I mean it, Amelia. You didn't just sit around and wallow. You stood back up and stepped onto a new path. I know you just got here, but you're *here* is my point—embracing the unknown."

"This is definitely going to be an adventure," she said, pulling back from his arms. Her dad always had a way of making her feel like everything would be okay, especially through his hugs.

"I meant what I said. We really are here for you with this project. Andrew and Diana are too. You're not alone."

"Just knowing my whole family is behind me helps me a lot. I don't know what I'm doing with a remodel like this, but I'm learning, and…" Remembering the way Ben jogged across the street toward her earlier made her smile.

"And?"

"I think I found a great contractor who really knows his stuff with historical homes."

"That's terrific. Just like your grandfather was."

"Yes." She nodded. "His name is Ben Walsh. He showed me so many of the past homes he worked on, and they were all so beautiful."

"We're all looking forward to seeing what's next for you."

His words landed on her like a heavy weight. What *was* next? With no clear answer, she felt increasingly unsettled. "I hope I made the right decision with this big change."

"Amelia? Steve?" her mother's voice called up the stairs. "Did I lose you guys up there?"

Amelia stood and walked out to the hallway. "Coming, Mom!" she hollered.

Her dad met her in the hallway and put his arm around her shoulder as they made their way to the stairs. "Dance is all you know. It's your greatest passion. But if you're worried about your decision to change your whole life because you think dance is over, then answer me this: Why did you, within an hour of being in this town, just happen to meet the local dance teacher?"

"Coincidence?" she guessed.

"Perhaps..." He stopped them at the top of the stairs and faced her. "Or fate."

"I don't know, Dad..." Amelia sighed. "Becoming a professional ballerina was the set path for me my whole life. It was fate mixed with a whole lot of hard work that led me to that destiny. And while meeting Ms. Sherry has been wonderful, I just happened to come across her because of an unexpected turn of events."

"You're right that you've been fortunate with your talent of dancing and have worked very hard to achieve what you have. But that same destiny can also have unexpected twists and turns. That's just how life is. But it's not all for nothing. There is a reason you're here."

"Unexpected twists like this?" She waved her hand around. "Jumping to buy the first home I looked at?" As her dad studied her, doubt started to creep in about her impulsive decision to buy the farmhouse, which she hadn't thought twice about until now. Suddenly, it seemed like a hasty choice to pack up her life and move without a plan.

"Yes, like buying this home *and* meeting Ms. Sherry the moment you came to town. Those chance encounters that feel like they're out of nowhere, that is fate at work—you just didn't expect them like you did becoming a ballerina. Lucky twists changing your direction and leading you to where you are meant to be next."

"It's bringing me happiness, Ava. How lucky am I?" She heard her own words from the night Ava told her about not wanting to disappoint her family and mess up her role as the Sugar Plum Fairy. She remembered how thrilling it was to see her face her fears and get back up and try again—especially knowing she had helped bring about that courage. But could she do the same now she was in White Bridge? Face whatever was next for her? Ben popped into her mind again —another unexpected encounter. But what did it all mean for her?

After hearing her dad lay it all out, that heavy weight felt as if it was pushing down on her chest. If this was a lucky twist in her path, redirecting her to where she was supposed to go, then why did she feel so adrift?

"Buying this home… meeting Ms. Sherry…" *Meeting Ben…* "Yeah, it's all an unexpected twist all right, but to where? I feel like I'm worrying you."

"Amelia," her dad said, putting his hands on her shoulders. "I know this is hard for you to understand, especially after years of moving down a very set path. And I will say it has been difficult for me to watch all these changes as your dad, and—"

"Then I am worrying you," she cut in, casting her eyes to the floor.

"No, let me finish. As someone who has a hard time making even the simplest choices every day… I'm learning from you as I witness this journey, and I'm putting myself in the shoes of your followers on social media and will watch it all unfold with excitement. I meant what I said before. I am so proud of you. So keep embracing the unknown like you have and let it open you to continued possibilities. Leaving

New Haven and what was familiar was difficult, but these challenges are where you find the ability to keep trusting what life has for you next. I'm excited to cheer you on. So is your mom, who has probably mapped out the entire first floor for decorating by now."

They both laughed knowing he was right.

"Thank you for being here for me, Dad." Amelia smiled appreciatively at him, but as they made their way downstairs, her chest still felt tight. Everyone was supporting her and enthusiastically watching her and waiting for what was to come. What if she disappointed everyone? She remembered Ms. Sherry's request for her to take over the ballet studio... *especially* her.

THE HOUSE WAS SILENT, EXCEPT FOR MOCHA PURRING NEXT TO her in bed. It had been a wonderful start to her visit from her parents. Her mother cooked her childhood favorite, chicken and dumplings, while Amelia made a quick trip to the store and picked up her dad's choice of apple crumb pie and vanilla ice cream.

After dinner, they talked for hours about the house, how Andrew was, especially since her brother was known to try to hide how he truly felt so he didn't worry her, and what her parents had been up to. All in all, it was a nice evening and she was exhausted, but her mind couldn't settle in the stillness of her room. Her dad's words from earlier kept repeating in her mind. *"Challenges are where you find the ability to keep trusting what life has for you next. I'm excited to cheer you on."*

After taking a sip of her peppermint and ginger tea, she sat back in her bed, staring at the ceiling. Her blind faith and the initial thrill of the farmhouse purchase seemed to be wearing off as her future faced her. Were her dad's attempts to boost her spirits just a way of distracting himself from his own uncertainties? She couldn't shake the feeling that perhaps buying this home was more of a way to hide in her sorrow over not dancing anymore.

The coin she'd found in the attic with its message of luck crossed her mind. Her dad had been right about one thing: years of hard work and help from her grandparents enabled her to buy this home. But how could she trust such a sudden twist of fate?

Clicking off the light beside her, she closed her eyes, and finally drifted off. She dreamed she was back on the stage—where she gracefully twirled with unwavering confidence.

CHAPTER 18

"*D*o you remember when we had that blizzard when we were ten? I think that was still the most snow I'd ever seen," Amelia said, barely above a whisper since she didn't want to wake her parents who were still asleep in the room next to her. Her early-morning talks with her brother tended to get rowdy if she wasn't careful. Laughing through all their memories was something they had been doing since he'd gotten sick—perhaps to avoid the reality of his present situation.

"How could I forget? Wasn't that the storm when you made tracks off the roof, pretending you already sledded on it?" Andrew laughed through the phone.

"Yup. I just wanted you to do it first so I could make sure we wouldn't land in those big bushes below." Sitting up in her bed, she sat cross-legged and put her pillow on her lap to lean on.

"Luckily this house is split-level and we had at least two feet of fluffy snow to land on. I'll never forget Mom's face when she ran outside after seeing us from the window, flying through the air on our snow tubes."

Amelia drew her knees up, trying to muffle her laughter in the pillow. "How is it living back there? I mean, you and Diana must be wanting to pull your hair out with Mom's interesting ways."

"You know Diana, always polite, but sometimes I can see her frustration, especially when Mom cleans…"

"'A clean house starts with us!'" Amelia impersonated their mother.

"'And by us, I mean you!'" Andrew finished off their mother's famous Saturday-morning-cleaning phrase.

Amelia heard shuffling in her parents' room. "Oops, I hope I didn't wake them. I think they're up." For a moment, the conversation made her feel like they were kids again, when her brother wasn't sick and everything felt safe.

"I'm surprised they slept this late. Mom's usually up with the sun, even on Saturdays."

"We were up late last night chatting. I'm glad they got to sleep in a bit."

"Living here really hasn't been so bad. Diana and I appreciate all the help, especially…" He paused.

"Andrew…" Amelia exhaled. "How are you feeling? And please don't push the question off."

Silence on the other end told her the answer. "I have good days, and I have bad days," he finally said.

"Will the good days come more as you move through this round of treatment?" Closing her eyes, she silently prayed against her now thudding heart. Being away from her twin brother while he battled cancer was harder than the day Dr. Reed told her that her ballet career was over. While she had wished they could stay in their childhood memories for the whole conversation, she needed to be present for what he was going through.

"To be honest, Amelia, we're not sure. The doctors are trying to remain positive. as usual, but we can't make any predictions at this point. The treatment isn't working like they'd hoped."

Her pulse began to race faster. Trying not to go into a full-fledged panic, which only made things harder for Andrew, she got out of bed. Holding her phone to her ear with her shoulder, she hoisted up the window as much as the old pane would allow and crouched down near the opening. The icy morning air instantly stung her face, but it helped her breathe against the anxiety so he wouldn't catch on. It was hard to hide anything from a twin, and the more emotion she showed, the less he would share with her. Even in his weak state, he was still protective of his "little sister."

Now the roles felt reversed, but she was in White Bridge and not at their parents' house helping him—which kept her at the edge of panic a lot. Knowing he was suffering felt like half of her was struggling right alongside him—their twintuition grabbing hold of her.

"Once I get these renovations rolling, I'll come spend some time at home. I need—" She turned around and slid down against the wall under the window, allowing her pulse to steady.

"What you need is to focus on your new life over there in White Bridge. Remember, I'm still waiting on the Sugar Plum Fairy."

"I could always come do some of the dance privately for you and Diana." A knock on her door hoisted her up from the floor and she shut the window. "I'll just do it without my pointe shoes so there's no risk for injury."

"Amelia?" her mother asked from the other side of the door.

"That's not what I mean," Andrew told her.

"Hang on, Mom is at the door." She walked over and let her mom in. "It's Andrew on the phone. We've been chatting awhile. I hope I didn't wake you and Dad."

"Hi, Andrew," her mother said, leaning toward the phone.

"Tell her hello," Andrew said.

"He says hi." Amelia sat on the edge of her bed.

"And no, you didn't wake us. It's half past eight, we needed to get up. Would you like some pancakes? I saw a box of mix in your pantry, which was a pleasant surprise."

"You bought pancake mix?" her brother asked when he heard their mom through the phone.

"Yeah, it's like a whole new me," she told them both.

"Well, I'd be happy to whip some up." Her mom squinted. "Why's your face all red?"

"I got hot." Amelia lied. Her mom was the same way as Andrew. If she knew Amelia was feeling anxiety from the impact of Andrew's illness, she'd probably stay an extra week.

"Oh. Strange. It's four degrees outside." Her mom shook her head. "Anyway, I'll be downstairs."

Amelia shut the door behind her mom. "Well, Mom's off making pancakes. Spoiling me some more. I better get downstairs."

"Jealous. Her pancakes are the best. But don't tell Diana I said that."

"Tell Diana I say hello, and I'll talk to you soon."

"Love you, sis."

Amelia hung up and put her phone on the bed, then got up to shower. She needed to look happy and fresh when she went downstairs and not like a nervous mess. Her parents were only there for two days, and she wanted them to enjoy themselves and so did Andrew. They both had been working hard to help Diana take care of him, and they needed this break. They didn't need to worry about her on top of Andrew's cancer.

After her shower, she was more awake and much calmer. Remembering how cold it would be, she threw on some jeans, thick socks, and a dark red sweater. Quickly curling her long brown hair, she secured it off to the side in a low ponytail, the waves bunched together and falling down her side. With one last check in the mirror, she felt satisfied and turned to leave the bathroom when her makeup bag stopped her. Remembering Ben's note about the train ride, she shrugged and walked back to the mirror.

"Might as well," she told her reflection as she spread on some blush—trying to convince herself she should just finish the look—and that it had nothing to do with whether or not she'd run into Ben.

"Thought you fell back asleep up there," Kimberly said when Amelia finally came into the kitchen. She put a plate in the microwave. "I'll heat up your pancakes."

"Thank you, Mom," Amelia said, pouring herself a cup of coffee and then sitting down, just as her plate of pancakes was placed in front of her at the table. "Wow, those look good. I could get used to this service."

"Well, you know I love doing this," her mom said, lightly touching her hair. "You look nice today. I love when you curl your hair like that."

"Gives it some life, I think, since it's as straight as an arrow." Amelia took a bite of her pancakes. The rich caramel flavor coated her tongue, nearly causing her to inhale the rest. "Why did I ever stop eating these?" she said, barely swallowing before the next bite.

Her parents laughed.

"I'm so glad you like them," Kimberly said. "So, it's a new day with all kinds of possibilities. Any ideas on what you two would like to do?"

"Whatever the two of you want is fine by me," Steve said, standing up to refill his coffee. "I'm just happy to spend the day with you two."

"We can do anything you want today, but tonight I have

an idea." Amelia lowered her fork. "There's a 'Holiday Express' train ride that leaves from White Bridge and circles through a few surrounding towns before it makes its way back, and from what I've been told, the town makes a whole event of it. They light a bonfire for everyone and serve hot chocolate while people wait, and it's a Christmas-themed ride with Santa and Mrs. Claus."

"That sounds like a scene right out of a holiday movie," her dad said. "I'm sure your mom would love it."

"Christmas anything is fine by me. Let's plan on it." Her mom sat down across from Amelia. "I just read online about a Christmas 'shop and stroll' in town when I was searching for things to do. There's supposed to be all kinds of deals in the local shops."

"Aren't you done with your Christmas shopping, dear?" Steve asked.

"Since when do I need to actually *need* something to shop?"

Her parents both chuckled. Amelia enjoyed watching their flirty banter.

Her mom glanced back at her. "And your dad and I were hoping we could treat you to dinner out. Would that be all right before the train ride?"

"Dinner would be wonderful." Amelia picked up her fork again. "I wish Andrew and Diana were here for all the fun."

"How did Andrew sound to you?" her dad asked. "Your mom said you two were on the phone earlier."

"The same, but a little quieter than his normal self. He told me treatment wasn't going as well as his doctors had expected."

"For now, but we're holding hope that will change as he continues it." Her mom eyed her over her coffee mug. "Did he mention anything else?"

"Not anything in particular, why?"

"Oh, nothing, just wondering what he said is all." Kimberly stood and took her mug to the sink without looking at her.

Amelia wanted to press her, but her mom quickly turned with a big smile.

"The sun is shining, and we have a town to explore. Your dad and I just need to get ourselves ready for the day and off we go."

Amelia stayed at the table to finish her pancakes while her parents went upstairs. Mocha wandered into the kitchen now it was quieter and rubbed against her legs under the table. Amelia got up to feed her and put her plate in the sink. Her mom's question about Andrew still sat with her. What else could he possibly have to say? Her twintuition must have blown right over any clues during their phone call due to her nerves getting the best of her. She'd have to check in with him again later. For now, her focus was on giving her parents a nice visit.

After she fed Mocha, she went to the living room to wait. She pulled out her phone and saw a text from Ms. Sherry wishing her a fun day with her parents. She had graciously understood why Amelia couldn't be at their first full dress rehearsal today, even though the performance next weekend was inching closer. As Amelia contemplated the upcoming week and the multitude of practices with Ava and all the dancers, she suddenly found her thoughts somehow marveling right back on Ben and seeing him later that day.

HOLDING THE LAST OF THE SEASONAL DRINKS SHE HAD WANTED to try—a hot chestnut praline latte—Amelia put her hat and gloves on before she and her parents exited The White Bridge Grind. The arctic air that came through overnight had taken hold, but with the sunshine, hopefully walking outside would be a little more bearable.

A sign ahead, *Saturday Shop 'n' Stroll*, pointed them down the main street where the sidewalks were already filled with shoppers. They followed the crowd and her mom stopped promptly at the first store.

"Let's try to check out every store. You never know what goodies we'll find in these small independent stores. All I have near me is big shopping plazas and malls."

Her dad groaned and Amelia grinned at him.

"Rethinking the whole 'I'm just happy to spend the day with you two' now?" she jokingly asked.

"Why don't you head over to a bar and watch whatever game is on?" Kimberly suggested.

Her dad paused at the door and looked down the street. "That sounds like a good idea. Happen to know of any?" he asked, facing Amelia.

"I think there's a restaurant and bar down the road near the ballet studio," Amelia said as her mom motioned for them to come see something she'd already found inside the shop.

"I may need to go find it soon," he said.

Two hours later, they grabbed a quick lunch at the deli and Amelia told her mom she'd catch up with her at one of the clothing stores after she walked with her dad over to the bar. Stepping inside the Bridgeview Tavern, Amelia felt her purse vibrate with an incoming call. It appeared to be a local number, so she held up her phone to her dad and stood near the corner of the entrance to answer.

"Hello?"

"Hi, is this Amelia Collins?" a male voice asked.

"Yes, it is."

"Hi, Amelia, it's Tom, the historian you met with last week."

"Hi, Tom. Sorry for the noise behind me. I'm at a place called the Bridgeview Tavern with my dad."

"That's a great place to eat and have some drinks. On warmer days, they have a nice deck to eat on behind the restaurant. From there, you head through an entrance to a trail that brings you to the river and the famous white bridge. It's a good walk because it runs in a big loop."

"This town is full of such nice things to experience."

"It sure is," Tom said. "The reason I'm calling is I finally got ahold of Lisa Allard. It took a bit of effort to track her down and get her on the phone. As I mentioned to you before, she's a tough one to find. Luckily, I have connections here in town that helped me."

"Wow, that's great," Amelia said, still puzzled by the woman's elusiveness, but she didn't have time to get into it standing in the doorway of the tavern. "So did she already know about the coin?"

"Yes, she did. We actually had a nice conversation. I told her about you and how the coin was found and what value it holds."

"I'm glad she knew about it. With how old the coin is and the dates on the letters, I wasn't sure she'd know the coin existed. What else did she say?"

"She thanked me for getting ahold of her, but then was silent for a long while before she asked me if the house was being taken care of. I wasn't expecting that."

"That's interesting. From what I understood she wanted nothing to do with the house."

"That's what all of us in town thought too. I just told her the basics of what I knew, which was that you were just getting started with the remodel. She also asked me if Ben Walsh was going to be the one to oversee the renovations. I found that to be sort of an 'out of the blue' question, but, nonetheless, I told her she could ask you all her questions about the house directly."

"That is a strange thing to ask." Amelia pondered on it for few seconds. "Maybe she knows of his work and just wants to make sure someone with experience is handling it."

"That could be…" Tom trailed off for a moment. "But then I recommended that we meet in person to give her the coin and not mail something so valuable, and she was really hesitant."

"Really? Where does she live? Maybe it's too far."

"I asked her and she said she was about an hour away, so it wasn't too bad of a drive. She said she had to think about it and that she'd call me back."

"So now you're just waiting?"

"Actually, no. Surprisingly, only a few days later she called back and confirmed she'd meet us."

"Great. I'm relieved I'll get to return the coin to its rightful owner."

"Would Monday morning in my office at the town's museum work? Lisa said she can get there around eleven."

"I'll be there."

Amelia dropped her phone back into purse and looked up to see her dad at the bar, holding up a beer and motioning with his free hand for her to "go on." That was her cue to go find her mom again, so she waved and walked back outside. The clothing store they had agreed to meet at was just across the street, next to the ballet studio. As she made her way over, she couldn't stop thinking about the coin and Lisa's question about Ben. Ben and Chris had a strong reputation for their specialized services in historical remodeling, but Lisa lived quite a way away from White Bridge these days. How had Ben's name gotten mixed up in the conversation with Tom… or rather, *why*?

CHAPTER 19

"*A*ll aboard the Holiday Express Train!" a man shouted into a megaphone from the platform.

The crowd of people who had tickets for the next ride lined up to get on, and Amelia clapped her hands together seeing all the adorable children dressed in their holiday pajamas with winter coats on top.

"How special is this?" Amelia turned to her mom who was just as delighted as she was watching the kids jump around their parents in line. The ticket booth had a big sign taped across it that said, *Sold Out*.

"Amelia, do we already have tickets?" her dad asked.

"I bought them on the website a few days ago and snagged some of the last."

Steve grinned. "It's a good thing we agreed to go since you bought them already."

"Oh, I would have just dragged you and Mom along if you hadn't," Amelia teased. "Look at Mom's face, she's so excited. I don't think I'd have to force her to partake."

They both glanced at Kimberly who was smiling from ear to ear at all the children.

"I know we don't have any kids with us, but I'm looking forward to seeing that train. I can see all the decorations from out here." Her mom pointed to the windows that had garland streamed across each one.

The three of them stepped up at the end of the line to get on.

"Wow! Check out that bonfire over there. It's huge!" Amelia pointed to the giant flames filling a large circle with people gathered around. She whipped out her phone and recorded the scene for her audience. "My followers who live in large cities will love this small-town holiday scene."

"I think it's so wonderful you still have so many supportive followers," Kimberly said.

"Me too. Especially because many of them have been following me since my college ballet days. I miss putting up dancing clips, but this will have to make up for it."

Her dad was still watching the people around the bonfire. "This is quite a gathering, and the cold doesn't feel so bad with all these heat lamps around us. The town thought of everything."

"Leave it to you, Steve, to see all the little details." Her mom smiled at her husband, who put his arm around her.

"Amelia!" a young voice called from behind them, and Amelia turned to see Julia racing toward her. Julia threw her arms around her waist and squeezed tight.

"What a hug!" Amelia said, reaching down to hug her back.

"Are you here for a train ride?" Julia asked.

"Sure am. Are you getting on the 7:30 one like us?"

"That we are," Ben answered as he caught up to them with Ava.

"Who do we have here?" Kimberly asked, looking down at Julia, who was wearing red-and-white pajamas with reindeer all over them and her hair in pigtail braids with red bows on the end of each.

"Mom, Dad, this is Julia and her dad, Ben, who is heading up the remodel on my house, and his other daughter, Ava." Amelia gestured toward her parents. "And these are my parents, Steve and Kim."

"Hi, Ms. Kim!" Julia grinned up at her.

Amelia's mom bent over. "Hello, Julia, I certainly love your pajamas. It looks like your older sister is matching." Her mom peered up at Ava.

"Unwillingly matching," Ben added as the group continued up the line toward a door of the train. "She's being a good sport about it though." He patted Ava's shoulder, and she zipped up her coat farther, clearly trying to cover her matching pajamas.

"Hi, Steve and Kim," he said, extending his hand out to her parents.

"Nice to meet you, Ben," Steve said. "Amelia already told me about you and your specialties with old homes. Glad to know she found you."

"Already talking about me?" Ben smirked at Amelia.

Her cheeks warmed. "Maybe," she replied and caught her mom quietly observing their exchange. "My mom here is especially excited to see the train. I'm sure you've been on it many times," she quickly said to Julia to pull her mom's attention off her and Ben.

"About a hundred!" Julia said.

Everyone laughed at the girl's excitement.

"I'm really looking forward to this," Kimberly said and continued chatting with Julia about everything they would see on the train.

Amelia turned to Ava. "Sorry to miss dress rehearsal with you today, but I will make up for it all week. We can squeeze in some extra time."

"It's okay." Ava drew her eyebrows together. "I gave it my all today, but I still messed up on that last spin. I'm so frustrated because last week we finally nailed it."

"Sometimes our nerves get the best of us right before the big day. Mine always did. I found myself messing up the most about a week prior to each of my performances."

"Really?" The tension in her face eased. "I think I'm much better off with all the practice we've done. I don't know where I'd be if you hadn't come to White Bridge."

"Remember, you've got this. I'm so proud of your improvement in the short time we've been working together. Your dad will be really impressed," Amelia said, sneaking a peek at Ben who mouthed "Thank you" above Ava's head.

They reached the platform, and a man dressed in an old-fashioned conductor's suit greeted them. "Tickets, please!"

Ben and Amelia held up their phones and the conductor scanned everyone in.

"Both parties are in Santa's Lounge. Go right and straight back through two cars until you see the sign."

"Look at that, we bought the same tickets," Ben said just behind her ear, sending a chill down her back despite the heat from the train.

Once inside, multi-colored holiday lights lined the ceiling and Christmas music played above their heads from the speakers. Families and children were getting settled in their seats as they made their way down the aisle.

"Here it is, Dad!" Julia nearly shouted from the front of the line after they crossed through two cars.

"She's right, Santa's Lounge," Kimberly, who was standing with Julia, informed everyone behind her.

The lounge was set up differently, with round tables lining the sides, and much more room than the thin aisles they'd just walked through. Amelia nearly laughed out loud when she saw the last two empty tables directly across from each other.

"And it looks like we reserved the same section too," Ben said.

"What are the odds?" Amelia held her arms up and shrugged.

"Interesting how things work," Ben said, holding her gaze.

"Julia has requested Steve and I sit with her." Kimberly came up next to them, drawing her attention.

"I'm sure she has." Ben cast his eyes toward his daughter. "I must warn you though, she is a talker."

"Oh, don't I already know it. She said she still has lots to tell me about the train." Kimberly threw her fingers in the air before taking a seat next to Julia.

"Come on, Ava, over here!" Julia called to her sister, patting the seat on the other side of her. "You don't mind, Daddy, do you?"

"Of course not, J-Bear. As long as Amelia's parents are cool with it." Ben looked at her parents and pointed his thumb toward Julia. "Looks like she's the boss tonight," he said behind the back of his hand.

Steve scooted in next to his wife. "We would be honored to sit with your girls."

"Ava, why don't you run over to get our table a round of cookies and hot chocolates." Kimberly handed her some cash and Ben touched his daughter's arm, leaning close to her ear, and whispered something. Ava nodded up at her dad before he turned back to Amelia.

"That seemed to perk Ava right up." Amelia watched her dash over to the food station at the back of the car.

"She's sort of outgrown all this Santa stuff, so it was a push to get her not only to come but to match her sister," Ben explained. "But cookies and hot chocolate will always do the trick. I had to remind her to be sensible and only have a bite or two. Sometimes the thrill of the Christmas season makes her indulge too much. Would you like some hot chocolate?"

"Yes, please. Hot chocolate sounds perfect. And I can only imagine how hard the holidays are with her condition."

"It is, but she is getting more mature and handling it much easier now," he said and went to get their hot chocolates.

Amelia took off her coat and hung it on a hook by the table and sat. She watched her mom's expression as she interacted with Julia—looking absolutely elated to share this experience through a child's eyes. It made her a little sad to think about how Andrew and Diana haven't had any children yet to give her mom the grandchild she clearly would love to have, and now with his latest setback… she wasn't sure when or *if* that would happen.

"She's going to make a terrific grandmother one day." Ben came back with two hot chocolates and set them on the table before shrugging off his coat and sitting down across from her.

Just as they looked over, Julia erupted into a fit of giggles.

"She most certainly will." Amelia turned back toward Ben. "That's probably my dad getting Julia all revved up. He loves to joke around." She placed her hands around the warm cup. "And I was just thinking about that."

"About her as a grandmother?"

"Yeah…" She picked up her hot chocolate and took off the lid to let some of the heat out, giving herself a moment to collect her thoughts, watching the steam rise. Sharing about her brother was never easy, especially since she didn't have a set answer to how things would go for him, but when she looked at Ben, his trusting eyes unleashed the words. "I was also thinking about my twin brother, Andrew, and his wife, Diana."

"I've always wondered what it would be like to have a twin."

"It's great, but it can be bothersome, particularly when nothing gets past him. Andrew always knows when I'm not telling him everything or when I'm upset even before I realize I am." Amelia smiled. "We call it 'twintuition.'"

"It's sounds like having a whole other half of you," he said, taking a sip from his cup. "I like that though. It's special. So, what brought them to mind?"

"I was thinking how much my mom had looked forward to their first baby. I remember on their wedding day it was all she could talk about—how she couldn't wait to be a grandmother."

"Had?" He pointed out.

She frowned at him.

"You said your mom *had* looked forward to their first baby. Are they not having kids?"   '

"Oh, right. Sorry, I sometimes get so lost in my thoughts, I forget details. My brother is battling leukemia and has been since about a year after they got married. The baby department is sort of closed temporarily until he gets better."

"That must be tough for everyone," Ben said. "Including you. How are you holding up?"

"It's torture," she said immediately, noticing how good it felt to say that out loud. "Sorry, I don't mean to dump this on you. Here we are on Santa's train and I'm bringing the vibe down."

"You're not," Ben said equally as fast, causing her to sit back. "Really, you're not. You know my story. Now I know some of yours. I like learning about you, even if it's not always happy information."

The sincerity in his eyes rendered her speechless, before the crackle of the speakers above jarred her out of her daze.

"Ladies and gentlemen! Welcome to The Holiday Express!

We are about to get moving in just a few minutes. There are food stations with cookies and hot chocolate in all the lounge cars, so please help yourself! And sit back and get comfortable because Santa and Mrs. Claus will be making their rounds in each car. A complimentary picture will be taken for everyone to download from our website. Enjoy the ride!"

"Dad! Ava said she will take the picture with me this year!" Julia cupped her hands to call out and sat up on her knees.

"That's great, sweetheart. Thanks for being so cooperative, Ava!" He gave his older daughter a thumbs up.

Amelia noticed the smile as the girl threw her eyes up.

"See? Even Ava can't deny the holiday magic on this train." She put the lid back on her cooled hot chocolate and brought it to her lips.

"This train ride magic sure has everyone feeling happy and comfortable," he gently said.

"Thanks for listening to me. It really feels good to share about my brother, especially because I try to keep my anxiety about not being with him from my parents. I don't want to burden them."

"I know I just met your parents, but from what I have witnessed so far, I think they would certainly understand how you feel."

"They are good parents, almost too good, and certainly patient. So, yes, they would. But they have a lot on their plate helping take care of Andrew, and I just don't want them worrying about me on top of it."

"Are you going to go home and see him for Christmas? Maybe it'll help once you're with him for a little while."

"Yes, I'll go for Christmas. I wanted to beforehand, but I don't know how much of a help I'd be." She left out the part about Andrew asking her not to and to instead focus on her next steps in her career—which instantly made her think of Ms. Sherry's offer. She didn't have an answer yet, but as she thought about her brother she knew exactly what he'd tell her to do. Yet something was still holding her back from taking that leap of faith.

The train began to pull forward and the cheers of all the children aboard filled the air around them. The Christmas music played a little louder as the train picked up speed.

"I think just seeing you would help him. Just like your presence in the studio with Ava has helped her." Ben peered at her from above the lid of his cup and she caught the gold and green in his eyes collide as their gazes met.

Laughter from the other table pulled apart their stare. Kimberly had her arms up wide and high, telling the girls something as animatedly as she could.

Not sure how to respond, Amelia switched subjects. "My mom is having a blast. Before my brother and I were born, she taught elementary school for years. She was a favorite among her students from what I heard back in my hometown in Massachusetts."

"I can see why," Ben said, watching Kimberly lean forward with the story as both girls listened intently. He looked at her again. "So back to you."

"Me?"

"Yeah… you. White Bridge's hottest new dance teacher. How are you liking being over there with the girls?"

Amelia's mind went blank, bringing out the same hesitation from only moments ago. Helping Ava and getting to know her had been wonderful, but she was far from a teacher.

"You know… I really don't have an answer, to be honest. I never thought of myself as a teacher. Working with Ava privately is one thing, but I sort of bombed the first attempt at teaching Julia's whole class."

"That's not what Julia told me."

"Really?" Amelia asked in amazement. She still cringed thinking about how Ms. Sherry had stopped the music.

"Yeah, she came home and bragged about how a professional ballerina helped in her class that night."

"I'm surprised because Ms. Sherry had to jump in when I got the whole class confused in a matter of minutes."

"Well, you impacted Julia regardless. Children always experience things differently."

"It's good to hear she enjoyed my being there. I hope Ava has too."

"Do we speak two different languages, or did you simply not *hear* Ava back in line before?"

Amelia grinned. "Yes, I heard her. I just wanted to make sure I'm helping her enough."

"Believe me, you are. You're a great teacher, Amelia, at least with Ava's role, from what I am witnessing with the change in her."

"One-on-one isn't as intimidating, plus I know the Sugar Plum Fairy's dances so well, I could practically do them in my sleep. And Ava is very easy to work with. She's a great kid."

"So what's the hesitation about teaching for?"

The memory surfaced before she had a chance to answer. Ms. Ruth's voice taking over her thoughts. "*Not good enough, Amelia! Aim for better than that! You have younger dancers watching! Perfection is all they should see!*"

"Amelia?" Ben said.

She blinked against a jingling sound from the car before them and looked at him.

"Ho ho ho!" Santa called in the distance.

All the children cheered again.

"Daddy!" Julia stood up in her seat pointing toward the car next to them. "Santa is almost here! Do you hear him?"

"I do, J-Bear!" Ben said to Julia and turned to Amelia again. "Are you okay?"

"Yes, I'm fine. I spaced out thinking about something is all."

"Was it something I said?"

"No. I..." Her normal response of brushing off her old dance teacher's verbal abuse didn't feel right anymore. The words lingered through her. *Perfection is all they should see!* Perfect dancer, perfect diet... no wonder she didn't think she had any teaching skills and couldn't give Ms. Sherry an answer yet—because she didn't think she was "perfect" enough to do it.

Ben's face reflected genuine care as he waited patiently for her to continue.

"I used to have this really mean dance teacher when I was a child. Her name was Ms. Ruth, and what's worse was that she was my first teacher. For years she zeroed in on me, often just me, at every dance class—criticizing my every move."

Ben waited before he spoke, evidently trying to find the right words. "Yet you still went on to become a professional ballerina. So whatever that woman said to you, it didn't stick." He glanced over at his daughters' happy faces. "And it's surely not sticking with how you motivate Ava and Julia."

"Except it *has* stuck with me, more than I've ever admitted," she said, trying not to sound frustrated. Talking about Ms. Ruth always drew up anger. "Ms. Ruth's words have somehow lingered—always finding their way to me, especially now, after such a mess up during a performance last spring when I injured myself. That injury cost me my career. And for months I beat myself up, thinking if only I'd paid attention more, was more careful, a more perfect ballerina, then it wouldn't have happened. That nasty teacher always made me feel less than, pushing me toward this perfection that is impossible to achieve."

Sympathy reflected from his eyes as distant laughter from the car before them filled the pause. "Of course that's impossible. Perfection doesn't exist. Ballet is an art," he said, reaching over and placing his hand on hers—the light gesture bridging them together. "It requires talent, yes, but also practice, and with that mistakes will happen."

"I guess I didn't realize how much that teacher's words affected my career... and my life... until I lost everything," she said, feeling him squeeze her hand before letting it go. She buried her hands together in her lap to smother the longing of wanting his touch again.

Ben sat back. "Look, Amelia, what happened to you last spring was unfortunate, but you are human, not a perfect robot. You will mess up, fall, and everything between, with dance and other things in life... just like parenting."

Her parents were enjoying the funny faces Julia was making when Amelia peered over.

Ben leaned toward her again. "Someone once told my girls that passion, not perfection, makes a dancer grow."

"I love that. Who told them that?" she asked, but had a feeling she already knew the answer.

"Molly did. She used to dance ballet too. In fact, I met her the night my parents dragged me to go see *The Nutcracker* when I was Ava's age at our town's high school. She was the Sugar Plum Fairy that year..." He took a breath and Amelia nodded, but kept quiet about how Ava had already shared this with her. "And I try hard to carry their mother's words, reminding them before every class. I want them to enjoy dancing, not worry over trying to perfect it. Just like you teach Ava every time you work with her."

"Molly sounds like she was an incredible mom." The truth

of Molly's statement suddenly made it all come together for Amelia. Ben was right. The way she encouraged Ava was what she'd been missing for herself up until this point. She never once pushed his daughter to perfect anything. Why was she still pushing herself?

Guilt pinged Amelia when she looked over at her mom continuing to entertain the girls. Her mom had been nothing short of supportive and positive all those years growing up, yet Amelia had let Ms. Ruth's voice overpower her. And she realized now how it even impacted her with not knowing what the "perfect" next steps would be. Her desire to prove that she could reach those perfect standards had blinded her to the beauty of her accomplishments and living life.

"She sure was," Ben said. "Trying to level up to how she was as a parent has been tough, but despite how hard it can be doing it all on my own, the experiences of parenting are always nothing short of magical."

"I can see that. Watching you with those girls has been wonderful," Amelia said, turning back to him. "And Molly was right. Perfection does not grow a dancer. Determination, practice, and a genuine love of it does. I wish I could go back and drill this into my younger self. Although, ironically, Ms. Ruth's words are what pushed me to keep going with dance. I wanted to prove to her that I could be that perfect dancer with the perfect image and everything. She's not even alive anymore, and I'm still under her spell."

A smile slowly spread across his face. "About done?"

"With?"

"Proving to some old woman who isn't on this earth anymore that you can dance?"

The impact of his honesty struck her, but before she could answer, the doors to their car opened, and Santa and Mrs. Claus walked in.

"Ho ho ho!" Santa waved.

"Come on," Ben said. "Let's go get some of that childhood magic."

CHAPTER 20

CHRISTMAS EVE, 1985

Lisa Allard

"*M*om?" Lisa called from the couch, swinging her swollen feet over to sit up. "Not sure propping up my legs helped the swelling. My ankles still look like water balloons are attached to them."

Brenda came in holding a large glass of ice water. "Drink up," she instructed.

"Drink more water? I'm blowing up like a balloon already. I can't fit any more water in me."

"I was just like this when I was pregnant with your brother. I swear Timothy came out filled with water too." Her mother held out the glass.

Reluctantly, Lisa took it and, despite how uncomfortable she felt, she drank it—holding her breath against another contraction.

"Are you all right, Lisa?" Her mother watched her hold the bottom of her large belly.

The pains had been coming on and off since the middle of

the night, and while they weren't regular, they were intensi-fying, especially since she'd seen her doctor earlier.

"I'm fine," she lied and fanned her face with her hand. "It's so hot in here. Why do we have such a huge fire going? The flames are practically burning my skin." She had a feeling labor was coming, but a part of her wanted to keep that to herself a little longer so she could relish in these last moments of pregnancy with her baby.

"Lisa, it's twenty-eight degrees outside. This old farm-house feels rather drafty, in my opinion. What you feel is end-of-pregnancy fun."

Lisa groaned and sat back, placing her empty glass on the table next to her. "The doctor didn't even care about my swollen ankles this morning. I just want the labor part over with."

But did she? The labor would end, but the agony for her would just begin when she had to leave the hospital with empty arms. She fought against the tears that stung her eyes, having no energy to battle her mother. The decision was already made. She would give birth and hand her baby off to the adoptive parents.

"Honey." Brenda came over and sat next to her. "He gave you a thorough check up. Everything is stable."

"Or he just wanted to get back to his Christmas Eve plans."

"No, this is his job. He's well used to being called out on holidays after nearly twenty years of practice. Like he told you, it's just some water retention, but the good news is he said you are expected to go into labor any moment. So it's almost over. Now we just wait."

Over for you. Lisa kept her thoughts to herself to avoid a repeated explosion. She had tried for months to change her parents' decision about adoption, to let her keep her baby, but to no avail. And at sixteen years old she felt powerless against them.

"Longest wait of my life," she said, trying to breathe through another sharp pull from down low. *Was this the real thing?*

"And then you can go back to your life. Your last year of high school, then college and everything else you want to do." Her mother patted her knee as if it would be that simple.

"When is Tim supposed to get here?" Lisa changed the subject. "I thought college exams were over last week. Why did he stay on campus?"

"He and his girlfriend, Christine, hung around to do a project with one of the groups they are involved in for the community. He'll be here soon... with Christine."

"I take it things are serious then?"

Her mother nodded. "I'd say they are growing more serious, especially since he's invited her for Christmas Eve dinner. She doesn't live too far from White Bridge, so he's even planning on going to her parent's house tomorrow for dessert."

"Well, don't they sound like the couple of the year," Lisa said, looking toward the window when she heard a car pull in the driveway. "I'm happy for them."

But she wasn't. For an older brother who had always supported her and been there for her, he had abandoned her during her greatest need. He never called her, never checked in, and had essentially told her she was a disgrace to the family when she first found out she was pregnant. Now she had to face him with his perfect girlfriend after nine months of silence.

"Lisa, don't start. Not now, during Christmas." Her mom stood up and peered out the window. "Your dad is back from the office."

"Working on Christmas Eve?" She'd been so uncomfortable since returning home from the doctor she hadn't even noticed he was gone.

"He was meeting with…." Her mom's face fell trying to get the names out, and Lisa knew who she'd meant. It had been months since her parents sorted it all out, and even though that was their final decision, her mother still couldn't say their names without crying.

"The adoptive parents?" she finished for her.

"Yes… and Brian's parents."

Lisa glanced at the crackling flames. Brian wanted to put the baby up for adoption too and his parents fully agreed that would be the best option. She was totally outnumbered.

"Why were Brian's parents there? There's nothing for them to do at this point."

"To be honest, I'm not sure. I didn't get a chance to talk to your father before we rushed out the door to see the doctor."

The tears brimming in Lisa's eyes finally fell and she quickly wiped them away. Brian was her first love, torn away from her by his parents since finding out they were pregnant —treating Lisa as if it had been entirely her fault. He was in the grade ahead of her and graduating the following spring. The one letter he wrote after his parents made him stop seeing her was still on top of her bedside table. He told her he was sorry how things turned out between them and said his goodbyes… She missed him terribly.

"Lisa, I want to have Christmas just for us and not have to talk about the adoptive parents, but your father needed to have them sign one more thing," her mother explained, looking away from her. She knew how much pain forcing Lisa to give up her baby had caused, but Brenda was in denial, thinking everything would go back to the way it was once Lisa delivered.

But it wouldn't. Everything about the farmhouse and her town would always remind her of what she'd lost. Lisa knew that once she graduated she would leave White Bridge and her family behind and start over.

Pushing off the arm rest of the couch, Lisa hoisted herself up to go to the bathroom to freshen up before her brother arrived and felt a pop below.

"I'm not sure your Christmas plans will happen." Lisa stood frozen in the middle of the living room.

Her mom looked at her. "What do you mean?"

"I think my water just broke."

PRESENT DAY

Amelia put her fork on top of her empty plate and picked up her orange juice. She and her parents had just finished a late breakfast at a diner Ben had recommended.

"Ben and his girls are just lovely," her mom said for probably the tenth time since they got home the night before. She was glad her parents had enjoyed themselves. "How do we get the photo they took of all of us with Santa and Mrs. Claus?"

"The website says we will be emailed a code today. Since I bought the tickets, it'll come to mine. Once I get that I can log in and download it, and I'll forward the picture to you." Amelia noticed her dad watching them quietly. "Something on your mind, Dad?"

"I was just thinking about the evaluation this week. I hope you don't mind, but I made a short list," he said, shifting to reach into his back pocket. "Just some things I happened to see as I walked through the house."

Amelia took the list and quickly scanned it, appreciating how invested he was. "Thanks, Dad. This is helpful," she said, even though she had a hunch Ben would have already picked up on the things he'd written down.

"I know he's experienced, but I figured the more eyes on a home this old the better." He shrugged before taking the check from the waitress. "I really like him." He held up a finger to stop the server from dashing off to the next table.

"Ben?"

"Who else are we talking about?" Her dad winked at her and put cash in the bill holder and handed it back. "No change needed," he said to the waitress.

"Yes, I agree with your dad. I'm so happy we got to meet your new friend. And that Julia…" Her mom chuckled. "She told me every fact she knew about the train and what it does when it's not Christmas time."

Amelia smiled. "She's a sweet girl."

"And Ava? What a beauty she is." Her mom stood, picking up her coat off the back of her chair. "She told me you have really helped her with practicing her role as the Sugar Plum Fairy." Kimberly came around and put her arm around Amelia just as she pulled on her own coat. "I know how hard that must be for you. Of all roles to have to work on with her."

"It was hard to swallow at first, but once I saw Ava I knew I couldn't let her down. She was terribly nervous about it when I first met her, and it made me remember how…" Amelia trailed off, not wanting to bring up Andrew and lower the mood. Diana had called earlier to let them know he was having a hard day so her parents would be prepared when they returned home.

"How Andrew tried to help you practice at home because you got the same way the first year you danced it?" her mom finished for her as the three of them walked outside to the parking lot. "And how we basically lost you to your room that year."

"What do you mean?" she questioned.

"Let's put it this way," her dad cut in. "When your mother would call you and your brother down for dinner, you'd always come rushing in at least ten minutes after we started eating."

Her mom laughed. "Oh, those were the days! You'd always say, 'Sorry, sorry, sorry! I just had to perfect what I was working on!'"

Perfection does not make a dancer grow. Amelia's conversation with Ben came to mind, but hearing her parents' memories had her suddenly feeling defensive. She may have been fighting to prove to Ms. Ruth and herself that she could live up to that perfect image, but stressing her parents with it was something she did not ever want.

"I remember that, too, but it wasn't *every* time. I was surely invested in other interests as well."

Kimberly scrunched her nose and shook her head. "No… it was nearly every night. But never mind that. You are now here, possibly with some great opportunities ahead with those young dancers. You should talk to Ms. Sherry about staying on to help teach after the holidays."

But is that the right thing? There she went again, letting doubt creep in.

Amelia just smiled in response. She hadn't told her parents yet about the teacher's retirement or the offer to have her take over. Like Andrew, she knew if she mentioned it they wouldn't leave her alone about it.

Her dad extended his arms. "Mom and I must hit the road."

Amelia hugged her parents goodbye. When she got into her car, she turned on her ignition but stayed in park, tapping the steering wheel, staring ahead in thought. Her conversation on the train with Ben had had her mind spinning circles all night around Ms. Sherry's offer, and after her mom's suggestion, it seemed like everyone saw it for her—but her.

Regardless of her decision, Ms. Sherry was waiting on an answer, so Amelia needed to talk to her soon. But for now she needed a distraction; an activity for the day to help her relax. Just as she was about to put the car in reverse to head home and figure out something to do, a message flashed up on her dashboard, picking her pulse up when she saw Ben's name.

> Good morning! The girls and I are going snow tubing and neither would leave until I asked if you could come. I told them your parents are probably still in town so I couldn't promise anything. Would sliding down a mountain in the freezing cold interest you?

Snow tubing? Amelia thought about the idea for a couple minutes and finally sent him a response.

> How could I say no to them? My parents just left to go home. Send me the address and I'll meet you there.

AMELIA SLID HER SUNGLASSES IN PLACE JUST BEFORE THE GLARE off the snowy mountain blinded her. Watching the people fly down on black snow tubes made her stomach flip, and hearing all the kids squeal and shout as they spun in circles made her think of Andrew. How could they have gone through their entire upbringing without partaking in this?

Ben had told her to meet him inside the café where people could change out of their wet clothes, get some food and drinks, and buy tickets. Inside, crowds of people filled the tables, sipping on hot drinks and munching on all kinds of treats. Wreaths hung from each window and twinkle lights lined the windowsills as well as the cashiers area. A giant tree glowed in the corner, wrapped in red ribbon from top to bottom, showing off its beauty from the window.

"Amelia!" She heard Ben's voice behind her.

Both girls were dressed head to toe in snow gear, and she giggled watching them try to get to her with their heavy boots weighing them down.

Julia got to her first and was out of breath. "It's hard to walk in all this snow stuff."

"I bet! But you will be nice and warm out there."

"I like your purple snow pants, Amelia," Ava said.

Amelia struck a pose, making them both giggle. "Thanks. They're brand new. Halfway here, I realized I didn't have any, so I made a stop. Judging by all the red cheeks in here, I'm glad I got them."

"We live in Connecticut, and you didn't own any snow pants?" Ben asked.

"The hours at the theater didn't leave room for this kind of fun," she explained.

"Well, then you'll definitely enjoy this. Let's get your lift ticket and go!" Ben waved at everyone to follow.

Julia tugged on Amelia's arm and practically dragged her through the crowds of people toward the ticket windows. A short while later, Amelia found herself on top of her snow tube being pulled up the slope as she held tightly to a rope. The higher she got, the more anxious she became.

"This is one tall mountain!" she called out to Ben, who was in front of her. "Here I thought we were just going sledding down a simple hill."

Ben gave her a thumbs up. "And a fast one!" he yelled out over his shoulder.

When they reached the top, Ben instructed them to

spread out among the lines so they could all go down at the same time. Finally, it was their turn and the staff directing people when to go told her to get in the front of her tube and sit down with her feet dug into the snow to brace herself. She stole a glance at Ben, who was laughing.

"What's so funny?"

"Your face!"

The person on staff must have noticed, too, and leaned down. "First time?"

"Yes," she replied, the butterflies in her stomach fluttering out of control at this point.

"Then hang tight! When I say go, lift your feet." He signaled to his co-worker on the other side of the lines. "One, two, three… Go!"

Amelia let out a scream and lifted her feet and her tube quickly gathered speed. Within seconds she was spinning down the track and wondered if her tube was nearly in the air. When she felt a bump, she realized she had been, as she then landed, followed by another jump. The knots in her stomach transformed into an exciting rush the faster she sped, until she finally reached the bottom and toppled over into the snow.

"Wahoo!" she heard Julia call near her.

Ben was laughing hysterically as he slid up beside her.

Amelia immediately jumped up. "Let's do that again!"

Ben stood, picking up his tube. "Fifty more times at least!"

The afternoon sun eventually disappeared below the horizon and before Amelia knew it they had been tubing for hours, with only one break for hot apple cider and cinnamon donuts. The now twilight sky made all the lights around the mountain brighten. After one of their runs, she looked over and saw the Christmas lights glittering from the café—a beautiful holiday winter scene.

Julia lay down in the snow after another run down the

hill. "Phew! I'm not sure I can get up that mountain anymore."

Pulling off his wet hat, Ben shook out some snow clumps from his hair. "I'm with you," he said. "I bet you girls are hungry." He looked over at Amelia. "And I bet you are too." His warm hazel eyes fixed on hers as the holiday lights illuminated his rosy cheeks, sending a tingle through her.

"Snow tubing definitely works up an appetite," she said.

"Can we get cheeseburgers, Dad?" Ava asked.

"Sure can," Ben answered, keeping his focus on Amelia. "Care for some cheeseburgers?"

"Don't need to ask me twice. I love cheeseburgers," she said without one bout of hesitation and winked when Julia beamed at her.

"There's a place we always go that's close to here. They have the best cheeseburgers," Julia said and began pushing her tube toward the return area.

When they reached the parking lot after changing out of their snow gear, Ben told the girls to get in his truck while he walked Amelia to her car.

"I'll text you the place we're going in case you lose us on the road."

"Sounds good."

"This was fun, having you here with us," he said, lingering by her car door.

"Yes, it was. I'm a new fan. I hope we can make it back again before spring," she suggested, nervously fidgeting with a loose strand of hair that had fallen out of her ponytail.

"We definitely will," he said without missing a beat. "We can also go regular sledding. It's actually a birthday tradition of mine on Christmas Day. We don't come here, but there's a secret hill in White Bridge where I take the girls to burn off their post-Christmas gift excitement."

"Your birthday is on Christmas?"

"Yeah, not the most ideal day, but it's grown on me, especially since I've lived in White Bridge. Let's put it this way, it's an easy day to remember, especially when you live in a small town where you get a lot of extra gifts."

Amelia grinned. "I bet."

"Come on, Dad!" Julia called out from his truck.

"We better get these girls fed."

"You are such a great dad, Ben." Amelia looked over at the truck and saw Julia hanging out the window making funny faces at them. "The girls are always so happy."

A flicker of uncertainty cast over his face.

"I hope so…" He started to say something else, stepping closer to her, but the girls broke his attention, causing her to move back. A puzzled look cast over his face. "I'll see you at the restaurant."

As Amelia followed them, the weekend's events swirled in her mind, quickly becoming singularly consumed by one thought: Ben.

CHAPTER 21

CHRISTMAS MORNING, 1985

Lisa Allard

L isa studied every feature of her baby's face. Voices grew closer as someone began to climb the stairs, and she leaned down, inhaling the sweet newborn scent—trying to somehow memorize it.

The labor had been fast and furious the night before, and while she hadn't planned on birthing at home, the baby had other plans—coming into the world just after midnight on Christmas Day. With it being her first time, she'd had no idea the contractions she'd been having the day before would intensify so fast. The paramedics arrived just in time, and minutes later it was all over. After, the paramedics stayed for a bit to check her and the baby over, they told her parents everything was fine, and Lisa opted to stay home to have these last hours with her baby.

Now in the stillness of her room, the dawn's gentle rays filtering through the window, looking at her precious baby, she wished she had more time.

A knock at the door pulled her attention away.

"Lisa?" Her mother popped her head in. Closing the door behind her, Brenda sat down on the bed next to Lisa, placing her hand over her daughter's. "It's time."

Before her mother got back up, Lisa gripped her hand. "Wait. I want to keep this swaddle."

Her mother wiped away a tear that escaped down her cheek and didn't argue as she went to get another one. She had been gripping something and put it down before retrieving the new swaddle.

"Is that the pouch with the coin?" Lisa asked.

Her mother glanced down at it. "Oh, yeah it is. I was just…" Brenda stopped, frantically wiping fresh tears that spilled out of her eyes. Lisa waited for her to collect herself. "I was just looking at it in my room before I came to get you. I was going to see if you wanted to keep it in here with you for a little while."

Lisa looked down at her baby, desperately trying to control the anger that began to boil. She didn't want to lose it in her condition… not before the adoptive parents came in.

"That's the last thing I want in here. A coin that supposedly brought our family luck and prosperity for over a century must have skipped right over me."

"Lisa…" Her mother came over with the swaddle. "I just thought it could be a strong reminder for you that when times seem bleak, like they do now, things can still turn around, and they will for you. You have a purpose in this world."

My purpose includes this baby. The anger simmering just beneath the surface threatened to spill over if she kept this conversation going. "Take the coin out of here and go get everyone."

Dropping the blanket, her mother stifled a sob and left the room.

Switching out the swaddle, Lisa leaned over, tears pooling

in her eyes, as she kissed every inch of the tiny face she would never forget. She whispered, "May we meet again, my little one. Thank you for a Christmas gift I will always remember. I love you."

∼

PRESENT DAY

Monday was welcomed with gray clouds hovering across the sky, making all the twinkle lights shine brighter in the farmhouse against the darkened morning. As Amelia roamed from room to room, the invigorating scent of coffee brewing in her kitchen began to pull her back into the present, giving her a boost of much-needed energy after a terrible night's sleep. With a heavy sigh, she furrowed her brow in frustration as she thought again how, after a wonderful day snow tubing with Ben and the girls, she may have ruined it when they said their goodbyes after dinner. But was there anything to ruin between her and Ben, or was she just imagining it all?

Pausing at the fireplace in the front room, she tried to focus on the new decorations her mother had added over the weekend. The beautiful pre-lit flocked garlands and the tall golden reindeer standing beside the fireplace were a blur against the depth of Ben's stare by her car the night before, which had sent waves through her entire body that hadn't stopped all night.

She went to the kitchen to get her coffee, exhaustion blanketing her all over again. She'd need a few cups to get herself moving. The day was just getting started and she had a lot to do, including meeting Tom and Lisa to return the coin, then practice with Ava, and without much sleep she wasn't sure how she would make it through. Sitting down with her mug, she tried to concentrate on the day ahead, but her thoughts stayed trapped in a never-ending loop. Everything had been going so well when they were at dinner.

"OH, AVA, ARE WE EMBARRASSING YOU?" BEN HAD ASKED HIS daughter at the restaurant while they were eating their cheeseburgers.

Amelia had tried not to laugh, but Julia had decided to put on a comedy act, making it nearly impossible. Ben, as patient as ever, had joined in on the laughter, causing Ava to nearly hide under the table.

With everyone content and full, the girls went to the truck after they ate, leaving her alone with Ben next to her car... once again. This time, her car was a little hidden behind the truck, and she found herself inches from Ben's face when he leaned over to open her door.

Amelia's pulse had thudded as he placed a hand against her car, stopping her before she got in the driver's seat, his eyes moving to her lips.

"Today was amazing," she quickly said against the tremble in her body, and just as she had done after they went snow tubing, she took a step back.

Sensing her hesitation, he straightened up a bit. *"Amelia..."* he'd started to say.

"Thank you for dinner and such a great day."

When she put her hand on the car door, he took that as a cue and moved aside so she could open the door.

What is wrong with me?

She rushed to call Lucy when she got home and spent nearly two hours talking through it.

"I don't understand," her friend had said. *"I think I forgot where I was when I saw him jog across the street that day, and you*

had him nearly locking lips with you yesterday, and you... hesitated?"

∼

LAUGHING TO HERSELF IN THE QUIET OF HER KITCHEN AS SHE thought about Lucy's comment, Amelia exhaled.

"He has the girls to focus on," she reasoned out loud.

It was the only excuse she could think of. Glancing out the window, the white landscape made the red barn pop in the distance, and across the yard she saw a mother deer with two fawns following closely. The protective doe stopped every couple steps to make sure her babies were still behind her. It was touching to witness, and before Amelia knew it the words just slipped out of her.

"And there is no way I can be as perfect as Molly was to those girls."

Perfect. There she went again, slipping right back into her old ways. But when it came to Julia and Ava, was that bad? They deserved nothing less than that and the last thing she'd ever want was to ruin the seamless bond they had in memory of their mom.

∼

WHEN AMELIA PULLED INTO THE SMALL PARKING LOT BEHIND the museum, flurries began to drift lazily down from the overcast sky. She hurried inside out of the cold wind that had picked up with the snow, but when she opened the door, she collided with a woman, causing all the papers she was carrying to drop to the floor.

Amelia immediately bent down to pick them up. "I'm terribly sorry, I—" She stopped when she saw the paper posters were for that weekend's ballet performance. She looked up to see Ms. Sherry watching her.

"Hi, Amelia," Ms. Sherry said. Her frown from nearly being knocked over turned into a smile as she took the posters Amelia handed her. "Thanks. I'm just going around town getting these hung. Figured I'd throw one up here at the museum too. Never know who will see it."

"Need help? I'm free in an hour or so."

"No, I think I have it covered. Just a few more stops." Ms. Sherry straightened her pile of posters. "I missed you all weekend. So did the dancers. They were asking for Ms. Amelia. It was sweet. How was your visit with your parents?"

"It was…" Amelia thought about her answer, but it wasn't her parents that came to mind. Ben's laughter as they flew down the mountain on their tubes, the festive train ride, and the cozy booth at the restaurant last night were what she thought of. "A really good weekend."

"I just ran into Rick Miller at the coffee shop. He was telling me about your tree and how he took his son snow tubing yesterday."

"Oh, yeah?" Amelia's face heated.

Ms. Sherry tilted her head, arching a brow. "Yeah. At this big mountain about an hour from here. It has a big rope that pulls you up and everything."

"I—"

"Are you all right, dear? You look rather flushed."

"I'm just going to be late for a meeting with Tom is all. I was practically running through the parking lot before I ran into you." She could tell there was more to Ms. Sherry's conversation with Rick, but she really needed to get to Tom.

"I see," Ms. Sherry said and put the posters under her arm to adjust her hat.

"But I was thinking all weekend about your offer. I think

we need to sit down and discuss it some more, if it still stands?"

Ms. Sherry frowned. "Oh, I was actually going to talk to you about that when I saw you at the studio tomorrow. I have some terrible news."

"Is everything all right? Are you okay?" she touched Ms. Sherry's arm.

"It's not about me. I'm fine…" Ms. Sherry's eyes glistened, her lip shaking. "But my studio isn't. The owner sold the building. So I'm not sure where you'd teach my students now this has happened."

"What? It was *sold*?"

"Yes. I've been silently dealing with this for the past week, praying it wouldn't be so, but alas, it's a done deal. It happened fast. The owner knew I was retiring and decided to take an offer that came to him to sell the building. The new owners aren't interested in keeping my studio." A tear escaped down her face. "I don't even know how to tell my dancers. It was hard enough to announce my retirement, but I had assured them everything would be okay. I thought we would just have to replace me, but now the studio will be gone too."

"Okay, deep breaths, Ms. Sherry. I don't know the answer to all this yet, but I am here for you." Amelia put her arms around the woman who suddenly felt frail with the sobering news. She wanted to fix this for her but didn't know how.

Ms. Sherry pulled back and wiped her eyes. "You have a meeting to get to. Go on. I won't keep you any longer. I'll see you tomorrow and we can talk more then. Also"—she started to turn, but stopped—"I hope you and Ben and the girls had a blast on the mountain yesterday." A weak smile formed across her face.

Amelia's eyes widened as she fixated on the door, not sure

what to make of what she'd just heard. Rick Miller must have witnessed something between her and Ben and was already making them the highlight of this morning's small-town gossip. But with no time to ponder, she went to find Tom's office.

After walking down a short hallway, she saw his name outside one of the doors. She knocked and waited and when he opened the door, she didn't see a woman inside with him as she'd expected.

"Amelia, you made it," he said, turning around to pull out one of the chairs on the other side of his desk for her to sit.

"And here I thought I'd be the last one. Sorry I'm a little late." She sat down when he gestured to an empty chair. "I ran into Ms. Sherry out front."

"Yeah, I saw her hanging a poster for *The Nutcracker* performance this weekend and meant to wait for you out there, but a phone call grabbed my attention."

The news about the studio still gripped Amelia's thoughts, but Tom's office, filled with history, distracted her. On the walls were old framed pictures of White Bridge and a map of the town dating back almost two hundred years. Various books on White Bridge and other pieces of the town's history were in every corner, including a flat block holding a dated feather pen and ink on the corner of his desk. The plaque read, *White Bridge School House 1746–1941.*

"Is that schoolhouse still standing?" she asked as she kept looking around at all the artifacts. She could have spent the rest of the morning going through his collection.

"Yes, it is. Our schoolchildren have tours in it every year," Tom said noticing her interest as he sat down. "You should see what I have at my house. And it's not just relics from this town either."

"I can only imagine with you being a historian. What a neat job you have."

"I love it. History never bores me." He sat back in his chair. "So, Lisa left me a voicemail early this morning, before I got here, explaining she isn't coming."

"She's not? But what about the coin? Isn't she interested in having it back?"

"She didn't say anything about it. Just that she was sorry she had to cancel."

"Huh… Well, that's too bad." Amelia shook her head. "You'd think she'd be excited to come get it. Especially since you said it's valuable."

Tom handed her the pouch with the coin. "It's very valuable, which is why I still had you come so I could give it back to you, even though I know you were hoping to return it to Lisa."

Amelia set the pouch in her lap. "I'm curious to know what you found out. Tell me about it."

"Remember how we thought we saw 1860 stamped over the 1859 date?" Amelia nodded. "Well, we were correct. If you want, you can put it in my magnifier to see." Tom reached behind him to pick up the device and placed it in front of her.

Amelia stood, pulled the coin out and placed it under the lens, then bent over to look. She clearly saw 1860 stamped over 1859. "I see it much better now."

"When I got ahold of my friend who specializes in numismatics, he told me this is the 1860 British penny, but it's an incredibly rare variety because of that stamped-over date. Otherwise known as the '60 over 59' variety."

"Why did they stamp over it like that?"

"That penny was discontinued in 1860 and this variety we have here was actually not intended for circulation, which is why it's so rare."

"Wow, how interesting."

"But what's even more important is how well the mint condition is graded, and for this one it's a sixty-three."

"Is that good or bad?" Amelia had no idea what the explanation meant, but she had tuned in once she heard "*incredibly rare.*"

"Very good. It basically means it doesn't have a lot of large scrapes. It's worth well over five thousand US dollars."

"That's impressive," Amelia said and put the coin back in the bag. "It just doesn't feel right that I have something that belongs to that family and is worth so much. Would it be all right if I get Lisa's phone number from you? I'd like to call her and see if I can reschedule meeting her. I really feel I need to get the coin back to her after hearing all this."

"Of course." He jotted down the number on a sticky note. "Good luck getting ahold of her. You're doing the right thing by trying to return it. She's all that's left of the O'Sheas. And what a lucky coin to have had in their family."

Remembering Ellen O'Shea's note inside the bag, Amelia nodded at Tom. "Yes, it is. I'll try my hardest to get it to her."

When she left Tom's office, she remembered she had her scheduled evaluation with Ben the next day. She got in her car and made a quick call to Ben's office to make sure the application she'd submitted Friday had cleared. The secretary told her everything was all set and the evaluation was a go for the next day. With a flutter in her stomach, thinking about being alone with Ben at her house, she dialed Lisa's number, but it went straight to voicemail.

"Hi, Lisa, my name is Amelia Collins. I bought the farmhouse on Maple Ridge and called for the meeting today. I understand you had to cancel. I just met with Tom, and he explained how much value this coin has, and I would really like to figure out a way to return it to you. I just don't feel right keeping it. If you like, you can meet me at the farmhouse anytime this week. I'll be home in the mornings. Or we can meet somewhere else. Just let me know. I hope to set up a time soon. Take care."

After rambling off her number, Amelia hung up. She'd done all she could to contact the woman.

CHAPTER 22

*B*en's truck crunched along her driveway the next morning, and Amelia did a quick sweep of the downstairs to make sure all the lights were on, including her Christmas ones. She even had a cranberry candle burning and the uplifting sweet aroma was already filling the front room. The truck door opened and shut, and she suddenly laughed looking around at her effort to make the house warm and inviting.

He's coming to do an evaluation, not for dinner... She chuckled at her thoughts and waited for him to get to the door, reminding herself to relax.

Ben knocked and when she opened the door, he was standing there with a toolbox, headlight on his head, and a clipboard.

"Good morning!" he said, playfully clicking his headlight on and off. "Ready for some fun?"

Amelia grinned and stepped aside to let him in. "You sure look like you are." Relief washed over her. She had spent most of the morning worried about how awkward it would be, given the way they ended their night on Sunday.

"Never know in these old homes when I'll need this handy light." He pulled the light off his head and scanned the room. "Well doesn't this feel cozy."

"You should have seen the place last week. It looked abandoned. Until my mom got ahold of it over the weekend."

Ben started to run his hand along the mantel. "After meeting her, that makes sense. She seems like the decorating type."

"She sure is. But it feels rather silly to get all this décor up knowing you and your team will take it all down soon."

"Actually, it's okay you have it out. We won't be diving into it until after the holidays anyway." He walked over to the doorway to the living room. "Nice tree. Where'd you get it?" he joked. His eyes glinted with amusement before he walked in.

"Not sure. Just showed up out of the blue!" she teased back. "Want some coffee?"

He came to the doorway again. "I'd love some in a bit," he said, gesturing behind him. "I'm going to start upstairs, and I'll have a cup when I come back down. You're more than welcome to join me, or you can wait until I'm done. Either way, we will go over everything."

"I'll hang back in the kitchen and let you do your thing. I have notes after yesterday's practice for things I'm going to cover with Ava this week, and I wanted to check them over. The big day is approaching fast."

"Yes, it is. I can't wait to see the show. Ava is still a little nervous about some spin thing and practicing nonstop. I even caught her practicing in her room after her shower last night."

"I used to practice in my room, too, when I was young. We've come a long way in timing the movement she's working on over the past couple weeks, and she is better at it than she lets herself believe. The 'spin thing' she's trying to get down is called the Italian fouetté."

"Italian who?"

Amelia burst out laughing. "Just know your daughter chose a version of the dance that takes that particular step and moves it right into a pirouette. A very tricky move, but I'm so proud of how determined she is."

"A piro-what now?" He scratched his head. "You know, I have two daughters who have been dancing for years, and I've never actually asked them what these moves are called."

"Let me show you." Amelia put her hands in position and gently stepped forward and carefully lifted her heels up and looked over her shoulder with a leg extended behind her before slowly turning her body. The rush of doing two simple movements overtook her. She'd given Ava plenty of demonstrations during their time together, but doing it for Ben felt different, as if she were performing for an audience again. "Gosh I miss the stage!" she nearly shouted against the thrill, causing her to lose her balance.

He reached out and steadied her hips. "Whoa there… careful. We don't need to visit your doctor down in New Haven explaining you reinjured yourself in your own house." His hands moved down and took hers. "This is what the internet is for, to look it up."

They didn't move, hands still locked together before she loosened one to brush her hair behind her ears, casting her eyes down at her feet. "If *that* reinjures me with how slow I did it, then my doctor would be pretty upset with his surgeries."

"Well then, let's keep your feet planted on the ground," he said, not loosening his grip on the other hand. "I may not know how hard all these dance moves are or what they entail, but I'm proud of her regardless of how well she does that spin. I know she's working hard. I can't wait to see."

"Me either," she said, lifting her head. The way he smiled at her aroused all her senses, leaving her craving for more when he finally released her other hand.

"Well, I better get started. This house will take some time to get through. And, Amelia?" His eyes were gentle as they rested on her. "I know how much you love dancing and miss it. Watching Ava dance this weekend will be like watching you on stage."

Amelia couldn't move after he got upstairs. She stood listening to the creaking of the old wooden floors above her head as Ben moved around. *Watching Ava dance this weekend will be like watching you up there*. His statement had struck something deep in her. And for the first time, she didn't question it. While she'd always miss dancing, working with Ava was starting to become an intricate part of her *new* identity as a dancer. Her thoughts immediately moved once again to Andrew's words. *"You haven't had your final curtain draw yet."*

She headed to the kitchen to get her phone and sent her mom a quick text.

> Hi, Mom, just wanted to check in. How's Andrew today? Haven't had a chance to call him this week, but wanted to know what you and Dad thought about taking him for a little drive this Saturday to watch the dancers here perform The Nutcracker. We can talk more about it later, but it's just a thought. I know it's not me up there, but having me behind the curtain is the closest thing we've got.

After opening her email on her phone, Amelia bulleted her notes from the day before and typed some additional thoughts in an email for Ms. Sherry. Tomorrow, Ava's male counterpart, performing as the Mouse King, was coming down from his college to have one last practice with her before dress rehearsal Friday, and Amelia wanted to make sure Ms. Sherry could articulate to him what she suggested to hopefully make the performance run as smoothly as possible.

After she was done typing it all out, she scanned through it once more and hit send. Sitting back in her chair, she felt triumph, but different to how she'd ever experienced it before. It was a victory that resonated much deeper than all her winning performances as a professional dancer, or success as a model and social media influencer. In a matter of weeks, she had led Ava through her challenges and fears, which had inadvertently begun to free Amelia from hers. Those early years of insults and verbal abuse from Ms. Ruth had blocked her from truly feeling successful and strong unless she could achieve some unattainable level of perfection, yet she'd spent her adult life up until this point convincing herself otherwise. Had she perfected Ava's skills in her role as the Sugar Plum Fairy? Amelia realized *no one* could do that, but witnessing Ava shine in her own way had been humbling after years of trying to prove herself to be the best, to be perfect.

She thought about Ben's comment from that night on the train, questioning if she was done allowing some cruel old dance teacher to continue to control her viewpoint and emotions. And, more importantly, was she going to let it dictate what was building between her and Ben? The girls only had one mother, and she could never be replaced. But why did she ever think she had to?

Her phone suddenly distracted her, notifying her of some new emails, and one caught her attention. The subject line said: "Thank you Amelia." Curious, she opened it.

Dear Amelia,

This is Maddie, Sophia's mom, who you met last month in the coffee shop over on Chapel Street. I wanted to reach out and update you on Sophia's progress in dance since meeting you. This weekend she will take the stage in her class's winter performance for the first time. Encouraging her like you did that day, "from a real ballerina" as she loves to brag, gave her the motivation and courage to step onto the stage. Her teacher said she's not afraid anymore, and as Sophia puts it, "will try her very best."

I can't thank you enough. Always remember that little dancing eyes are watching you, whether you are performing or not.

Take care,
  Maddie

Amelia closed her eyes against the sting of tears. A thud from above startled them open, followed by Ben's footsteps right over her head. Then it suddenly hit her. She jumped up and ran upstairs to Ben. She found him in the guest bathroom, just as he was closing the window.

"I'm done!" she said, touching the wall to catch her breath.

"Well, I'm not. I still have downstairs and even the barn to get through. Unless we're keeping the barn the way it is. You know... with all that space out there—"

"Ben!" Amelia laughed. "That's not what I mean. I mean I'm done with Ms. Ruth. You asked me when we were on the train if I was done letting that old lady haunt my emotions, and I'm here to tell you *yes*, I'm *done*!"

A smile quickly spread across his face. "And it only took you three days to give me an answer."

"Wait." She drew her eyebrows together. "There *is* a lot of space in that barn."

"*I thought we would just have to replace me... now the studio will be gone.*" She shuddered against the heartbreak Ms. Sherry wore on her face the day before.

"Can you pause up here and go out there with me?" she asked.

"Sure, let's go."

As they made their way across the snowy grass, Amelia slipped, and Ben reached over and slid his arm around her waist, just as she was balancing herself.

"I'm okay, thanks."

"I know." He cast a flirtatious look her way.

When they reached the barn, Ben pulled open the heavy doors. This wasn't the first time she'd been in the barn since moving in, but it was as if she was looking at it with new eyes. Walking in a little more, she glanced up at the loft and the ceilings as Ben stayed silent, curiously watching her.

Finally, everything since the day her brother told her that her dance career wasn't over had a clear answer, and she swung around. "Ben, I know this may make your job a whole lot bigger, but something in me is pushing me to make this barn a—"

"Dance studio?" he finished for her.

Walking closer, she saw his expression stay steady, as if he was not surprised. "How did you know that was what I was thinking?"

"A hunch I just got. But also..." He looked around the space himself. "Judging by the fact that not only would this be the perfect barn to transform into a studio, but because the studio was sold."

"Ms. Sherry told everyone?"

"Yes, she did. It's going to be a bookstore by next summer."

Amelia watched him look around the barn, his builder's eyes clearly taking over as he studied the space. "When did she share the news?"

"She came to me privately the Saturday your parents were in town. She didn't know who else to turn to and thought my expertise in remodeling could somehow convince the new owners that it wouldn't be easy to convert the studio into a bookstore. But it didn't work."

"Did the new owners give her any time?"

Ben stood next to her again. "March. Which was rather gracious of them considering they're from out of town and have no idea how much Ms. Sherry's ballet studio means to White Bridge. They had wanted to get started on the bookstore remodel right away."

"March isn't a lot of time, but it's better than nothing."

"So if you want to convert this barn, I take it you will be accepting Ms. Sherry's offer to be the new dance teacher?"

"You knew about that too?"

"Why else do you think I nudged you about being a teacher on the train?" He motioned around the barn. "You're going to save the day with this idea."

"You think it's a good idea?"

"It's more than a good idea." Ben took a step toward her.

"I really hope so because—"

He put his finger to her lips. This time her feet stayed planted, unwavering as he stepped closer, their faces merely inches apart.

"Amelia, you haven't just impacted Ava. You've been the answer Ms. Sherry was waiting on." His fingers brushed along hers, shooting a tingle down her spine. "And mine." His eyes found her mouth, but before he could place his next move on her, the sound of a car in the driveway broke them apart.

"Now who could that be?" she said.

They both went outside. A lady had stepped out of the car and shut the door. She stood in the driveway, staring up at the house.

"Do you recognize her?" Amelia asked.

Ben shook his head. "May we help you?" he called out to

her, and she turned to face them, appearing startled to see them come out of the barn.

As they started across the lawn, the woman stayed quiet, letting them get closer. Amelia guessed her to be somewhere in her fifties and noticed strands of her dark blonde hair catch in the breeze.

"Hi, I'm Amelia Collins. I own this house," she said, offering her hand.

The woman gave her hand a slight shake. "Hello," she said before moving her attention toward Ben.

"And I'm Ben Walsh," he said.

"I know who you are," the woman said.

Amelia looked over at Ben who kept his eyes on the woman, clearly confused. "Have we met before?"

The woman hesitated before reaching for her sunglasses. "Yes," she said as she slowly slid them down, revealing the same hazel eyes Amelia had come to know so well. "I'm Lisa Allard. Your birth mother."

CHAPTER 23

CHRISTMAS DAY, 1986

Lisa Allard

"*A*re you ready to see it?" Lisa's mother appeared in her bedroom door and she could hardly look at her.

"Ready isn't the right word, Mom. No other choice, is more like it."

Brenda came into her bedroom and sat down at the edge of the bed, holding an envelope to her chest.

"Now remember, this is the only update we're going to get, per the adoption agreement." Her mother paused, watching her. Lisa's eyes were already swimming in tears, a few escaping down her face. "Are you sure you want to see it? It's your choice."

"Just like it was my choice a year ago?" Although twelve months had passed, the anger had not fully abated, but rather transformed in her heart to a constant dull ache.

"Lisa…" her mother started.

But Lisa waved her hand. "Forget what I said. If I don't

see the update, then I'll always think about it. What he looks like. His name. Everything."

Closing her eyes for a moment, her mother took a breath and then handed her the envelope. Lisa took it, wiping her eyes with her free hand, and opened it. She pulled out a folded piece of paper with typed words and felt the picture within. When she unfolded the paper, the picture dropped out, and she picked it up before reading the letter. She covered her mouth when she saw him, nearly choking on the lump that formed in her throat. Sandy-blond hair and hazel eyes, just like her.

"He looks like you," her mother gently said. "Read the letter, sweetheart. You'll be comforted knowing how loved he is." She patted Lisa's knee and stood up to give her some privacy.

Loved, yes... but not with me.

With shaking hands, she opened the letter.

> Dearest Lisa,
>
> Well, here he is... our sweet little Ben. Growing fast and strong, Benjamin Edward Walsh is now one! He is walking, saying "mama" and "dada" and "more" (he always wants more food!). But most importantly, he is healthy and happy. Since the day we took him home, he has filled my empty arms and given his dad a purpose—a son to shape into a proper young man one day. Ben has been nothing but a joy, and it's all because of you, Lisa.
>
> One day I will tell him all about you. How

beautiful you are, how brave you were, and the gift you gave us. How you made us a family. We aren't too far from White Bridge, so when I tell him about you, I will also tell him about the town that means so much to us.

Every day we think about you, pray for you, and hope you go on to do great things that your future is waiting for. Ben will always hold a part of you. No one can take that away. Remember that.

Forever grateful,
Melissa and Jeffrey Walsh

Lying down on her pillow, Lisa held the picture in front of her as she turned to the side. Spent from emotion, she closed her eyes, holding on to his picture as she drifted off to sleep—dreaming of the day they would meet again.

～

PRESENT DAY

Amelia stared at the woman while Ben took a step back. His birth mother? Who had passed away? Amelia immediately reached for him, equally stunned, but he put up his hands.

"Can we go inside to talk?" Lisa asked.

But Ben shook his head. "How… are you…?" He backed away from her. "I don't understand."

"Ben, I know this is shocking. But you need to know the

truth. This house…" Lisa hesitated. "It means more to you than you realize. It's where you were born."

Ben's mouth fell open and he stepped back farther. "What are you talking about?"

"Please, if you would just let me explain," Lisa pleaded.

"What's there to explain? My mother told me you had passed away over ten years ago."

"And that was supposed to stay the story, until Amelia moved in, found the coin, and both Tom and Ms. Sherry reached out to me."

"Wait, what? *Ms. Sherry?*" Amelia said. "I only spoke to Tom about contacting you." Suddenly she remembered what Tom had told her about getting some help from people in town to find Lisa. "Wait, Tom mentioned something—"

"You knew about her too!" Ben's voice rose.

"What? Ben, no…" Amelia tried to approach him again, but he backed further away. "I knew nothing about her being your birth mother."

Lisa stepped forward to intervene. "I know none of this is making sense, which is why we have to talk."

"Ms. Sherry knew you were alive? I… I can't do this." Without another word, he took off to his truck and left.

"Amelia," Lisa said, coming closer to her with tears now rushing down her face. "I didn't know he'd be here."

"I don't believe that. Besides the fact that he thought you were dead, you *knew* he was working on this house and could possibly be here. I know because Tom told me you asked about Ben."

Lisa looked down. "Yes, I did ask him."

"So you knew he was in White Bridge." Amelia's defenses rose, piecing it all together and wanting to somehow shield Ben from further hurt. "So, what? You decided to show up to let him know you were alive and drop all that on him three seconds into seeing him?"

"I... I don't know why I did that. I've spent thirty-eight years, since the day I handed him to the Walshes, trying to figure out what I'd say if I was lucky enough to see him again. I got nervous and it all just started to pour out." Lisa kept her eyes to the driveway, wiping the tears that kept dropping off her cheeks.

"How did you even know Ben was in White Bridge? And *Ms. Sherry* called you? This isn't adding up."

Lisa stayed quiet for a moment before looking at Amelia again. "I've known he was in White Bridge since the day he bought his house with Molly."

"Wait... How did you know about Molly? Were you in contact with Ben's parents or something?"

"Yes."

"What a mess of a situation... I don't even know where to begin." Amelia threw up her hands. She was glad Ben hadn't heard that part... not yet at least. His parents must have lied to him about her passing... but why? "And now Ben's clearly upset." All she wanted to do was get in her car and go find him.

"I need to talk to him," Lisa said as she struggled to keep her composure.

"Well, he obviously doesn't want to talk to you right now, and I don't blame him!" Amelia lowered her voice when she saw the woman bury her face in her hands. "Okay, we both need to calm down. Would you like to come in?"

"Yes, thank you."

Lisa followed her up the porch steps. When they got inside, it dawned on Amelia that this could be the first time the woman had been in the farmhouse in a long time. When she looked at her, Lisa was standing still, looking around the room.

"I never thought I'd be back here again..." she whispered.

"Have a seat in the living room," Amelia said, leading her

to the couch. "I'm going to try to call Ben." She went to the kitchen where her phone was and dialed Ben's number—but only got his voicemail. After leaving him a quick message, she called his office and asked if he or Chris were there, but the secretary said Chris had just left in a hurry for an unexpected meeting. *Ben… Chris must be with him.*

Not knowing what to do next, she walked back to the living room and sat down next to Lisa, who looked lost in thought as she stared at the fireplace.

"Would you like something to drink?"

"No, thank you. I just need to figure out what to do now."

"So does Ben. He needs to absorb what just happened." Amelia remembered the reason Lisa most likely had come to begin with. "You came here for the coin, right?"

"Yes, but it doesn't matter now, given what just took place."

"Still… let me go get it." Amelia went upstairs and retrieved the felt pouch and brought it down to Lisa. "I'm glad it's back with you. It didn't feel right keeping something with so much value that belongs to your family."

Lisa opened the bag and pulled out the coin, holding it in her hand as she looked at it in silence. "Thank you," she finally said and put it in her purse.

The sound of a car coming down the driveway caught their attention, and Amelia stood up to peer out the window, hoping to see Ben returning. Instead, she saw Ms. Sherry getting out of her car.

"Ms. Sherry?" Amelia said out loud and went to open the front door.

Ms. Sherry came up onto the porch. "That's her car, right? Is she here?"

"Lisa? Yes, she's inside."

Ms. Sherry touched her arm. "Good. Come on in. There's a lot to tell you."

"I'll say." Amelia followed her inside.

Lisa stood up when they came into the living room. "I take it Ben called you?"

Ms. Sherry eyed Lisa without greeting her at all. "Oh, yes. I answered to a very angry Ben. But understandably so. Lisa, I told you *years* ago this would happen. That lying to him would backfire because there would come a time when the truth would need to come out. And here we are."

"I should have listened to you…" Lisa said, barely able to look at Ms. Sherry.

"And after I'm done here, I'm giving Ben the letter. I'm not playing with this lie any longer."

"Letter?" Amelia sat back down, as did Lisa. "Well, now I'm officially lost."

Ms. Sherry sat in the armchair opposite them by the twinkling Christmas tree—it's soft glow soothing among such a heavy topic—and looked at Amelia. "Do you know about his adoption story?"

"I only knew that he had been adopted and that his birth mother had passed away from the little he told me," Amelia said, glancing at Lisa. "Which is obviously not the case. Ms. Sherry, could you please explain what's going on? What letter are you talking about?"

"I sure can, and I'm sorry you had to witness all this, Amelia. Gives small-town gossip a whole new meaning, doesn't it?" Ms. Sherry gave her an apologetic look.

"Makes city life back in New Haven seem boring now."

"I bet. This town is small, but packed with history." Ms. Sherry took a moment before she began. "I'm going on seventy-five next year and have lived in White Bridge my entire life. I knew Lisa's mother, Brenda. We went to school together and were the best of friends."

"Where is your mother now?" Amelia asked Lisa.

"She passed away about five years ago. Both my parents

are gone, and now my brother, Timothy, whom I assume you heard about with the sale of this house."

"I'm sorry for your loss," Amelia said.

Lisa looked away. "Thank you. But Timothy and I had become strangers by the time I graduated high school and left this town."

"I'm sorry to hear that," Amelia said.

"Don't be. It was my choice. I left this town and this house for a reason." Lisa looked at Ms. Sherry. "But you were right in the voicemail you left me last week. That living with such resentment for as long as I had would only make me emotionally decline. I've really been struggling with this since my parents and brother passed… it's as if knowing everyone is now gone somehow made me really start to reflect on everything."

"I was hoping when your mother left White Bridge to be closer to you years ago that you two would make amends. Did you?"

Lisa's eyes misted over as she tried to hold back her emotions and shook her head. Amelia got up and got her some tissues.

"I see," Ms. Sherry said.

"Thank you, Amelia." Lisa took the box. "But you were right again, I *have* been declining. And Ben doesn't deserve to sit with this lie for the rest of his life… thinking I'm gone."

"It's why I made the call to you," Ms. Sherry said. "It wasn't just to tell you that Amelia found your coin. I just couldn't carry this lie any longer, seeing him all the time… but the truth had to come from you."

"Why did you lie about your death in the first place?" Amelia asked. "Did Ben's birth father know about this lie too?"

"No, Brian didn't know. In fact, I haven't spoken to him since I was pregnant, and I don't know where he is today. His family left town after he went to college." Lisa turned in her seat toward Amelia. "My parents forced me to place Ben for adoption against my will. His birth father and family also agreed to their plan… so I was outnumbered and only sixteen years old. My brother, Timothy, sided with my parents and had become ashamed of me for the pregnancy and for putting our parents through that. The wounds of being so ignored and having what I wanted—to keep my baby—dismissed ran so deep that I left this town and them when I finished high school."

"That's devastating. I understand now why you were so angry and left back then…" Amelia shook her head. "But the lie still doesn't make any sense. Ben told me he wanted to meet you when he was older. If you never wanted to give him up… Why didn't you meet him then?"

"I guess shame trickled into me after leaving so angry. And a part of me felt like I *did* die when I had to hand Ben to his parents. By the time Mrs. Walsh contacted me, I had been out of White Bridge for so long, absorbing years of sadness, that I convinced myself I didn't deserve to meet him. What's worse… I convinced his parents to go along with the lie. But after I heard Ms. Sherry's voicemail… I realized I had been inadvertently punishing Ben with all of this by allowing him to believe that lie. He deserves to know about me and his birth family if that is what he wants."

"It *is* what he wants, Lisa," Ms. Sherry said to the woman, but Lisa stayed quiet and stood up by the window, facing outside.

"Now I get why Tom warned me multiple times it would be hard to get a hold of her," Amelia told Ms. Sherry. "How did he know to ask you to call Lisa?"

"He didn't know about Ben's adoptive story, but he had a hunch I could get through to Lisa because of the friendship I had with her mother and get her to come here for that coin.

After I left you that voicemail, Lisa, I knew it was either going to be me telling Ben the truth or you." Ms. Sherry looked up toward Lisa, whose shoulders were slumped forward.

"So from what you've explained so far, Ms. Sherry, it's clear you knew Ben was Lisa's biological son when he first moved to White Bridge," Amelia said.

"I did. I knew right away the first day he introduced himself to me that he was Lisa's Ben. I was one of the few in town who Brenda and her husband told what his name was after they got their update, with the letter, from his adoptive parents. The letter that Ben should have read a long time ago, when he first was interested in meeting you."

"Oh, so that's what you meant by a letter..." Amelia glanced at Lisa who still wouldn't move from the window. "How incredibly hard to know all of this and keep it to yourself."

"More than you realize..." Ms. Sherry straightened up in her chair before continuing. "I reached out to Lisa to let her know he had found his way to White Bridge and married a woman named Molly and that she needed to try to contact him—to get the truth out then—but I never heard back from her. Then I let it just sit... for far too long."

"I got your message back then," Lisa said, finally turning around to face Ms. Sherry. "But I was a coward. I'm sorry I put you through all this." The woman could barely look Ms. Sherry in the eye. "It even cost you your friendship with my mother."

"I would stand up for you all over again if I had to. Forcing you to adopt your baby was a decision I never stood by. I'm sorry you had to endure that. I know how painful it was for you to hand him over. I couldn't imagine being in your position."

Lisa's eyes shone with fresh tears again. "And years of

continued pain since. Which is why I'm here now. It's time to fix this."

Ms. Sherry looked right at Amelia. "Go find Ben. Get him to at least listen to Lisa. He will talk to you."

"I'm not sure about that. He left pretty upset."

"Amelia… since you've come into his life, it's the first time I've seen him looking so… alive again. Like the old Ben coming back. He's angry with me right now, so you're the only one who can get him to talk to Lisa."

STARING OUT THE FRONT WINDOW FROM THE COUCH, AMELIA sat in the oppressive silence that only amplified her thoughts after Lisa and Ms. Sherry left. She wasn't entirely convinced she was the best person to reach out to Ben, but someone had to, and after going back and forth on the matter, she finally picked up her phone. It wouldn't hurt to try. Calling him again was the only solution she could think of for the time being, but when she looked at the screen she saw two missed calls from her mom and a text saying to call her as soon as she could.

It only rang once before her mom picked up. "Amelia?"

"Mom, is everything all right?"

"It's Andrew."

"What?" She immediately jumped up. "Okay, give me time to pack. I'll be on my way as soon as I can."

"No, no. You don't need to come. Besides, we got your text. We're coming to you this weekend."

Confused, she sat back down. "Wait, what? Then what is going on?"

"We were at the doctor with him earlier, getting results from the latest scan to see if any progress was happening with the new treatment."

"He told me already it wasn't working."

"We had a hunch based on how much weaker he was getting, but didn't know for sure until we got his scan results."

"What did the doctor say?"

"That the cancer"—her mother's voice cracked and she took a deep breath—"has spread to his spleen and liver."

Everything in the room spun, but she kept control for her mom. "Which means?"

"We don't have an exact answer. But Andrew said he knows one thing—he is coming to White Bridge. So we will arrive on Friday. I wanted to tell you first, even though he planned on speaking to you in person."

Placing her trembling hand against the windowsill, Amelia tried not to cry. The shock sliced through her, even though she'd had years of preparation for this possibility.

"Thank you for telling me. It gives me time to process."

"I know how you need that…" The pause stretched on, neither able to speak. "Hang tight, honey," her mother finally said. "We will all be there Friday. I love you."

"Love you, Mom."

Amelia still needed to call Ben, but all she could think about was Andrew. Before she put the phone down, another call came through and she recognized Ben's office number.

She hesitated, but wanted to make sure he was all right. "Hello?"

"Amelia? Hi, this is Chris, Ben's partner. Have a minute to talk?"

"Yes."

"I just spent over an hour talking to Ben. I understand something happened during the evaluation."

"Yes, but it was not his doing."

"No, it wasn't. But I told him I would call you… I just…" Chris sighed.

This was not a typical bump in the job, and she could tell he was struggling to remain professional.

"No need to explain. I couldn't imagine dealing with what he just did."

"Me either. But I just wanted you to know that I will be the one coming to finish the evaluation. That house is…" He trailed off again.

Not wanting to sound flustered, she gave herself a moment before cutting to the chase. "So you will be taking over the entire job?"

"I really don't know. I'm thinking for now, I will be. If you would like to seek out other services, I completely understand. I have some recommendations I could give you."

She thought about that idea, but it didn't sit right with her. "That won't be necessary. You are the best ones for the job."

"That means a lot, especially after what happened today. How about we meet tomorrow morning at your house. Would ten work?"

"Yes, that will be fine."

"Great. It won't take me long. Ben gave me his notes on the second floor. So I'll get the first floor done and have a look at the barn. He mentioned you wanted to remodel that into a ballet studio."

"Yes." She thought about Ben's daughters. Would he send them somewhere else to dance now? She wasn't sure he'd ever be able to come to this house again. "Sounds like a plan. And, Chris… is he okay?"

"He will be. Ben Walsh is one of the strongest people I know." Chris paused. "But between you and me, Amelia, and after hearing what just took place… perhaps this needed to happen."

"I agree."

When they hung up, she immediately called Ben again. Voicemail.

"Hi, Ben. It's me, Amelia, again. I just spoke to Chris, and I wanted you to know that I'm perfectly fine having him finish the evaluation if that's what you need. I'm not concerned about the house... It's you I care about. Please call me."

All she could do now was wait.

CHAPTER 24

*T*he exhaustion burned through her fatigued eyes when Amelia looked at her reflection in the bathroom mirror the next morning. Lying wide awake the entire night, she hadn't been able to relax for one minute. The only place she could find peace was in the living room, where the Christmas tree's gentle radiance offered a glimmer of hope against the lonely darkness of the night.

If she wasn't thinking about Ben, she was thinking about Andrew or her parents and what they must be feeling. And here she was, sitting in a farmhouse in the country, feeling useless. She wanted to fix everything, but didn't know where to start.

It was already after eight and Chris was coming soon to finish the evaluation. Suddenly, all the repairs didn't seem important, but it was too late to cancel. She had texted her mom before the sun came up to check on Andrew, not realizing just how early it was. Her phone lit up next to the sink with her mom's response as she held a cool rag against the dark bags under her eyes.

My are you up early! Did you get any sleep? Andrew is still sleeping. I think he just needs a few days with Diana to process everything, especially before seeing you this weekend. I'm here if you need to talk. XO

Turning on the shower to make herself presentable for Chris, Amelia fought to keep herself from crying. She'd already done her fair share of that through the night, but her heart sank every time she remembered the day before in the barn with Ben and how excited he seemed about her idea... and how he had peered down at her, getting closer...

As she stood in her bathroom, she couldn't help but wonder what room he was born in or what the house looked like when Lisa was pregnant with him. Steam began to rise and she got in. After a shower and coffee she'd be good as new to fake it through an hour or two.

A short while later, all clean and dressed, she made her way downstairs when she heard the crunching on her driveway. Thinking it was Chris showing up early for their appointment, she went to the front door and opened it, but only caught the backend of a car turning out of the driveway... and at her feet, a gift. She picked up the box wrapped in dark green with a silver bow and took it inside. The envelope on top poked out from under the ribbon. She sat down on the couch to see who it was from, starting with the letter.

Dear Amelia,

There isn't an easy way to begin a letter to a woman I only met yesterday, but knowing you are the one who bought my family's farmhouse makes me feel connected to you in a special

way... like kindred spirits.

I'm deeply sorry you had to witness such emotional turmoil yesterday. But inviting me in and allowing me to share my story meant a lot to me. And you were right, I did think there was a possibility that Ben would be there. And despite your invitation to come by in the voicemail you left me, it was wrong of me not to call you first because you had no idea who I was.

After Ms. Sherry and I left, we went to town and talked for a while. I later strolled around Main Street, trying to calm myself, and inside one of the antique gift shops I saw this and thought of you. Ms. Sherry told me you are a ballerina and an answer to her prayers... as you are to mine.

I may have given up the farmhouse, but I always prayed the right person would buy it and love it like my family did. Thank you for returning the coin, and I wish you nothing but years of happiness and joy in your new home.

A token of my appreciation.

Warmly,
Lisa Allard

Amelia opened the green wrapping and gasped when she

saw a round heirloom porcelain music box. When she opened the top, her eyes widened in disbelief. It was the Sugar Plum Fairy from *The Nutcracker*. She twisted the metal knob, tears pooling in her eyes as the "Dance of the Sugar Plum Fairy" played and the little plastic ballerina spun about. The back of the lid showed Clara holding the nutcracker doll next to her brother, Fritz.

The conversation with her father at the top of the stairs the weekend before came to mind as she cradled the music box in her arms, letting its melodious tune serve as a gentle reminder that life continued to be full of unexpected blessings.

The sound of a car again in her driveway caught her attention and when she heard the knock, she placed the music box on the coffee table.

Opening the door, she expected to see Chris for sure this time. "Hi, Chr—" She stopped short when she saw Ben standing on the other side. "Ben?"

"May I come in?"

"Of course, yes, please come in. Chris is supposed to be here any minute to finish the evaluation."

He stepped inside. "No, he won't be coming."

"He won't?"

"No. Because I'm here to finish what I started. That is, if you still want me to."

"I do want you to, but I really won't be upset if you can't do this job given the circumstances. Are you sure?"

Ben didn't answer her, instead stepping into the room and looking around. The same way Lisa had the day before.

"I wonder if I was born in this room," he said.

Amelia walked up behind him. "I was thinking about the same thing earlier."

When he turned to face her, his eyes were red. "Do you mind if I just get to the rest of the evaluation? When I keep moving, it helps."

"Absolutely. In fact, I'm the same way. Except now that I can't dance anymore, I need a new way to move through my emotions." She offered him a smile, but his face stayed even. She couldn't imagine how strange being here was for him.

He walked away to get started and, not knowing what to do with herself, Amelia went into the kitchen to make breakfast. She scrambled some eggs and made avocado toast, poured coffee into a mug, and sat down to eat. The winter landscape out her window filled the time as she gazed outside.

The same red cardinal she and her dad had spotted suddenly flew by, landing on a tree right outside the window. While she sipped her coffee, the bird made its way from one branch to the next. The cardinal was known to be a comforting sight to those who had lost loved ones, but she also understood it to be an uplifting symbol, conveying strength to those who witness it. Given the cardinal's reputation, Amelia suddenly felt the history of this home wrap around her, holding her with generations of love and loss through the bird's bright-red presence.

"What a pretty bird," Ben said, appearing in the doorway of the kitchen.

"Very. It's the second time he's come to visit me."

"Those birds are known for showing up when people in your life have died and are coming to visit."

"I know, and for some reason I feel like there is so much to unravel with this house that the bird is trying to convey about your family who have passed."

"My family…" Ben repeated the phrase.

"I'm so sorry, that just sort of came out. The Walsh family is your family."

Ben pointed to the chair. "Do you mind if I sit down?"

"Not at all. Are you hungry? I can make you some eggs."

"No, thank you, but some coffee would be great."

Amelia stood up to pour him a cup and he quietly sipped.

"How many rooms did you get through?"

"Just the dining room so far. It's the biggest problem area down here. I read the inspector's report and took a look. My suggestion is hiring someone who has experience with fireplaces in a home this old. We've used masons from a company that specializes in historical homes. I'll give them a call if you'd like."

"Yes, that sounds like a good idea."

Ben shifted in his chair, pulling his phone out of his pocket. "Phone call coming in, let me just make sure it's not Chris." He stared at the screen without answering.

"If you need to take the call, go ahead."

He put the phone on the table. "It's my mother. She's been calling nonstop since last night."

"So she knows what happened?"

"Yes. I called my parents yesterday and didn't exactly sugarcoat my message about how upset I was."

"Have you spoken to them yet?"

"No." He tapped the side of his mug and looked out the window.

"Ben, I'm so sorry about what happened yesterday. I want you to know I spoke to both Lisa and Ms. Sherry."

"Yeah, I heard," he said, his hands still moving over the mug. "That's another reason I came back here today, not just for the evaluation." His gaze fell back to her. "I feel like I should be the one who is sorry. Storming off the way I did and leaving you to deal with the aftermath. You got thrown into this mess, and for that I'm sorry."

"I meant what I said in my voicemail... I care for you, Ben," she said, placing her hand on his, steadying his fingers. "And I'm here for you, but... I think you need to call your mom."

"I know. But right now, I'm too angry. They told me my birth mother… was *dead*, Amelia."

"It's understandable you feel that way…" She looked at their hands joined together on the table. "To be honest, I had a hard time listening to Ms. Sherry explain all she knew and learn she kept this from you for so long."

Ben let out long sigh, let go of her hand, and ran his through his hair as he sat back. "I was pretty stunned to learn that too, but the more I thought it through last night while pacing around my living room after I spoke with her on the phone, the more I realized what a hard position Ms. Sherry had been put in. She told me it wasn't her business to share something like that… and she's right. This falls on my parents and Lisa."

"That's true… but what a lot to hold in. I'm not sure I would have been as quiet about it as her." She watched him look back out the window, his face so distraught, and she folded her hands together to suppress the urge to put her arms around him. "I'm curious though. What made you move to White Bridge?"

"Molly and I drove through here one day. The house I live in now was for sale and something in me just… felt *at home* here in White Bridge for the first time, even more than my childhood home. Now I understand why." He reached into his back pocket and pulled out a folded piece of paper, then slid it across the table to her. "She left this on my door at some point last night."

Amelia opened the paper.

Ben,

I understand if you don't ever want to speak to me again, but please do one thing: tell

279

*your girls about me. About that house. Their
heritage. Everything. And just know how much I
have loved you from the moment I held you in
my arms.*

    Lisa

Amelia put the letter down and stood up. "She made a visit to me too." She touched his shoulder as she walked past him to get the music box and letter. When she returned, she showed it to Ben, who read the letter and quietly stared at the music box for a couple minutes.

Amelia broke the silence. "I can't believe she found such a perfect gift."

"And I can't believe she thinks she can show up like this, give us all letters and a music box as if that will make everything better!" he nearly shouted, taking her by surprise at his outburst.

"Ben, I don't know what to say. But her words shook me a bit. I can see the pain you both hold."

"If she was in so much pain, then why did she lie? Why didn't she agree to meet me when my mother reached out to her?"

Amelia remembered Lisa's words. *"I was a coward."*

"Maybe she was just afraid."

She reached for him, but he stood up, nearly knocking the chair down.

"No excuse!"

"I can't even imagine how shocked you must be still. Seeing her standing there in the driveway yesterday must have felt like encountering a ghost from your past that you hadn't even met. Like a missing puzzle piece was just found."

"I wish she hadn't come." He turned to the window, crossing his arms in defense.

"I know you're angry now, but maybe later you will change your mind. You wanted to meet her before and now you can. You can learn a whole new part of your identity that maybe felt a little lost before."

Ben kept his back to her, and she desperately searched for comforting words. She stood up and moved next to him.

"Look, Ben, when I lost my ability to dance—"

"You lost the stage, not your mother, Amelia," Ben snapped.

She took a step back when he scowled at her.

"My mom told me Lisa was gone. That I had no chance to meet her, and I had put that part of me to rest and let her go. Now it just exploded in my face! Don't you understand?"

"I know our stories are different. I'm just trying to say that despite how hard this is, Lisa made a really good point in her letter. That your girls don't need to be in the dark about your family heritage. Your parents are a part of them, but so is Lisa. Just like how I've helped Ava with dance, it's been showing me a part of myself that I never embraced."

"Or you're just using this opportunity to seek solace from your own pain. And I'll handle my girls myself," he said slowly, his face flushed with anger. "I need to go." He stormed off once again.

When he slammed the door, Amelia sat on the couch, trying to stop the shaking. What just happened? Did she mess this up even more? She suddenly felt like a trespasser in her own home. Was it her place to buy a random farmhouse in a small town that held six generations of memories? She stood up and walked to the window, watching Ben's truck leave. Was he right? Was her time at Ms. Sherry's studio a cover up from the pain of losing her career... and now possibly her brother too? Was she just trying to redefine her identity in order to hide?

Amelia turned from the window. It was all too much to bear. Running upstairs, she went to the attic and pulled down one of her suitcases. She threw in whatever clothes she could grab quickly, ushered Mocha into her travel carrier, picked up the bag of cat food, then dashed out the door.

Shortly after leaving, she called Ben and got his voicemail.

"You're right, Ben. I am hiding. I don't even know what I'm doing in White Bridge to begin with. I'm leaving for a while. I'll be at my parents' house, but please tell Ava I'm sorry I won't be there this week to finish practicing with her and that she's more than ready to dance that part. They both will do so great this weekend."

Biting her lip, she knew the next call would be harder. She racked her brain trying to draw up some kind of excuse. *Andrew...* she thought and hit send on the studio's office number. She got another voicemail.

"Ms. Sherry, it's Amelia. I'm heading out of town to my parents' house, and I wanted to apologize for the short notice. My brother is sick and I just got news he's gotten worse. I'm so sorry to miss everything. Give all the girls my love, and good luck this weekend."

She silenced her phone and disconnected it from her car's Bluetooth, then got on the highway and zoned everything out.

CHAPTER 25

*T*he drive to her parents' house was much easier from White Bridge than New Haven, saving an extra hour of time, which was a relief with Mocha yowling in the back. She had been sleeping peacefully in her new favorite spot by her bedroom window when she was thrown into her carrier, so she was not going to let Amelia drive in much-needed silence.

Amelia pulled into the driveway and stopped the car as she admired her mother's work. All the windows glowed with battery-lit candles, and wreaths with big red ribbons hung from every window—including a larger one on the front door. Lit-up garland also wrapped around the door, which glowed perfectly next to all the twinkling lights in the front bushes. The porch was small, but the tall wooden sign leaning on the side of the door featured a picture of a rustic Christmas tree with snow and the words *Merry Christmas* under it.

She pulled in the rest of the way and parked. Just as she was getting her suitcase out of the back seat, the front door opened, and her mom and dad came out.

"Amelia?" her mother said, hurrying over.

Placing her suitcase on the ground, she looked at her mother with weary eyes. "I just needed to come home."

"You can always come anytime. Here, let me help you with that."

Her mother picked up her suitcase, and her dad reached in to get Mocha and the three of them walked inside. Andrew was standing next to the bottom of the stairs, waiting on her. The first thing she noticed was how much weight he'd lost and the second was the port for his meds and hydration. None of that mattered as she watched him. She couldn't hold it in anymore and burst into tears as she went to hug him.

"Okay, who told you?" he asked. "I swear this family can't keep any secrets."

Amelia pulled back. "I'm your twin, remember? You don't need to tell me. I already know."

"Amelia?" Diana appeared at the top of the stairs. "This is quite a surprise. We were all going to leave Friday morning to come see you at your new house."

"She just felt left out from all the excitement here," Andrew said, nudging his sister. "Come on, let's go dry those tears and pig out on all the cookies Mom just baked. She was going to pack them up and bring them Friday, but since you're here now… let's eat. Unless cookies are still a black-listed food item?"

Amelia smiled. "Not anymore. Where are they?"

"Andrew, you know most of them are for the dancers."

"The dancers?" Amelia looked at her mom, who was hanging her coat in the closet.

"Mm-hmm. Ms. Sherry gave me the exact number of them, so I made enough for each girl to have two."

Her dad stepped forward. "Let's all go sit in the living

room. I'll make coffee and get some water out for Mocha," he said and took the carrier into the kitchen.

When they sat down, Amelia turned to her mom. "You talked to Ms. Sherry? How did you know where to find her?"

"White Bridge has a population of about two thousand people and has one ballet school. It took about fifteen seconds to look up online," her mother said. "I wanted to bring the girls a treat for all their hard work. And Ms. Sherry is lovely. We exchanged numbers. I can't wait to have coffee with her next time I'm in White Bridge."

"I guess my estimate of fifty for the population was a bit off." Andrew winked at her. "But we still need to teach you how to get a homestead going over there."

"I'm not sure that will be necessary. And, Mom, thank you for thinking of Ms. Sherry's dancers, but we won't be seeing the performance."

"Now wait just a minute," Andrew cut in. "I've missed every opportunity to watch you dance in *The Nutcracker* our entire lives. Your favorite performance. It's like an omen has been hanging over our heads to keep me from it. You spent the last few weeks working tirelessly to train their Sugar Plum Fairy— and now you're saying I'm going to miss seeing that too?"

"But, Andrew, it's still not me up there."

"So? When I watch… What's her name? The girl you trained?"

"Ava."

"When I watch Ava leap and spin and twirl and do whatever else you dancers do, I will be first to stand and cheer because my amazing sister is the backbone of her every move."

"What Mr. Dramatic is trying to say, Amelia"—Diana came over and sat by her—"is that he told your mom to specifically tell you not to come home because he was still

LINDSAY GIBSON

waiting on *The Nutcracker*. We were looking forward to seeing that show and also your home."

"She never listens," Andrew said, shaking his head as he sat back. "But that's nothing new."

Amelia picked up a cookie from the tray their mother placed on the coffee table and tossed it at him. "Eat a cookie and hush." She turned back to Diana. "I'm not sure that home and White Bridge are for me. I'm wondering if I should remodel it and then put it on the market again."

"No, you're not selling it," Andrew said before taking a bite of the cookie.

"Andrew, let me explain—"

"You're not because Diana and I will not fit into that tiny apartment you and Mocha lived in down in New Haven."

"What are you talking about?" Amelia eyed her twin and knew from the look on his face he had something up his sleeve.

"Mom and Dad's house is wonderful, but I'm tired of the same scenery I've had since I was a child." He smiled. "No offense, Mom."

Kimberly put up her hands. "None taken," she said, picking up one of the mugs of coffee.

"Amelia, you are my twin sister. We came into this world together, and there's nowhere I'd want to spend my time before I exit besides with Diana and you." He glanced at his parents. "Okay, fine, you two can hang around too sometimes."

Amelia watched her mom pick up a napkin to wipe her eyes.

"Now you made Mom cry. Nice."

"I'm actually really happy witnessing this conversation," their mom said. "You two never change, and it's a joy to see how close you are."

"Happy watching us... but also really tired," Andrew

286

continued. "I'm sort of a pain right now. So Diana and I would like to put all this on you for a while. What do you say, sis?"

Amelia stood up and nearly crashed into him as she hugged him. "Of course you two can come out to White Bridge. I would love nothing more."

"Good. Because Diana has spent the last day packing us all up," Andrew said.

"Diana, what about work? You love that school you teach in."

"I've been doing a little digging, and there happens to be an opening in White Bridge Elementary in January for one of their second-grade classrooms. The teacher is going on maternity leave. I can figure it out from there," Diana said.

"Didn't the school already get back to you?" Kimberly asked.

"Yes, just this morning. Amelia"—Diana looked at her—"I gave my notice already to the school here, so you can't say no."

"No, you can't. We will just move to a farm by ourselves if you do. Maybe Diana will get a knack for gardening."

"Nope." Diana giggled. "Not happening."

"Honey, you look extremely tired," her mom said to Amelia. "Go on up and get some rest. This was a lot to take in. Sleep helps everything."

Amelia didn't argue. Just as her mom suggested the nap, she noticed the pounding in her head and her body felt heavy. The second she got upstairs and lay on her bed in her childhood room—she was asleep.

Amelia's eyes peeked open and the burning exhaustion from earlier had eased. Sitting up, she noticed the room cast a radiant glow from the setting sun. She wasn't sure how long she was asleep, but it was enough to replenish her. The heaviness she'd felt on the drive over was gone and her headache had dialed down.

She headed to the bathroom to splash her face and as she passed the top of the stairs, she heard voices below. It was good to be home with her family, and the idea of having Andrew and Diana stay with her for however long they wanted brought much-needed relief. The anxiety of being away from him while he was ill had been so hard, and over the years she had felt as if she didn't help enough, due to her endless schedule at the theater.

Now she had the time and the room with her new home. They'd need to work out the logistics with his medical team, but he was going to love being out in the countryside, watching nature. What better place to be in his condition? If anything, buying the Maple Ridge farmhouse was perhaps meant for him. She was really looking forward to being by his side.

Once she'd freshened up, her energy rose even more, and she padded down the stairs to see if her mom needed help with dinner preparation. Smells of garlic and herbs engulfed her as she reached the bottom of the stairs, bypassing the living room and going straight to the kitchen.

Her mom was bent over the oven, checking on the dinner when she walked in.

"It smells heavenly in here," Amelia said.

"Beef lasagna and garlic bread will be ready soon," her mom said and closed the oven. "You were asleep for nearly three hours, so I hope you feel better."

"Wow, that long? Yes, I do, much better. I didn't sleep at all last night."

"I know!" a little voice burst in behind her. "Daddy said you looked like a ghost this morning."

Amelia recognized the voice and whipped around to see Julia wearing one of her mom's aprons and holding an unopened salad dressing.

"I think I found it, Ms. Kim." Julia handed her mom the dressing. "Italian dressing, right?"

"That's the one," her mom said, taking the bottle.

"Julia?" Amelia went over and hugged the girl. "Why are you here?"

"Because you up and left White Bridge. We weren't done practicing," another young voice said, and when Amelia turned, Ava had come into the kitchen.

"Ava... I'm so sorry. I felt terrible the whole way here thinking about you."

Ava walked over and hugged her. "It's okay. Ms. Sherry said we just have to practice double-time tomorrow."

"So that means we need to hit the road first thing in the morning," a low voice said from the doorway.

Amelia closed her eyes before facing him. "We do?" It was all she could think of to say.

Ben joined her where she stood near the kitchen table, the hints of gold in his eyes becoming sharper as he got closer, keeping his gaze fixated on her. He grabbed her hand, and Amelia's mom ushered the girls out of the kitchen.

"We absolutely do."

"Ben, what happened yesterday was more than most people could handle. And I didn't help—"

"Like I said when we were in the barn, you have been nothing but helpful. With Ms. Sherry, Ava... me. The way you tried to comfort me this morning meant everything to me, even though I lashed out. I turned around when I was halfway home, but when I got back, you had already left." He stepped closer to her. "Amelia, I am so sorry for how I acted this morning."

"You're angry and rightfully so." She felt his fingers wrap around hers.

"Doesn't excuse how I behaved. I was wrong to explode my anger on you. I'm not sure what will happen between me and Lisa, but staying angry doesn't help anything. I will work through this for myself and for my girls. You were right, they deserve to have a chance to learn about their heritage… about our family's history with our town. White Bridge is part of them… and now a part of you. Our next ballet teacher. I can't wait to get my hands on that barn."

Amelia looked down at their joined hands. "Do you mean that?"

"More than anything," he said, running his hands up her arms. "I see your talent when Julia spins around the living room, shouting out that she's a ballerina like Ms. Amelia, and when Ava excitedly comes into the kitchen after practice to show me something you taught her. Your days on the stage will live on with every young dancer you come across."

"The girls mean the world to me. All I want is for them and all those students to feel nothing but joy when they put on their dance shoes; and to give them the guidance as the loving teacher I only dreamed of as a child." She let go of his hand and brushed away the tears that slid out.

"You do all of that with nothing but grace."

"And I want you to know just how amazing you are," Amelia continued. "Like me, life has given you a path that is hard to see at times, losing ourselves to only—"

"Be lucky enough to somehow find who we are through each other."

He lifted her chin. His fingertips traced the contours of her cheek, his touch feather light as he leaned in and his lips brushed against hers, until they finally met in a collision of passion. He pulled her against him as they danced in perfect harmony.

Breathless, they broke apart. Amelia reached up, running her hands through a piece of his sandy-blond hair that fell forward.

"I guess that coin you found didn't lose its luck yet," Ben said.

Amelia smiled, thinking of her mom. "We created our own good luck." She stood up on her tippy toes and kissed him once more.

"Are you two done being all gushy?" Julia peeked her head in, and they both laughed.

"For now," Ben said, glancing at Amelia.

"Good, 'cause we're starving!" Ava said and walked in with everyone else behind her.

"We better eat and get a good night's sleep. We have to get back to White Bridge and show that town what the Sugar Plum Fairy is all about!" Amelia said, giving Ava a stern nod.

"And bring the Maple Ridge farmhouse back to life," Ben added. "And a new dance studio."

"Does this mean what I think it does?" Ava asked.

Amelia saw both girls cupping their mouths.

"I still need to fill in Ms. Sherry, but I'm converting the barn on my property to a new ballet studio. Your teacher may be retiring, and the old studio is closing down…" She looked at her dad who was standing in the doorway. "But a lucky twist of fate has opened a new path for all of us."

Both girls jumped with excitement and Amelia soaked it all in. She saw her brother light up next to Ben as he watched everything transpire. She couldn't wait to finally show him *The Nutcracker*.

CHAPTER 26

*M*ocha was unusually quiet on the drive back to White Bridge the next morning. Perhaps she felt the tension ease from the night before, but she was happily content the whole way.

"We're home, sweet girl," Amelia said, pulling into her driveway. She had woken up with boundless energy after sleeping soundly and was more than ready for the weekend. As she got Mocha out of the car, Diana and Andrew came down the driveway.

The moment she parked the car, Diana jumped out. "Wow! Look at this place!"

Amelia went to Andrew's side and opened the door, helping him out. "I'm so glad you two are here. I hope you brought enough clothes until the movers get here next week."

"I think I packed enough for a month." Diana smiled at Amelia before she put her arm around Andrew's waist and turned to observe the fields, the barn, and the house.

Amelia stood next to them and held Andrew's hand. "Feels like home having you here now."

"I gotta hand it to you, sis, this is incredible."

"Diana, I'll help you get all your stuff. Take Andrew inside. The living room is to the right when you walk in."

Diana walked over to Amelia, hugging her tight. "Thank you for having us. There's so much I need to do to get things organized, like getting homecare switched over and…"

"I'll help you. And whatever the cost is, please don't worry. My parents offered to help and so will I. Keeping Andrew comfortable and—"

"Fed," her brother cut in. "Anyone else starving?"

Diana laughed. "And yes, fed."

Amelia put her hand on her sister-in-law's shoulder. "We will get through this together."

While Diana got Andrew set up on the couch, Amelia got all the suitcases inside and showed Diana the room they would stay in.

"While you two settle in, there's something I have to do. It won't take long. The pantry is pretty stocked. Help yourselves to whatever you want."

Amelia wasn't sure why she was nervous when she got back in the car, but her stomach was doing flips by the time she pulled into the driveway at the studio. She found Ms. Sherry sitting at her desk, counting something on a sheet of paper in front of her.

Amelia stood in the doorway and knocked softly.

Ms. Sherry popped her head up. "Amelia, you gave me a fright! I didn't hear you come in."

"I see that. You looked pretty absorbed there." She pointed to the papers on the desk.

"Yes, I am. I was counting how many VIP tickets were sold and sorting out where to place them on Saturday."

"VIP?"

"Every year I sell a certain number of VIP tickets. Past students of mine, family of the dancers, etc. They don't cost more or anything since this isn't Northeast Performing Arts."

Amelia grinned and sat down across from her. "Ah, I see."

"Anyway, enough of that… you're back."

"I'm back." Amelia suddenly felt foolish for running off to her parents like she had. "I'm sorry for all the drama."

Ms. Sherry waved her hand. "No, don't apologize. I don't blame you for needing a bit of a breather. You were sort of thrown right into all of that."

"I take it you gave Ben my mom's number to get my parents' address."

"Guilty."

"I'm glad you did. I feel for Ben. This situation is going to take some time to work through, but I think he's willing to try."

"That's great to hear."

"Yeah, it is. I wasn't sure at first because he was so angry. It was part of the reason I scooted off to my parents' house so fast. Things got rather heated between us… but we're okay now." She smiled to herself. "More than okay."

"Not surprised he's so angry. I would be too. Looks like you got the second hit, after he called me with some choice words. We're okay now, too, thank goodness."

"He mentioned you two spoke that night for a long time."

"We did and while it was an intense conversation, the man needed a good release. I was afraid he'd hold things in and put a wall back up…" Ms. Sherry eyed her for a moment. "But that wall seems to be crumbled for good now."

"Yes, it is." The kiss from the night before flooded her mind. "We've—"

"Realized you're perfect for each other?"

"How did you guess?"

"Because you are probably every shade of red." Ms. Sherry waggled her eyebrows. "You two work together so well."

"I think so too." Amelia felt her past melt away, unable to grab hold anymore. "But no one is perfect."

Ms. Sherry smiled. "And sometimes they are… together."

"I just hope I can help him move forward with Lisa and that they find a way to connect."

"Me too. Wounds that deep take time, but I think a path forward is always possible. I have a hunch it's going to be okay."

"I hope so."

"It will." Ms. Sherry looked at her desk. "Now I just need to figure out a path for my dancers."

A burst of enthusiasm swept over Amelia. "That's actually why I'm here. I have a solution."

"Oh?"

"Ben is not only heading up the remodel of the farmhouse, but he's converting the old barn into a ballet studio—that is, if the town allows for it."

Ms. Sherry nearly tripped on the leg of her chair she shot up so fast. "Oh, Amelia… this is fantastic news!" She came around her desk with her arms extended and Amelia stood to hug her. "And don't worry about the town"—she leaned back—"let me handle that. The town may have specifics for their historical homes, but this is one they will not dispute, especially if I have a say in it."

"Everything was meant to be then."

Amelia felt Ms. Sherry embrace her again before she stood back with her hands on her shoulders.

"Like I said when I met you—Christmas wishes do come true."

"I better get going. I have a few more pirouettes to get out of Ava before Saturday."

"Thank you, Amelia. My heart is full knowing my girls will be in good hands."

~

BACK HOME, AMELIA SAT BY HER CHRISTMAS TREE AND HELD up her phone. Her followers had been out of the loop for over a week now.

"Hi, everyone! Thank you for your patience as I have been silent for a little while. But there is so much to catch you all up on." She took a deep breath and beamed at the camera. "As it turns out, my ballet days are not over after all…"

When she was done, she clicked her phone off and went upstairs to change into her dance clothes to meet Ava for practice. It was time to get ready for the big show.

CHAPTER 27

*A*melia stood on the side of the stage on Saturday night, the curtain still drawn and the hum of the audience chatting in their seats echoing around her. Walking out to the center she looked at the scene. For a high-school stage and props, she was thoroughly impressed, and that was when it hit her—she was on stage again, but this time filled with happiness instead of heartache.

The sounds of giggling girls nearby as they waited for the show to begin brought all the challenges from her early days with Ms. Ruth, to her hard work rising to the top as a professional ballerina, into a bright future set before her now. A new dance had begun.

Ms. Sherry's voice broke through on her headset. "It's time."

Amelia heard Ms. Sherry in front of the curtain addressing the audience, and that was her cue to get the girls positioned on stage. Minutes later, as the music began, playing Tchaikovsky's iconic overture, the curtain slowly rose, revealing a lavishly decorated living room within the Stahlbaum residence. The set design perfectly represented a nineteenth-century European household with opulent furnishings and even a fake fireplace offering coziness to the scene. Soft, warm lighting cast a gentle glow on the girls, enhancing the inviting atmosphere. The adult volunteers playing the Stahlbaum family, elegantly dressed in their finest attire, gracefully began to move about the stage, engaging in joyful conversation and exchanging presents.

The audience was dark, so Amelia couldn't see anyone from where she stood as she thought about her family. She had been swamped all day with preparations and hadn't checked in once with her parents since they arrived in White Bridge earlier, or with Andrew and Diana, but she had left their tickets on the kitchen table and knew they would all be out there. Focusing back on the performance, she helped the girls change into new costumes and set them up to go onto the stage for each scene. For her first time backstage, she found herself instinctually getting into the rhythm like an old pro.

Finally, the second act came, and it was time for Ava. As Amelia stood next to her, she noticed the girl looking pale as she watched the stage, waiting for her cue to go on.

Amelia leaned over to her. "If you weren't nervous, I'd be concerned."

Ava looked at her with surprise. "You would?"

"Yes. You're human, you're supposed to be nervous with something like this."

"I just want it to be perfect."

"Ava," Amelia said. "Perfection does not grow a dancer."

Ava's eyes glistened at hearing the exact words she'd needed in this moment—the words of her mother. Amelia watched with pride as Ava mouthed "Thank you" before gliding onto stage and hitting every move with ease. Tears began to fall as Amelia feverishly clapped alongside the audience who were in a standing ovation for Ava's first dance.

"Saying I'm proud to call her my granddaughter is an understatement," a woman's voice said behind her.

Amelia looked back and saw a woman she didn't recognize. "Hi there," she said.

"Melissa Walsh," the lady said, keeping her voice low so as not to disturb the show. "I wanted to get the perfect view. And to meet—"

Ava nearly knocked them over with excitement as she came off stage.

"Did you see me!" she exclaimed in an excited whisper. She hesitated when she saw Melissa, but a smile instantly broke out. "Grandma?"

"You nailed it, Ava!" Ben said in a low tone as he walked up beside them. "I can't wait to see you kill it with the Prince soon."

Melissa gave her granddaughter a hug. "Knock 'em dead."

"I will, thanks to Amelia," Ava said before rushing off to change for the next dance.

Ben looked at Amelia. "Amelia, meet my mother, Melissa," he whispered.

Melissa extended her hand. "We were just about to. Thank you for helping Ava shine out there."

"It was my pleasure. And it's so good to meet you," Amelia quietly said.

Ben looked past his mom and motioned someone else forward. When Amelia turned, she saw Lisa.

"Mind if we have someone else get a special view for the rest of the show with us, Mom?"

"Of course not," Melissa said and smiled at Lisa.

Ms. Sherry came over to stand with them, and Amelia gave her an incredulous look. She laughed under her breath when Ms. Sherry mouthed "Told you" and nodded toward Melissa, Lisa, and Ben.

Lisa opened her purse and reached for a tissue. "I knew

I'd need these here. Amelia, if you hadn't found that coin, none of this would have happened. I would have stayed where I was… hiding from White Bridge. There are no words to thank you for returning the coin."

Ben put his arms around Amelia's waist. "I feel the same way." He gently pulled her back, so they could talk away from the wings.

Lisa's face lit up watching them together and Ms. Sherry took over directing the girls to give them a minute.

Looking up at Ben, Amelia's heart was full… fuller than it ever had been before. For so long she had leaned on ballet to fill a void she hadn't realized was missing. Up until this moment, dancing had felt like a competition to always do better, work harder, and prove herself. Her love of ballet had been unknowingly controlled by someone else's words that had shaped her beliefs, her thoughts, and her true self. Watching the girls move freely on stage and soaking in the music and movements had her now twirling alongside them —fully liberated from her past.

"Ben," she started, her pulse picking up when they locked eyes. "I'm so proud of you."

"Oh, yeah?" He held her tighter. "What for?"

She nodded toward Lisa and Melissa. "For keeping your barriers down…" Her father's words popped into her head again. "And giving this unexpected encounter a chance. Forgiveness is hard…"

"But it leads us forward." He placed his lips on hers before they turned to enjoy the rest of the show.

"It's time," Ms. Sherry said when the end of the show came.

Amelia walked deeper into the wings, holding her breath as Ava and the Prince got into position—the pas de deux with the Nutcracker Prince had been Ava's biggest worry. Ben came up behind her and took her hand. *Nice and slow…*

you've got this… she willed her thoughts toward Ava, who carefully raised her leg in front of the Prince. Ms. Sherry stood on the other side of Amelia, holding her other hand as Ava began to spin… faster and faster… without one single slip.

As soon as the audience was on its feet cheering, so was Amelia as she turned to hug Ms. Sherry.

"She did it!" Amelia jumped up and down.

"That she did!" Ben couldn't help himself and ran out just as the curtain slowly began to fall. The audience cheered even louder when Ben scooped up his daughter.

Amelia's heart soared watching them. Getting to this moment had taken many twists and turns, just like her time on stage as a ballerina had always been—and none of it perfect. Life was never perfect, nor should it be. It would take her down new paths that were unknown and sometimes scary, but with a little faith and the courage to forgive, fate could spin things into a lucky turn of events… leading her forward to where she was meant to be.

Amelia stepped out on the stage, and the house lights came on. As the audience continued to cheer, she saw him— Andrew in the front row, wildly clapping. And just as the curtain fully dropped, he saw her, too, and blew her a kiss. Her final curtain call… was still yet to come.

EPILOGUE

DECEMBER, TWO YEARS LATER

"Remind me why we chose December for this wedding? I went out to my car, and I cannot feel my face now." Diana came into the room, rubbing her hands together. "But at least my makeup is frozen in place now." The sparkles on her long red maid-of-honor dress glittered against the setting sun through the window.

Amelia laughed at her sister-in-law through the mirror as she touched up her lipstick. "Today will make up for the years of birthdays and Christmases in this house he missed."

Diana sat down on the edge of Amelia's bed. "Which makes this Christmas-themed wedding perfect." She looked out the window. "Look, Amelia, the red cardinal just flew by the window."

Both women went to the window to peer outside. The cardinal perched on its favorite branch just below them. A two-parted whistle came from the bird, loudly at first before its singing faded.

Amelia glanced at Diana, her eyes swimming with tears, and reached for her hand.

"Hi, Andrew," his widow whispered.

"He knew he'd never hear the end of it had he not come for his twin sister's big day." Amelia turned and pulled Diana in, hugging her in silence as they both thought of Andrew.

"I need to get it together. This is your day and Andrew would want nothing but happiness," Diana said, walking to the bathroom to retrieve a tissue. She gently leaned into the mirror to dab around her eyes.

"You better not ruin your makeup, Diana." Kimberly appeared at the doorway. "If I see tears, then mine will start, and her father hasn't even walked her down the aisle yet."

Diana straightened. "I better stuff some more tissues in my dress for later."

Her mother walked over to Amelia. "There are no words for how beautiful you look." Kimberly held her hand and stepped out, admiring her wedding gown. "The lace is simply perfect."

The dress hugged Amelia's figure just right, its romantic v-neckline complemented the long sheer sleeves and the laced bodice that sparkled with beads, before the train extended out from the mermaid-style skirt. Amelia's long brown hair was swept up elegantly to the side, her lipstick the color of Christmas poinsettias.

"Bridal bouquet delivery," Lucy said, coming into the room with the same color bridesmaid dress as Diana, holding vibrant red roses and stopping short when Amelia turned around to face her. "You are beyond gorgeous. Okay, now I'm going to start crying," she said, fanning her face.

"*Don't!*" Diana and Kimberly said in unison.

"Enough with all the tears… it's time to say I do to the love of my life," Amelia said.

"Your father is at the bottom of the stairs, ready to take you to Ben for his first look before he hands you off," her mother said, holding her hand out to escort her out of the room.

When Amelia reached the top of the stairs, she ran her hand down the brand-new railing Ben had just finished polishing the week before. Her father stood at the bottom, his eyes reddening as he watched her come down.

"See, now I can't control mine anymore," she heard Diana say behind her when she saw Steve crying.

The smell of vanilla wafted up the staircase from lit candles, and soft lights cascaded in her direction. For the past two Christmases while Ben completed the remodel, she had gathered decorations that were up to both her mother's and Ms. Higgens's liking. She'd never forget the previous Christmas when she and Ben threw a holiday party, and Sam and her old ballet master walked through the door—a look of pure delight on Ms. Higgens's face. It was the same night Ben got down on his knee before her and everyone they cared about.

"As a father, I've dreaded this moment," her dad began, wiping away fresh tears. "But it's also a moment I'll cherish forever." Her engagement ring glistened as he took her hand and kissed it.

"Is everyone seated in the barn, Steve?" her mother asked.

The barn had been converted into a ballet studio beautifully. The size nearly doubled the studio Ms. Sherry had, with more than enough room for their intimate wedding. Amelia couldn't believe the transformation from ballet studio to wedding as there was nowhere else she and Ben wanted to exchange their vows.

"Ms. Sherry made sure everyone was accounted for and quietly seated while the violinists continue until we arrive," he answered, making Amelia laugh.

"Once a teacher, always a teacher," she said.

Her father pointed toward the closed door of the living room. "Ben is waiting."

Her father stuck out his arm and walked her to the doorway. She had originally not meant to let Ben see her before she walked down the aisle, but he said he had something important to do with her first. When her father opened the door, Ben's back was turned, but his parents were facing her when she walked through. His mother cupped her mouth when she saw Amelia. Behind them, Lisa stepped forward and held Melissa's hand, gripping something in her other.

Ben slowly turned around, taking in the sight of his bride —his face a reflection of his heart as he slowly inhaled, struggling to keep his composure. "Wow…" he finally managed.

Lisa came over to them. "Here you go, Ben."

Amelia saw her hand him a familiar little felt pouch.

"Is that…?"

"The coin?" Ben opened the bag and took Amelia's hand, placing it in her palm and closing her fingers over it. "May it always bring our family good luck."

Looking into his eyes, she leaned close to his ear. "It already has." She kissed his cheek, holding on to him as she lifted a leg to carry on the tradition of placing the coin in her shoe.

Lisa came closer, taking each of their hands. "There aren't words to describe how blessed I am not only to be here witnessing your wedding, but to know that our family and this coin…"

"Is back home," Ben said, kissing Amelia's hand.

"It is known in our family," Lisa started, glancing back at Ben's parents with a smile, gesturing for them to come stand next to her, "that this coin was first presented during a Christmas wedding in 1869, and today that special tradition continues."

"It's become… the *Christmas Coin*," Melissa said.

"The Christmas Coin…" Lisa repeated, taking it in. "I love that."

Ben turned to Amelia. "Ready?"

"More than ever." Amelia reached for her father's arm.

Ben escorted his parents and Lisa to the barn and everyone else followed shortly behind them.

As Amelia and her father waited outside, she held on to him in the icy air. The violinists ended their song and the music switched before the door to the barn slowly opened. Julia and Ava were on the other side, standing next to their new yellow Labrador puppy who wore a black bow tie around his neck. Ava held his lead securely, beaming at them.

"You look gorgeous, Amelia," she said.

"Like a princess!" Julia giggled.

Amelia's father nodded at Ava who took her sister's hand and began to lead her and the dog down the aisle behind Lucy and Diana who were already at the end.

Faces from Amelia's past and present gazed at her as she walked by them toward Ben, who was poised to take this next dance by her side. In their own pas de deux fashion, their eyes met, and they made their vows, holding the Christmas coin in their hearts, knowing they would add to its timeless history together.

A LETTER FROM LINDSAY

Hello!

Thank you so much for picking up my novel, *The Christmas Coin*. I hope it whisked you away to the New England countryside and filled your heart with Christmas cheer.

If you'd like to know when my next book is out, you can **sign up for new release alerts here:**

https://www.harpethroad.com/lindsay-gibson-newsletter-signup

I won't share your information with anyone else, and I'll only email you a quick message whenever new books come out or go on sale.

If you did enjoy *The Christmas Coin*, I'd be so thankful if you'd write a review online. Getting feedback from readers helps to persuade others to pick up my book for the first time. It's one of the biggest gifts you could give me.

Until next time,

Lindsay

ACKNOWLEDGMENTS

To all of my amazing readers—you are what keeps me going! I wouldn't be able to bring you another heartfelt story without you. Your enthusiasm, reviews, and all the connections I've made both online and in person have meant everything to me.

I am forever grateful to Jenny Hale and the team at Harpeth Road Press for their unwavering dedication and continuing to pave the way for my career. Your expertise, support, and tireless efforts have once again brought my work to life and out into the world for all my readers to enjoy!

To my editors: Karli Jackson for taking my concept and shaping it on the page. To Elizabeth Mazer for helping me bring the past to the present once again with the storyline, and Jodi Hughes for sharpening every important detail and tying it all together. And finally, Lauren Finger for her meticulous attention to detail and Lottie Hayes-Clemens for polishing it up to perfection.

To Kristen Ingebretson, you've created another visual masterpiece! Thank you for another magical Christmas cover that shines with every romantic detail this story holds.

A special thanks to the doctors, dancers, and historical society of my hometown in Connecticut that have been there for every question. In special memory of Dr. Laser, who brought my middle daughter into the world and always told me during that difficult pregnancy while on bedrest that I would 'be dancing soon enough'. Your words of encouragement stayed with me while developing Amelia's character.

And finally, to my Irish love, Jason: As I look back on all the 'twists and turns' of my own life... I am reminded that through it all—it led me right to you. Your unshakable strength and love have never left my side. Thank you for taking my hand during the writing of this story and knowing just when to pull me in for a dance—reminding me that the 'luck of the Irish' is always within my reach.

Made in United States
Orlando, FL
28 October 2024

53224723R00193